OF WOLVES AND STAGS

Ria Parisi

Of Wolves and Stags

Inked in Gray Press

InkedinGray.com

ISBN

ISBN Paperback: 978-1-952969-15-7

ISBN Ebook: 978-1-952969-16-4

Cover Design by Danielle Kane

For every girl whose dress size tried to tell them they couldn't be the hero in their own story. Don't listen and be bold.

TRIGGER WARNINGS

Of Wolves and Stags has trigger warnings. In full transparency, we will list them here if you need them. 🩶

Trigger Warnings: Death on page including animal death, violent and disturbing imagery, minor depiction of gore, PTSD flashbacks and dealing with trauma, medical experimentation, insinuation that a nonbinary character had a disapproving family, off page violence against children

PART ONE:
TIDESEND

CHAPTER ONE

Over and under. Twist and through. Dalia's fingers moved deftly over the knots as she worked, a practiced routine which came to her as simply as breathing. She was not made for the sea, so she earned her keep in the village in other ways, like mending the tatters of a fishing net spat back from the waves.

A storm rolled its way through the night before, leaving behind plenty of work. A distraction as she waited for the one thing she looked forward to every week.

Stories.

Tidesend was about as isolated and as boring as a town could get. Exactly what Dalia Arrowood needed some ten years ago, when a scraggly little thing with nowhere else to go appeared on the village's doorstep. It was, if nothing else, a quiet and safe town. Perfect to keep her from harm, but her soul begged to be fed with tales of beyond this paltry existence.

Often, she would work on her nets out by the cliffside just on the outskirts of town. Perched on the rocks there she had the perfect view of when the wagons came back from market, carrying with them not only goods, but the gossip she so desired.

With the sound of wooden wheels and hooves against the cobblestone, the next step in her well-practiced sequence was forgotten. Rolling her net up into a manageable ball, she leapt up to intercept the incoming girl leading a wagon back into town.

"You're late."

"I'm not late." Mollie chuckled, mud kicking up around the swaying hem of her dress as she walked. "You're just impatient."

Very few were willing to leave the safety net a village such as Tidesend offered. It was nestled just about as far north as possible on the continent, beyond even the reaches of elven rule. Still, the half a day's journey to the market offered more danger than the near zero they lived at, and most were unwilling to make the trek.

But someone had to do it. Someone needed to be the brave soul and courageously travel down the well-worn road tog bring back supplies, and Mollie was the one person in this damn place who seemed as restless as she was. Though, unlike Dalia, the woman before her bore this courage beyond just her imagination, making her suited for the task.

"It's almost dusk. Nora's going to be looking for you," she chided with a smirk tugging at her lips.

"Of course she will," Dalia replied, rolling her eyes, flinging the half-mended net into the cart. "But there's enough work thanks to the storm that I have plenty of excuses not to be constantly by her side."

Mollie snorted.

Dalia could easily be described as her dark-haired friend's opposite. She was all supple curves where Mollie was sharp edges. Her face and jaw were soft in a way people often said was gentle or pretty, her manner more reserved than her tempestuous friend. The thing they bore in common was their spirits.

The two of them were often described as wild in their own ways. Things to be tamed, perhaps even some kind of challenge. But while Mollie's family held good standing, Dalia was an orphan taken in by a widow with little more to offer than a roof over her head. Therefore, the women in town would try to get Mollie to comply to social norms, while Dalia was more often than not overlooked.

Thank the Gods.

Falling in step with the cart, Dalia reached out to stroke the chestnut gelding's warm neck. Despite the mess on his owner's attire, Henry's coat was always glowing. Mollie would often decorate his bridle with wildflowers or lavender, making him look and smell delightful. The mixture of sea air and sweet floral notes left a familiar inviting tone to their stroll.

"Well, go on then," Dalia pushed.

"If you're so desperate for gossip, why do you never come with me?"

"Nora would never allow it."

They both knew it was a lie. The woman who took her in would have rejoiced to see Dalia contribute more to the village, but it was an easy enough excuse to give. One Mollie simply shrugged off.

"You know, you could just leave," Mollie suggested. "You're almost eighteen, you could simply leave all of this behind and find adventures of your own."

The suggestion gripped her heart, Dalia's words catching in her throat as she gave the only answer she could. The only one she knew how to give.

"You know I can't leave. I'm waiting for someone."

A promise, uttered between two sisters, held her tight within their village.

Go as far north as you possibly can. Wait for me there.

So much of Dalia's past was lost to her. In the space her memories should occupy, there existed a giant blur, created by a child in pain. Perhaps this was her mind trying to protect itself, erasing the bad so only bits and pieces remained. Fragments she tried to weave together, much like the nets she mended. Yet, all that seemed to be left were frayed edges of twine — nightmares of her childhood and a promise which dictated her every move. They bound her within the tangles of their net.

Mollie frowned but dropped the subject all the same. "Well, on to the gossip then. You won't believe it! Apparently White Stags have been spotted along the traveler's road."

"The human resistance? This far north?"

Her heart kicked against her ribs. Dalia had, of course, heard stories of the band of humans who came together against the elves. They were the stories she loved best. Tales of daring rebels attempting to do the impossible. But the elven occupation of Belestara was concentrated in the south. The north was mostly out of reach thanks to the expansive mountain range at their continent's center. The humans living north of the Medan Mountains paid their tithes to the elven king and were ultimately left alone.

In the south, the roads were often patrolled by small dangerous bands of elven soldiers called Hunts. Cloaked in darkness they roamed the southern countryside — a nightmare incarnate. Humans so unfortunate to live within the clutches of the Elven regime knew the terror an Elven Hunt carried with it. Dalia once knew that terror for herself. Now such horrors were buried somewhere deep within the recesses of the void which should have held her memories.

But Hunts didn't travel beyond the mountains. At least, not usually.

It was why she came here so many years ago. Why her sister made her promise to travel north and find refuge.

Mollie's voice bubbled up in excitement as she continued on, each word dripping more dread into the pool in Dalia's gut.

"Yes, but there's more. I hear elves were spotted just a few towns over."

"Elves?"

The question was barely a whisper as she sucked in through her teeth, the air cold as it shook down in her throat. Mollie simply nodded and said the words Dalia had dreaded ever hearing since coming to this isolated place.

"Not just *any* elves. A Hunt! I heard they were looking for one of those *things*. Can you even imagine? One of those monsters with magic. I thought they were only myths . . ."

Mollie's voice faded as a ringing sparked up in her ears. For ten years, Dalia carefully constructed a world where she was insignificant. A relatively simple task by saying nothing and clinging to her promises. All she needed to do was stay small. Quiet. A member of the village and nothing more.

With Mollie's simple words, all of that crumbled around her.

"Dalia?" Mollie paused. "Are you okay?"

"I'm sorry, I completely forgot I told Nora I would check the beach for any washed-up nets that need repairing. If I don't do it, she'll have my head. The words tumbled from her lips in a flurry. "You go ahead. I'll catch up with you and hear the rest of the story later."

The expression on Mollie's face fell. "Yeah, okay." Concern clouded her gaze a moment, though she gave a gentle smirk all the same.

"Hey, you know," Mollie teased, reaching out, brushing

some copper curls off Dalia's shoulders and making a show of taking a good look at her. "If you ever did leave this place, I'm sure you could convince some handsome gentleman to take you where you wanted."

A scoff was all Dalia needed to give. Mollie never could handle ending a conversation poorly, and her attempt at soothing over the awkwardness was welcomed.

"You are ridiculous, you know that?"

"Or beautiful lady. That's an option as well."

"Mollie . . ."

"Oh, come on, with those cute freckles and those curves. I'm sure you could manage."

Dalia rolled her eyes, but the hints of a smile were upon her lips, earning one from Mollie in return. With the subject dropped, her entire posture was more at ease.

"I'll tell Nora you're still combing the shore. Don't stay out too long, yeah?"

"Where was a Hunt even seen?" Dalia asked.

"Down by the old temple. But you know that's just gossip. People like to make up stories to feel more important. I'm sure it's fine, but still . . . can't be too careful."

Dalia nodded, the rumors sitting in her stomach like lead. She forced a smile onto her face for her friend's sake. The act was enough for Mollie, as she turned on her heels back to the village.

The distance between them stretched out. Once Dalia was sure her friend wasn't about to turn back, she dropped her smile. Nora was sure to be furious she stayed out so late, but she needed to get away, put space between her and that conversation. Let the woman scold her later, but Dalia couldn't face anyone when she felt like she might scream at any moment. The gossip she so longed for now hung on her heart like an anchor. For Dalia always knew what she was, what they let into their homes so willingly. The thing these people so easily spoke of as a monster was hidden in plain sight with them all along. They fed it. Clothed it. Treated a desperate monster as if it were one of their own, while she hid away behind the visage of a meek girl.

A home, they called it when they welcomed her. Not even knowing what they were inviting into their lives. But this wasn't a home. Tidesend was a woven cage. A temporary holding place until her reunion with her sister. A community to hide behind. So long as she didn't wriggle her way out of the weave and did what was expected of her. So long as they didn't know the truth, Dalia at least found some peace. But after ten years, the netting so meticulously traced around her promises threatened to unravel.

CHAPTER TWO

The shoreline of their little village was carved from the stone of the cliffs. There lay a few spots of soft white sandy beach taken up by the docks to launch fishing boats from, but mostly the water crashed right up against a steep cliffside.

The storm may have passed, but the air still hung thick. The waves crashed against the rocky shores as though threatening the weather might pick up again at any moment. That was the thing about Tidesend, the sea here had a mind of its own, acting often as if it possessed moods, swinging from lows to highs at barely a moment's notice.

The chaos of those waves worked for Dalia. It was the perfect place to hide. The town was so far north few already dared to tread this way, and even fewer dared those tides.

The village proper sat aloft those high walls, far enough away from the waves and their fits of rage that even the worst storms barely touched them. Dalia often found herself wandering away from the safety of the town, deft steps taking her down one of the slippery paths towards the icy water below.

She'd done it ever since she was a child. Whenever she needed to escape from the stagnant life she'd gotten far too used to, she would arrive here. Bouncing from one careful step to the next as she made her way down to the craggy shoreline.

Sand finally gave way under her boots as she wandered farther down a stretch of beach where no boats docked. It was an often-unused area, with nothing but a small shed at the end, farthest from the village before it lifted back up into cliffs again. The perfect spot to come and not be disturbed. One both she and Mollie used to escape the mundane responsibilities thrust upon them many times before.

Monster.

She knew exactly what Mollie really meant: those who wielded magic. In truth, those like her were known by another name: Crystalline. Most at this point thought of them as a simple bedtime story used to frighten children. People who were once humans changed into something else by sheer force and cruelty. All hunted, either for their abilities or in spite of them.

Monster.

That was all the world would see if they knew what she was. Dalia heard the word used in reference to someone like her so many times she almost accepted it as truth. Humans were not meant to have magic.

Only the Gods were.

Wait for me. Her sister's voice rang in her head. The final begging demands made by a protective sister haunted Dalia's days. *Wait for me. And promise me, you will never use your power. Not ever.*

In theory, she understood why her sister made her promise those things. Crystalline were more than just feared — their very existence was seen as an offense to the Gods. The stories and insults alone were enough to tell her what would happen if her own people found out what she was. An elf finding her would be worse. Being found by one of them came with the lingering threat of unfinished business, that she might be taken and used for the very purpose she was created for. The purpose she and her sister fled from.

For most people, elves were dangerous for their mere cruelty. Humans caught stepping out of line were always in danger of finding themselves run through by an elven blade. They were seen as beneath the long-lived elves, but Crystalline, they were seen as tools.

Living weapons created merely to be used. The how or why of it was still fuzzy, but enough gossip and deep-rooted instinctual fear told Dalia her sister was right to send her far away from elven kind.

Stars started to twinkle, pushing away the dusk for night. It was time to turn back or else Nora's wrath was not going to be worth this small moment of reprieve.

Shifting her weight, Dalia moved to turn around, when a loud wet slap stilled her feet. A wave, smacking against hard wood, half lodged into the sand and half rocked by the tide.

A boat? What was a boat doing out here?

The pounding in her chest was like a drum. Steady, but enough to rattle her. The sea had a way of claiming things and then spitting them back at random, but she never found something like this before. As far as she knew, none of the fishermen were searching for a lost vessel. Nor did this even look like one of their fishing boats. Meaning it couldn't have come from the village. Some poor soul must have gotten lost in the weather and then been swallowed up by the turbulent tides. One big question still hung in the dimming light: Was it empty? Or was someone still within the wreckage?

Forcing a swallow, Dalia summoned up her courage and moved forward, her pace picking up as she propelled herself towards the craft. Sand kicked up around her skirts the whole way, dancing in gritty sprays around her legs. If someone was in there, there was no telling what state they were in. She couldn't run back for help, not without risking the life of whatever soul washed up on their shore.

Reaching the edge of the wreck her blood ran cold, the chill biting sharper than the northern winds ever could. A hand draped over the lip, the rest of the body it was attached to laying in an unnatural pose within the frame.

For a moment she just stood there, looking everything over and trying to assess the situation. At first glance, she might have thought this person was dead. Yet, something within told her not to move. Her feet kept firmly planted in the sand she waited, the one thing she was truly good at. She waited one second, then another. What she was waiting for, she didn't know, but it finally came in an answer that caused her breath to catch in her throat.

Fingers curled and then unfurled.

This person was alive.

Dalia scrambled to her feet, grasping the edge of the boat and ripping against the tide. Logic beat at her skull, singing of the danger in this, but she didn't heed the warnings. Not when this stranger needed help.

With a final pull the boat scraped against the sand. With a frustrated cry, Dalia crashed down beside the vessel. The hull stuck firmly in the sand, no longer willing to budge. Her now soaking skirts entangled her legs as she scrambled, not caring about the grains of sand and shells clinging to her clothes and peppering her hair and face.

Her only thought was of time. How much time would this person be able to cling to life?

She grasped the side of the boat hauling herself up, looking over the side. Desperately she scanned the body within its wooden walls. For the first time, she got a real good look at the man. Burns marred his body from the tip of his head to his practically melted boots. His clothes fused to his body in places, and the left side of his face had been charred beyond recognition. His chest rose and fell in shallow uneven breaths that shook with each exhale. That and a few involuntary twitches, were the only indication of any life left in his body. Dalia could not be sure if he was conscious or not, but it was clear as day the thread holding him alive was fraying. Pulled tight, ready to snap at any moment.

It would be so easy to turn away from this. He wouldn't last much longer. It would be so simple to just deem him as too far gone and to go back and report a dead body, just another casualty of their dangerous shores.

Dalia would uphold her promise. Her life and cage would remain intact, no matter how much she hated it. Safety mattered more than adventure and purpose, a sentiment she would do well to remember.

Carefully she reached out, pale fingers ghosting over the man's body as if trying to see exactly where he had been broken. Her mind turned as she tried to assess the situation and avoid any of the burnt flesh. Something seemed odd. Dalia had seen burns before, but never anything like this. His body was as black as coal in places. The heat it must have taken to leave a wound such as this was unfathomable.

She should have turned away, leaving this man to his fate, but the pounding in her chest begged to stay. It was impossible to ignore the truth she had hidden for so long — she could save him. It was within her power. This man had been sent to her in some way — by the Gods or by luck. A pray answered. One she never dared to utter aloud.

The magic Dalia tucked away and hid would, at times, rebel against the leash tethering it away. Like an itch begging to be scratched. Any time she saw someone in need, the weight of it all grew heavier. Piled on her day after day. The specifics may have been a haze, but Dalia knew in her bones exactly what her magic could do. It was less a memory than an understanding of self, etched upon her very soul.

Someone was hurt. Someone was sick. The people around her would suffer, as any person might suffer within their life, and Dalia would watch. The need growing in her chest to do something. Anything. For a girl who so longed for adventure, she was an utter failure, standing stagnant at every chance presented to her.

Continuously she would deny herself, pushing down some fundamental part of who she was in a desperate attempt to keep the safety her sister so wished for her intact. Dalia could not allow another chance to slip through her fingers. Not with the threats of a Hunt already at her doorstep. If they were truly so close, what good had her promises done? Besides allow those around her to suffer when she could have done more.

No more.

She was done doing nothing. She was done *being* nothing. It had been so long since she flexed that muscle, allowing herself to tap into the power clawing inside of her to be free, after ten years of captivity.

"I'm sorry."

The simple words were a quiet release. After a decade, it was time to let her promises go. At least a part of them. Dalia did not have the courage to fully step out of her cage, but she could reach out a hand. With a dangerous rebellion, she stretched her fingers through the widening holes in the net entangling her soul.

Her hand stilled over his shoulder and found a purchase

there. Her fingers rested against a bit of exposed flesh intact just enough for her purposes. Heart pounding, her eyes fluttered closed. She could do this. She had to do this.

For a moment it felt like stumbling blind in the dark, searching for that place inside her locked away for so long, until she tripped headfirst into its warm glow. Something deep started to blossom and sing, and a heat pooled in her chest. Magic surged forth, and with some coaxing, she bid it to do her will. Light directed through her veins towards her fingers and finally into the man before her. Lifeforce spilling out of her and given to him.

Her eyes snapped open, their usual blue hue taking on a faint glow — a step toward freedom. Dalia's gaze drifted down to him, and a smile tugged at her lips.

His skin knitted itself back together, stitching up those places she noted earlier. Angry burns faded. Reds and blacks gave way to the raw pinks of healing. Through her excitement, caution was demanded. This power didn't come without a price, and a tremble in her hand as well as the nausea roiling in her gut screamed warnings she would do well to remember.

The lifeforce she was giving, it came from somewhere. From her, to be more precise. An exchange, some of herself for him. Dalia couldn't fully recall where she learned how to navigate the treacherous line, how to give just enough of herself for it to work, but not so much it cost more than she was willing to share. But some part of her remembered. Muscle memory kicking in, a great reminder in the void of her past that she'd done this before. He was not the first person she'd used magic to drag back from abyss. Only the first whose face was whole in recesses of her mind.

Her shoulders sagged, breath quickening. Time to stop. Quick surveillance told her it was okay to let go. His burns had healed, leaving behind angry red patches of skin but no scars.

Dalia could sense internal damage lingered, but that would have to be healed the old-fashioned way. He would be weak, need care, but he would be alive.

Dalia did one final check, closing her eyes and trying to discern anything she missed. Running her senses throughout his body to seek any lingering damage.

The taste of magic and freedom fluttered in her chest filling an aching hole there.

This was who she was meant to be.

Not a monster.

A healer.

She shut down the exchange, letting loose a breath. One that for the first time in a long time escaped her chest unburdened. Dalia opened her eyes once more, the man before her following suit. His eyes just barely cracked open, like a heavy weight wanted to hold them shut. Without the burns, she was able to get a better look at him. The angles of his face were sharp, but not at all unpleasant. His hair was a sandy mop upon his head that almost threatened to conceal the pale blue struggling to show behind his drooping lids. Dark short hair speckled his jawline in well behaved stubble. It was clear he took care in his appearance when he wasn't half dead covered in sand.

Dalia stayed silent, staring. Words failed, until his expression twisted. Fear etched upon every feature.

"It's alright," she said quickly but kept her tone soft and even. Wanting nothing more than to comfort him. "You're safe now."

His expression softened at those words. Confusion instead clouding his features, as a muscle worked in his jaw.

Dalia did nothing to explain fully, she couldn't. Not without exposing what she was. Danger was already invited by using her abilities, tempting fate even more by trusting a man she barely knew would not be wise. No matter the choice she just made.

Quietly, the man lifted a trembling hand, reaching towards her. His expression could only be described as something of awe. Briefly, his fingers brushed her curls. Barely grazing them, stopping short of pressing forward. Did he think her an illusion of some kind? It would be hard to blame him given the circumstances.

Her own hand reached out to meet his, bringing it down to rest on his chest, not wanting him to overexert himself. She leaned towards him, a gentle smile gracing her face before repeating those three calming words.

"You're safe now."

CHAPTER THREE

S oot coated the back of her throat, muddling her senses with the sharp smell of smoke as she struggled forward. Tiny feet in shoes worn past the sole struggled with each step, the hard path biting against her. One foot after the next, she kept moving. The hand on her wrist was a tether — the only thing keeping her from giving up and falling on the ground right there and then.

"Ammy, slow down," Dalia begged, but her sister merely shook her head.

Ash clung to her tiny frame, choking her, yet the elder girl tugging her along seemed wholly unphased by the inferno they left in their wake.

Blonde curls were illuminated by the reds and oranges the flames cast into the sky, like a crown anointing her sister's head. Dragging behind her, Dalia was desperate for a break, but Ammy was a vision of strength. At ease in the flames. Always ready to look for another fight. Always ready to keep punching until the end.

Screams erupted in the night air around them, sounds that

made Dalia's stomach twist as she forced herself forward. They wouldn't all make it out this night, a thought neither of the sisters could dwell on. Their focus had to be on themselves alone, or their own screams would soon join that haunting chorus.

Without warning, Ammy changed course. Throwing them both down into some overbrush, a hand clasped over Dalia's lips before a single complaint uttered forth.

Hoof beats.

A band of elves dressed in all black rode right by them, as the pair held their breath. A Hunt was looking for them now. Looking for their weapons who had escaped into the night. Once the clopping of hooves sounded far enough away, Ammy dropped her hand, cursing under her breath.

"Ammy . . ." Dalia begged softly.

"Listen to me."

Her sister squared off to face her, grasping both of her shoulders firmly. "I'm going to draw them off. I need you to run, Dalia. Alright? Run, and don't look back."

Panic swelled in her chest, constricting the ability to breathe. "No! No, I can't! I can't!"

"You can."

For all her panic, her sister was a stone wall. "Go as far North as you possibly can and wait for me there." It was an order. One that would stick with her no matter what else was lost in those flames. "Wait for me and promise me that you will never use your power, not ever. Promise me, Dalia!"

"I promise."

Two shaky words, a kiss to her head, and then her sister was gone. Dalia was utterly alone. Flames sprung to life in the darkness around her, as she was left with nothing but that promise. Clinging to her vow, she ran. In the end, the urge to look back always won out. Behind her was nothing but a blaze of devastation. Fire and somewhere within it, a set of dark eyes that she didn't recognize. Sad and *piercing, they stayed in the wreckage of the woods as it all burnt down. If she looked at them much longer, she would be swallowed whole. The intensity of the gaze threatened to drown her within its deep sadness.*

So she kept running, plunging into the darkness that lay before her.

DALIA AWOKE in a sticky sheen of sweat. Another nightmare. Another memory? It was so hard to tell.

It was the same every time, or close enough. Often, she dreamt of the night she and her sister parted. The night of the fire which allowed her to take flight from her elven captors. Yet, so much was still a blur. What always remained the same was the fire, the promise, and those eyes.

She didn't know whose they were or why they stuck with her so, but they were always there — waiting in those flames to haunt her.

Swinging her legs over the side of her bed, she pressed her hands to her temples, humming against the growing headache. Now was not the time to dwell on her past. Not when her future was finally unfolding.

One more breath in and out then she burst out from her covers, making sure to grab her cloak and throw it over her plain brown wool gown, not bothering to so much as braid her hair before heading out. Silently tiptoeing to the door, she threw her satchel over her shoulder. She collected some things the night before for her patient, stuffing them there for safe keeping.

No one could know what she had been up to. Not Mollie, and especially not Nora.

The woman would be furious if she knew, and it would

become harder to sneak out if the elder woman caught any inkling of her intentions.

"I need a favor."

Dalia rushed over to Mollie, keeping her voice hushed so in their closeness only the two women could hear what was about to be uttered between them.

"Tell Nora I'm going to market with you today." Mollie paused packing her cart, turning to take in her friend with a raised brow. They both knew this wasn't like her. Dalia was one to push the boundaries sometimes, sure, but this was an outright lie. It wasn't something she would usually pull, and the confusion was written all over Mollie's face.

"This is the second time this week you've asked me to cover for you," she said, raising an eyebrow questioningly. "Care to share what's going on?"

"Later," she promised sweetly. "Maybe I'm taking your advice. Finally living life a little."

Mollie's smile stretched, and Dalia could tell she was already jumping to conclusions. Sure, none of them would come close to what was really happening, but it felt good to hold this mystery. She was finally becoming more than a sad lump just waiting for something to happen. Something *had* happened, and now her life was tumbling out of control towards a kind of beginning.

"You owe me."

"I know." Dalia giggled back, practically bounding up and hugging her. "I'll tell you later. I promise."

"You'd better. I want all the juicy details."

Dalia nodded but couldn't help but wonder if she would actually do that. The story she told was going to have to be a curated one. One that didn't give away what she had done fully. Something she could devise later. For now, she needed to get back to her little secret.

THE DOOR of the old shed creaked as she opened it, the musty smell of the place filling her nostrils in a familiar comforting way.

"You're up."

The words left her lips delighted. She had set up a makeshift cot for her patient. Piling nets and blankets atop one another to try and keep him safe and warm through the night. Now, for the first time since finding him a week ago, the man was sitting up on his own accord. He leaned against the wall for support, but it was still a sight to behold after witnessing his wreck of a body left to die in a rowboat.

Her magic could only do so much. The past few days had been a game of touch and go as he drifted in and out of consciousness. Dalia hadn't dared to use her abilities again, frightened it would give her away. Instead, she settled on stealing medicines and salves. If she finished his healing as any doctor might, she would hopefully be able to play off the rest of it without too many questions.

"You came back."

His voice was a low pleasing gravel. Now clean and dry, his mop of hair still stubbornly sat in messy curls which veiled his eyes in a brunette curtain. He still looked barely pieced together, his clothes holding on in tatters, but at least he wasn't the scorched mound of flesh she'd found two nights prior.

Glenn was his name. He told her as much the last time he'd been awake. Glenn Cahill. That and the fact he was nineteen were about all she managed to learn. When he wasn't fitfully sleeping, he seemed to just stare at her in a haze. Suspicion clouded his sharp features but often gave way to the same reverence he'd shown before, not quite sure what to make of the woman who saved him.

"I keep doing that, don't I? You just can't get rid of me," she teased gently.

Her steps towards him were careful, her voice sweet. Treating him like a scared animal who might turn on her or try to run at any second. Dalia knew she needed to be gentle. This man endured something horrific, even if she didn't quite know what it was yet.

"I managed to get you fresh clothes, as promised." She produced a pair of trousers, a coat, and a simple cotton tunic snagged from one of the fisherman's bags while he was enjoying lunch. "Also, some more food, water, and fresh bandages."

He studied her with pale blue eyes, and Dalia couldn't fault him for his continued hesitancy. A young woman caring for a wounded stranger was an oddity to be sure, and he couldn't have known what truly transpired between them. The waking moment they shared on the beach was so brief, and for her sake, Dalia hoped he might have forgotten it entirely or considered it a fever dream.

All she told him was she found him injured and tried to patch up his wounds. It wasn't entirely a lie. She had indeed patched him up, just with magic instead of bandages and medicine. Then she dragged him here, hiding him in the shed she found solace in escaping to so many times.

"Why are you doing this?"

Despite the suspicion of his gaze, his low voice grew softer. A gentle edge emerged as he stared down at all she laid out before him. Something told her Glenn had not known much kindness in his life. At least not from random strangers. Something she could relate to all too well, from the time before she stumbled into Tidesend.

"Here, hand me your coat." Out of all his clothes it was the most marred from whatever attacked him. Dalia hoped with a soft voice and gentle treatment, she would be able to convince him to trust her. First, starting with getting him to wear a new coat which might protect him from the elements of the northern shore, rather than the shreds of fabric which slightly resembled his former coat. Hopefully the fisherman she'd taken it from would not miss his spare set of clothes too much.

Glenn paused for a moment, his silent gaze once again upon her, flittering between hesitation and intrigue. He didn't look at her like everyone else did. Like something to be passed over, just some girl from a fishing village. No, he looked at her like she was *someone*.

"Please," she pressed. "It's cold and your current one is ruined."

He seemed to consider for a few more seconds before finally stripping off the offending jacket and holding it out to her. Her lips pulled into a thankful grin as they swapped the two pieces of clothing. She got up to take the torn and burnt jacket over towards a pile of broken fishing lures in the corner of the shed before glancing back at him. It was nice to see him able to put on the new coat on his own — a testament to his returning strength. Pulling her gaze away from him, she went to drop the jacket on the pile, when her fingers brushed over something hard within the lapel.

Halting a moment, she turned the fabric within her hand, trying not to draw attention as she flipped the lapel of his jacket, finding a pin hidden there. It was small, something that wouldn't have caught someone's eye unless they knew where to look. Just a round wooden pin with the form of a stag carved into it.

Dalia's heart tumbled as she brushed her fingers over the curves of the animal engraved there. Daring a glance back at him, she tried to compose herself before tossing the jacket as though she hadn't just found something incredibly incriminating hidden within. Luckily, it seemed he was too busy trying to get comfortable to really notice the scene playing out.

He was a White Stag. A part of the stories which sustained her for so long. If the tales were true, the group only had one goal: to earn back the freedom stolen from the humans by the elves. A noble goal in the stories she clung to, but most of the gossip warned of them being dangerous. Mainly because they were targets for Hunts and so misfortune would often follow them. The elves were indiscriminate in their killing. A White Stag being found in a village would be likely to condemn anyone and everyone who lived within its limits.

"Everything alright?"

His question cut through her thoughts, and she turned to face him with an easy smile on her face. Dalia was used to hiding turbulent emotions, putting on a fake smile was simple enough. "Yes, sorry, I was just thinking."

"About what?"

A cool wash of surprise fell upon her. Anytime she gave an excuse of that nature it would usually be brushed away. The conversation would move on without anyone inquiring about what was on her mind. Never had anyone pressed her or showed enough interest to continue questioning. It was refreshing.

"You, honestly." Her voice was tentative. After all, they didn't really know each other. Names were exchanged and she had been nursing him back to health the last week. But, in truth, she knew next to nothing about him. Well, besides the fact he might very well be a White Stag and involved with something that nearly gotten him killed.

Those pale eyes chuckled right along with him as he caught her gaze. In the dark of the first night, she hadn't gotten a good look at him, but now, it was easy to admit in the moments his eyes met hers, she liked it. There was a casualness about his appearance, an ease. From his shaggy hair to the way he held himself, even if he must have been in pain. Being around him felt easy despite the fact he was a stranger, and she soaked in the way he looked at her.

"What about me?" he finally asked, his voice clearly entertained.

Dalia bit the inside of her lip before daring to play this game. He was still injured; she had the upper hand here. If he did turn out to be dangerous, she could easily flee. Expose the secret of him hiding here and that would be that. The town would handle it, run him off, and she would likely never see him again. Curiosity though, had a way of spurring her forward and blurring logic. She wanted to know about him. Glenn, this person who seemed to have sprung right out of the stories she held so dear.

The person whose circumstances finally broke through her voluntary stasis and allowed her to awaken her powers once more.

"Well, Glenn," she said in a slightly teasing tone, coming to sit on the edge of his thrown together cot. "I really know nothing about you. Well, besides the fact you showed up on these shores in terrible shape. I have so many questions. More than I can count."

"Funny, because I have one of my own." His voice was sweet, but the furrow in his brow and sharp gaze sparked apprehension.

"Oh?" she managed, her throat tightening. "And what's that?"

"What happened to my burns?"

Her stomach twisted.

The question was innocent enough, no ill intention seemed

to hide in those simple words, and yet it was like he'd set her spiraling off a cliff. By some miracle, Dalia kept her breath steady, praying her face was neutral enough to hide the way his question struck her.

"What burns?" Dalia wasn't sure if he heard the tremble in her voice, but his gaze broke off. Clenching his jaw, he stared up at the ceiling for a moment.

"I know I was as good as dead. You did something to me, to keep me here."

Swallowing, she stood up from the bed, ensuring some distance between them as if it might make this easier. Dalia worried her hands as she listened to him continue.

"I was burnt. I know I was. Whatever you did to fix it didn't come from those bandages and salves you keep bringing."

"You've been through a lot." Dalia was quick to reply, but he was quicker.

"No. No medicine in the world could do what you managed. Not in one night. Not in a hundred nights."

Fighting the quiver in her lip, she forced herself to turn back to him. What she expected was for this man to look at her like she always feared someone would. She expected the look of a brave rebel facing down a monster. Yet, it was not fear or even determination she saw now. It was confusion. Hope, even.

"I don't know what to say." Her calm voice blanketed the storm of emotions brewing within her. "I just, found you and brought you here. Did the best I could. Nothing else."

It wasn't a lie, but it also didn't answer his question. Still, Glenn nodded.

"I'll leave you to rest," she said quickly, cutting her visit short to prevent any further questions. "I'll be back tomorrow. Finish getting changed if you can and enjoy the food."

Before he could say anything more, she turned on her heels

to go. Dalia wanted to believe this was not a grave mistake. She couldn't bear to, not when in saving him she finally felt like the person she was meant to be. Yet, her actions invited danger by breaking her promise, stupidly allowing herself to believe she had been sent some gift.

A White Stag wasn't a gift. It was a curse if it attracted the elves here. The chances this endeavor could get her killed had risen greatly, but she wasn't ready to let go of all this. Not so long as he looked at her with hope in his eyes. Everything she wanted for as long as she could remember seemed to be wrapped up in a pair of blue eyes that sized her up as someone important. Somehow, that felt worth the risk.

CHAPTER FOUR

"And where in the world were you yesterday?"

It took everything in her to keep from rolling her eyes. As thankful as she was to the woman who took her in as a child, Dalia couldn't help but feel resentful with just how utterly nosy Nora was. When she was younger, Dalia needed her. As a budding adult, she was overbearing.

True, Nora was kind to her, and over the years given her so much, but it was not charity fueling her actions. It was to fill a void. The sting of loneliness and loss was no stranger to Nora. She often spoke of the daughter she'd lost many years ago, making Dalia feel like nothing more than a replacement on more than one occasion. A constant aching sting which kept her from getting too attached to the older woman.

Her caretaker was a slender, aging woman that in her childhood Dalia had been glad to play the role of dutiful daughter for. She played the part Nora required of her and waited for when her real family would return. Yet, time flew by, and the longer Ammy didn't show, the more Dalia strayed from what was expected of her, and what Nora couldn't seem to abide was her willfulness. When Dalia no longer pretend to be the perfect daughter Nora so longed for and lost, their relationship fractured.

Dalia's budding desire for freedom threw an even further wedge between her and her parental figure.

"I went with Mollie to the market. She's been begging me to go with her for so long now."

"So she said," Nora snapped back. "I would have expected you to have brought back something to show from such a trip."

There was an edge in her voice, something Dalia wasn't accustomed to from her. Nora was not one who often looked for a fight, but now she looked like a woman with her hackles raised. Nora would often ignore her. Often treat her as though she was useless, but she would go out of her way to avoid confrontation. Something must have happened to bring forward such ire.

Dalia sighed, grabbing a bowl of hot porridge and taking the seat across from her at their table. The cabin had a cozy warmth to it. Its wooden walls did their best to keep out the biting chill as the rain beat against their roof in sheets. A comforting breakfast like this would do wonders on such a day. She made a mental note to try and steal some away for Glenn. She'd only seen him once since he'd questioned her and it was a rather awkward affair. Dalia changed his bandages in almost complete silence, wishing every second that she might think of something to say to mend not his wounds but the fracture between her and this practical stranger. She longed to know him and understand what twist of fate brought him to her. Good food had a way of bringing people together. Perhaps a fresh meal would set things right and get him talking again.

"You clearly have something you want to say," Dalia said

before shoveling a piping spoonful into her mouth. "Have out with it."

"You would do well to be more respectful, girl. Don't forget who it was that put a roof over your head."

Her next spoonful paused in midair; the retort hit with such a force that she found herself staring back at Nora wide eyed.

For a moment she was silent, meeting the older woman's gaze in confusion, but a defiance threatened to spark there as well. The silent roar inside of her that she pushed down along with her magic, allowing it to curl in the pit of her belly rather than expose who she truly was. No matter her quiet nature, Dalia was no meek mouse to be ordered about. No matter how well she played the role.

"Please, just tell me what is wrong," Dalia pressed. Her words were polite, but her tone and stature stiffened.

The woman across the table from her let loose a sigh, fingers idly playing with the rim of her mug. "Dalia, you are no longer a child. I have spent the last week doing my responsibilities as well as your own. I should be asking you what is going on. Not the other way around."

Dalia shoved the spoonful of the porridge into her mouth.

"You're seventeen years old. It's time you got your head out of the clouds and took your position here the village more seriously. You'll need to settle down and make a home of your own soon enough."

Her stomach flipped into knots at the suggestion. By some miracle she had been able to avoid this topic for quite some time, besides the occasional suggestion that it was odd she never showed any interest in any suitors. By her age, most eligible ladies in Tidesend had secured at least *some* prospects. Dalia had done nothing but shun the one or two gentlemen who tried to look her way. Not because they were not well off or considered a poor match. It was just . . . Dalia didn't have any interest in the subject.

She tried to. She really did.

But any time Dalia tried to talk about boys or even girls with Mollie, it just never felt right. Mollie and all the other girls in town could giggle and flirt and blush when suitors glanced their way — not Dalia. There was just something different about her. She needed something else, something the others didn't. Something she couldn't quite put her finger on, but it hadn't mattered. Not till now.

"Why now?" she questioned quickly, clenching her spoon tightly. "Mollie hasn't found a match yet, and she's older than me. Why must I?"

Before she could ask any more on the subject, Nora quickly cut in. Slamming her own spoon down on the table.

"Mollie has money! A luxury that we do not!"

That silenced her. Nora rarely, if ever, raised her voice. Mollie would be allowed to live her life as she wished because of her financial situation. Dalia was nothing but a beggar here, an outsider who somehow managed to get by without fully assimilating into their way of life.

Nora composed herself, shifting in her seat before taking up her spoon and gingerly taking a bite of her meal, as if anger hadn't just spilled out of her, revealing what was brewing and bubbling beneath her usually calm exterior.

"You daydream and run around like a child. And it's not safe anymore, Dalia. I know you've heard the rumors. There's talk of Hunts just outside our borders. Worse, talk of monsters as well. We need you settled as soon as possible. It's what's best."

They both knew Dalia would have little say if she stayed in Tidesend. Nora was the one who made the rules in this house. The choice was laid before her: Stay and allow this woman to find her a match, or leave this place and throw away the last of her vow to her sister. That was the one thing she couldn't do. Some part of her needed to cling to the last lingering bit of her oath. Her magic was once again free, but she could still stay. She could still wait.

"There's no point," Dalia said softly. "I've told you. My staying here was meant to be temporary. My sister— "

"Your sister is never coming back!" The words hung in the air between them like an arrow. Aimed at her heart and poised to deliver a blow she might never recover from. "It's been ten years. She abandoned you. She's probably off with a life of her own. Or more likely dead."

Dalia stared at the table, not daring to look at Nora while she couldn't control the tremble in her lower lip. Nothing she was saying, she hadn't thought herself. But it was one thing for her to question and to doubt. It was another to have it thrown in her face like it was a fact.

"It's time you grew up and accepted that this is your home now. No one is coming to take you away."

A suffocating silence filled the cabin. What Nora presented as truths threatened to strangle her, to pull her down in that silence and never let her go, wrapping her in the nets she so diligently weaved and claiming her for this place. Cemented as not just a place to simply lay in wait, but now a permanent fixture.

Home.

This place could never be home. Not for her.

"You're wrong." The words burst from her softly before she could think better of them. There was a quiet strength in her denial. Something she could cling to.

"She's coming back. I just need to keep waiting."

Dalia shoved back from the table, practically ripping her shawl off the wall and running into the rain. Vaguely she could hear Nora yelling her name, commanding her to come back, but her feet didn't falter. She moved along the slick ground back towards the shed which concealed all her secrets.

BY THE TIME Dalia managed her way down the cliffside to the little shed, the rain had soaked through to her bones. Something Glenn certainly didn't seem to miss, a wide-eyed stare meeting her as she burst through the door.

He was not the only one to look surprised though. What Dalia expected to find was her patient in his cot as always. What she found instead was a man standing by his bedside. His clothes completely changed and his curls tamed back away from his sharp features.

"You're standing!" Dalia exclaimed, her hands clasped before her chest in what could only be described as pure and utter excitement.

"You're soaking wet," Glenn retorted, raising a brow.

"Glenn . . ." Her voice softened, the fight with Nora completely forgotten. "You're standing."

It needed to be repeated. Honestly it was a miracle, even with magical intervention, Dalia had her doubts and worries. What if she hadn't been enough? Now, what she saw confirmed that she was. Glenn Cahill would live to fight another day, or whatever it was White Stags did when they weren't simply characters in a story. Considering the courage to mention the pin she'd discovered to him never found her, she still didn't have much further insight.

"I am. Thanks to you."

His thanks brought a gentle heat to her cheeks. Dalia knew he wanted more answers, but even if she couldn't give him those, she had given him this. A chance again at life. One that might have come in a way he would never understand, but it was a chance all the same. What he gave her in return meant more than Dalia knew how to express. It was a chance in her own right. One to finally be herself, even if only once.

"Did you really just run all this way through the pouring rain to come see me?" A smirk played on his lips as he took to teasing her. "Didn't realize I was so important."

That heat flared a little in her cheeks. "You're my patient. Besides, it's just rain."

"Just rain? You're soaked to the bone."

It was a good point. It truly wasn't an oddity for her in all honesty. With so much of her life spent bottling herself up, sometimes it was nice to be reckless. The feeling of rain on her skin and heavy fabric on her limbs was sometimes a blessing. Even if for no other reason but to escape the mundane.

"What? You've never danced in the rain before?" It was a challenge, given with a smile and a mischievous glint in her eyes.

"I can't say that I have."

"Well then," Dalia said snagging his hand in her own. "We're going to have to fix that. Doctor's orders."

Glenn raised an eyebrow at her, amusement dancing along his sharp face. "Doctor's orders, huh? And what if your patient catches a cold on top of everything else?"

"Then I'll just have to nurse him back to health again, won't I?"

Something passed between them. Something small but meaningful all the same. It was as if a great weight lifted off them both. Dalia didn't know what he was carrying around with him, but his shoulders loosened, a half smile making a grand appearance on his lips. It was enough for her to forget all of her own worries, and when he nodded, she tugged him forward.

The rain certainly was cold. A warm shower was not something one was likely to find on the northern coast, but Dalia liked it that way. She loved how the water nibbled at her exposed flesh and how her nose reddened as the chill thrilled goosebumps down her arms. Relief flooded along with the cold her as she let loose a long breath.

Glenn was more hesitant. His body language once again tightened as he squinted up at the sky like he was questioning his choices in life. And perhaps more than simply the choice to come out into the rain.

"Oh come on!" she teased, dropping his hand as she ran forward, sand kicking up around her feet as she threw her arms up. "It's just a little rain."

Her head tilted back, and her eyes closed, letting the rain pelt at her face a moment, before she spun. Droplets and sand whirled around her as the fabric of her skirts swirled. There was nothing intricate about the movement, but the elements playing around her hem added a mesmerizing grace. Glenn said nothing, his half smile simply remained as he leaned back against the frame of the shed.

Nora would have called this behavior childish and given her yet another scolding. But it wasn't immaturity that drove her out into the rain — it was freedom. Freedom to make her own choices, no matter how insignificant. The fact she could choose to do something silly like spin in the rain, it made her feel a little less trapped.

"You are an odd woman," Glenn remarked. Despite his words, his tone was not unkind.

Dalia stopped her spinning, looking at the man who was still mostly dry thanks to sticking next to the shed's overhang. She couldn't help but feel like he was missing out. The beach really was beautiful when it rained. The sand collected in clumps and the sea got so worked up that those tempestuous tides seemed like they could swallow up anyone who dared to enter. Being able to coexist in such chaos was thrilling.

"I wouldn't have it any other way," Dalia answered unshaken. "They all say that about me here. I wear it as a badge of honor."

He stepped forward finally, allowing the water to wash over him. Messy curls pressed down by the force of the drops as he made his way out towards her. A somberness settled over him as he too let his head fall back, the ghost of a smirk leaving him as a sigh joined the water in washing over his face.

"I never thought I would feel the rain again. I thought I was well and truly dead."

Dalia just stood there, the rain pattering around and between them as she drank him in. Here he was, the first person she had allowed herself to grant a second chance. She didn't want him to be the last. Dalia wanted to be able to help so many more people. It might have been impossible, but that want gnawed at her all the same.

"You could come with me."

The suggestion cut between them and it was her turn to adopt a straighter stance as his eyes met hers.

"What?"

"I can't thank you enough for saving me, but we both know I will need to leave soon. You can't keep me a secret in that shed forever. Something tells me you want to leave too. Maybe find a place where you don't consider it so much of a compliment to be different from those around you."

He was leaving. Of course he was. Dalia knew this day would come. The pin on his jacket cemented that. He had a place to be. A purpose. He couldn't just waste away in some fishing village. Not like her.

"And where would we go?"

He shrugged. "Don't know. You don't even have to stay

with me if you don't wish but . . . I think a girl with a heart brave enough to dance in the rain and take in a stranger all on her own deserves some kind of adventure in her life."

It felt like being seen. The path she longed for was laid before her. She'd taken the first step in saving this man's life. Now, all she needed to do was keep walking and follow him. One foot after the other until her life was something more than just waiting. Yet, all she could think about were those flames, those eyes staring at her in the distance in her nightmares, and her damn promises.

Nora was wrong about her sister. Ammy was a fighter, one who wouldn't stop until she gave her last breath. In what little memories remained scattered in her mind, Dalia knew that much was true. Her elder sister, her protector, would stop at nothing to find her. Ammy would never stop fighting, so she could never stop waiting.

"I can't."

Those two words were so soft and broken, nothing like the vibrant girl she just allowed herself to reveal. Instead, she played the part of the meek mouse she pretended to be just to survive.

"I'm sorry," she explained further, seeing his expression drop. "I'm waiting for someone. My sister. I can't leave without her."

Silence stretched between them, painfully tugging at the place within her that begged to burst free once more. She wondered if Glenn felt the same. If his sad expression meant he was pained by her answer as well.

"Then in a few days' time, I shall miss you, Miss Dalia. And thank you, for all you have done for me."

Her chest ached in a way so familiar to how her powers clawed to be free. She hardly knew this man, but she felt attached in a way. He was her charge, her responsibility. The one thing that made her feel a sense of purpose, and Dalia didn't want to give that up.

His hand twitched, starting a climb up towards her cheek with the seeming intention to touch the soft skin there. Her heart kicked against her ribs, breath stuttering. Was this what the others felt? This anxiety that somehow, she wanted to feel again and again? This man she barely knew had managed to awaken a part of herself she'd not even known existed. This very morning she'd questioned it. Yet now, standing in the rain, so close to touching, it screamed to life inside of her.

Something new and exciting. Something she wanted to touch and explore. A want so treacherous it railed against the wall her promises erected around her heart and mind.

Drawing her lips into a tight line, she turned from him. Just her luck, to finally find herself attracted to someone and know she would have to watch him leave in just a few days. It was best not to entertain something so fleeting. She held no judgement towards women like Mollie who could give into desire and bed a man simply for a night. But such things were not what she desired. If this could not blossom into something more then her attraction and want would falter. It was best to nip in the bud whatever was aching in her gut.

"Come on, let's get inside and get warm."

Glenn dropped his hand, nodding. The sad acceptance twisting down his lips made her question her decision more than she would have liked. "Of course."

As they walked back to the shed in silence, Dalia found herself glad he'd not pushed the subject. The cracks in her resolve might not have survived.

CHAPTER FIVE

If only her magic could slow down time. Dalia felt like she was finally getting a chance to know this man who she had pulled back from the brink, and now, he was leaving.

Since the day they spent in the rain, she'd seen Glenn one more time. Once again, he suggested she leave this place with him. And once again, she refused. Dalia cursed herself for her cowardice in not being able to accept his offer; even more so, for not finding the courage to ask him about the stag pin she discovered. Her time with this mysterious stranger was ticking away and so many questions still lingered, begging to be asked.

The idea of spending her entire day with him just to finally ask those questions was tempting but came at the risk of angering Nora once again. Her caretaker was starting to press Mollie more and more for answers, and Dalia knew her friend couldn't cover for her forever. She was going to have to be able to show some proof she'd spent time in the market with her friend, helping with her duties there. A fact she made sure

Glenn knew, so he wasn't concerned when she didn't show up till late in the evening.

Besides, Mollie had been begging Dalia to come to the market with her for what felt like forever. It was finally time Dalia took her up on the offer.

Taking those first steps outside of the village threatened an odd nausea in her gut. It was just for the day; the tether between her and Tidesend still existed, and yet a strange sense of betrayal rumbled deep within her. As if those tiny steps finally severed her vow, even if it was only for a short while. Opposite of that, the pieces of her she'd learned to tame, were screaming. To the power within her, those first few steps were a victory. One she was utterly ashamed to revel in.

Dalia helped to lead Henry, as he pulled their cart along the well-worn path. Mollie chattered next to her, excitement riding on every word. It was enough for guilt to claw its way from her gut up into her throat. Her friend was so joyous about this venture between them, and Dalia's mind was elsewhere.

It floated back to the little shed on the shoreline, and to her dreams filled with fire.

When they finally arrived in Bluewater Market, she fell back into the here and now. It was hard to comprehend that she was in the place she had heard so many stories about. This was the source of all the tales she consumed so greedily. Compared to the dull fishing village she had gotten so accustomed to; this place was vibrant. A spectacle of brightly colored canopies over stalls as people bustled about.

Dalia could practically feel Mollie's smugness at how her eyes widened.

"Well go on," Mollie said, her elbow connecting with Dalia's ribs playfully. "Go look around. I can handle business."

"Are you sure?"

Dalia wasn't in a rush to abandon her escort, but she also

had to admit she was fighting the urge to go run around and look at everything she possibly could. It was all exactly as Mollie described and each new sight called to her sense of adventure in an intoxicating jumble of noise and life.

"Absolutely. You've been cooped up for too long. Go take it in." Mollie gave a sly smile before adding, "In return, you just have to tell me more about who I've been covering for you to go see."

Before Dalia could so much as protest, the brunette gave her a wink and walked off.

It had been easy to allow Mollie to think she was having some sort of affair, but how she was going to explain the truth eluded her. Honestly, it was probably for the best he was leaving so soon. Then she could come up with the lie of some torrid romance to satisfy Mollie and the truth could be buried along with the rest of her secrets.

Now was not the time to dwell on those anxieties, if she was going to be here, she was going to make the most of it.

Slowly, Dalia meandered through the lines of stalls. They were hardly half a day's walk from Tidesend, and yet everything: the smells, the sights, the wares . . . all of it seemed so foreign. With the majority of her childhood memories lost to her, the small fishing village was the only thing she truly knew. Now, after seeing how much more their world had to offer even just a few steps outside of the confines she'd grown to accept, it was easy to admit the wild part of her was right. She was missing so much.

Her wandering stopped by the stall full of spices. A sharp and earthy scent penetrated the air in such an oddly pleasant way. She'd never seen so many colors when it came to food. Strings of red, crushed powder so yellow it would probably stain her fingers, and pungent seeds all made her mouth water. Where did all of this come from?

"There's not much further we can run."

Panicked hushed tones struck out from not far beside her. Dalia knew better than to try and overhear someone else's conversation, but it was so hard to ignore. Even as she tried to focus on the array of bright colors before her, bits and pieces got through. Enough to make her glance over her shoulder at the couple.

They were dressed differently than anyone she'd ever seen. Multiple layers of gauzy fabric covered their bodies with small colorful stitching details. Hoods made from that same gauze rested upon their dark hair. In the north, the fabrics were thicker, the designs simpler. No one from her small village wore anything like that.

"It's not polite to stare."

Dalia drew in a sharp breath and turned forward. Coming face to face with a sour-faced shopkeeper.

Their short-sworn hair, stout figure, and heavy aprons only made their scowl seem more severe.

"I'm sorry," she muttered, embarrassment creeping into her cheeks hotly.

"Refugees. From the South," the shopkeeper explained, seeming to sense her confusion and disquiet. "Most likely driven up this way by the Withering."

"The what?"

Dalia had heard of a lot of things in the gossip and stories Mollie brought her from each trip, but the Withering was a term she never heard uttered before. A fact which seemed to only annoy the person before her.

"The Withering, girl. What, do you live with your head under the sand?" Before Dalia could explain, the shopkeeper spotted Mollie making her way over and a frown quickly formed. "Oh, I see. You're from Tidesend, yes? Easier to stay up there and forget about the rest of the world than to actually do anything to help."

Dalia bristled a little. It was hard to know the reputation of their isolated village when she'd never taken a single step outside its borders. By blocking out the rest of the world, her town was resented in a way she had not been prepared for.

"I don't understand . . ."

"Of course you don't," they scoffed. "While the south struggles to eat because their crops are turning to ash, you seashore folk don't look at anything outside yourself. So long as the Hunts are kept at bay who cares who else suffers, right?"

Mollie came up behind Dalia, placing a hand on her shoulder and giving a little tug. "Ignore, them. Valen is particularly prickly with strangers."

"Only when they don't pull their weight," they shot back, causing a frown to set on Mollie's face as she tugged once more.

"Come on, leave them. They should know better than to try and scare off potential customers."

A look shouting the chance of confrontation passed between them and her friend, before Mollie simply scoffed and turned to go.

Following her friend's lead, Dalia turned away. A deep silence fell over the two for the rest of the visit. Only once when they were alone on the path back, did they speak again, tittering about all the wares on offer that day. About how it felt to get to experience the market rather than imagine what it would be like. It wasn't until they were nearly through the path back home, wagon empty and pockets full, that Dalia finally found her voice to question what just transpired.

"Have you ever heard of the Withering before?"

A sigh escaped the slender girl and she nodded. "Here and there. Apparently, it's some kind of sickness affecting the crops and forests in the south. A lot of refugees have been coming to Bluewater lately in search of better places to live. Valen is one of them."

Dalia could hardly believe what was coming from her friend's mouth. All the tales Mollie spun for her and never once was this mentioned. Dalia didn't understand. The idea that Mollie never brought this piece of information back to the village when people were clearly in need and instead brought back idle gossip tasted foul in her mouth.

"But why didn't you ever mention it?"

"You wanted fun stories. There's nothing fun or adventurous about people losing their livelihoods."

"But—"

"It's nothing to worry about," she cut in, waving her hand as if she was shooing away a bee. "People are always worried about something. Hunts, White Stags, Monsters, now the Withering. In the south, it's always something. The elves don't come this far north. We have nothing to worry about. Even those rumors about a Hunt close by, they're just stories. Stuff like that doesn't really happen around here."

The sheer audacity and detached nature of her statement hit Dalia square in the chest. Mollie was just like the rest of them. She may have enjoyed playing outside of their walls, but she didn't care for the suffering of others. Dalia could sympathize. Maybe she was no better. After all, she hid herself away from the perils of the world too, just trying to survive.

But Tidesend did not exist separate from the world. She had found her way there, and she was exactly what they feared most. There was no saying the elves or the Withering would not eventually make their way up too.

No sooner had that thought entered her mind, did she realize just how justified it was. Ahead of them, reaching the peaks of the tree line, loomed a column of smoke. Oranges painted the darkening sky, but it wasn't from the setting sun. Dalia knew all too well what was before them.

Fire.

"Oh Gods . . ."

Tidesend.

It was burning.

Something sharp and sour clawed at the back of her throat. Guilt, with a heavy mixture of fear. This was her fault. It was the only explanation. Either due to her own presence in the village or by her rescue of a White Stag, only a Hunt would do such a thing.

"Find Nora!" Dalia yelled. Mollie's face was white as a sheet as she took in the blaze on the horizon. "Find as many people as you can. I will come find you as soon as I am able and help. Just get people out."

"Wait, where are you going? Dalia?"

There was no time to answer the shriek of a question as she fled through the trees, trying to bypass the village and go straight to the shore. No time to explain to Mollie just what was at stake.

Only a single path led in and out of town through the forest, but Dalia knew the cliff sides and rocky shores well. She hiked them time and time again when she wanted to escape their sleepy town, pretending it was some grand adventure rather than wasting her life away.

This time, as she scaled those rocks, her feet remembering the treacherous slippery path well, there was actual danger afoot. The orange glow in the distance kept trying to capture her attention but she kept moving. A tunnel formed in her vision, cutting her off from not just the blaze but the memories threatening to consume her. She needed to get to Glenn before anyone else did. Before the only soul she ever saved was snuffed out.

CHAPTER SIX

The shed was empty. Dalia's heart crept up into her throat. The vacant room evoked such a panic within her that her chest heaved from more than just the physical exertion of running all the way there. Looking around she didn't see any signs of a struggle. The blankets on his cot were amiss but nothing else was out of place. Without seeing him though, the lack of chaos offered little comfort.

"Dalia."

She jumped and slapped her hand over her mouth to keep herself from screaming before turning to find him standing in the doorway.

"Glenn, thank the Gods." Without thinking she ran over to him, frantically scanning his body for any indication of harm. His hair and clothes were a little disheveled but otherwise he appeared fine.

"Where were you?"

"I saw the smoke and went looking for you." His eyes were wild, panic dancing alight behind the pale blue. "You'd said you were going to the market today, were you in the town when this happened?"

"No." Dalia shook her head quickly. "I ran back here as soon as I saw. I worried that they might have come for you. But we don't have time, we need to go back. We need to see if we can't help."

Glenn stiffened, confusion gripping hold of his face.

"For me? What do you mean? Why would someone come for me?"

She drew in a sharp breath through her nose, halting her attempt for the door. They had never discussed the pin she found, and now it was clear it was meant to be hidden after all. This was not something he wanted to get out, regardless of how vital the information might be at the moment. He was putting on a show. Just how much of their short time together was just that? A show? Dalia needed to break through the act — she needed to know the truth.

"Because you're a White Stag."

His eyes widened for a moment before his gaze darted over to look at the pile in the corner where his ruined jacket lay.

"Well, aren't you a clever girl," he mused softly. It all shifted so quickly. Those words left his lips and the curtain lifted. The stoic man washed away with the coming of a new tide. His whole demeanor loosened, and his face rested into an expression Dalia could only describe as impressed.

"Alright then." He leaned back against the door frame, a comfortable smirk appearing on his lips. He looked like a fox caught trying to steal from a chicken coop. Sly and maybe a little dangerous, but she wasn't afraid. Dalia had found him out and backed him into this corner. Maybe now she might learn what brought him to their shores in such a state. "Yes, they may very well have come for me. I didn't see much but I know well enough the mark of a Hunt."

It seemed that was all he was willing to give her; Dalia felt the frustration boiling in her gut.

"What, that's it?" Her voice raised as she took a few steps back from him. "No explanation at all? The village is burning! People could be dying! I need to know why. I saved your life, Glenn. I ran here before going to anyone else. You owe me at least that."

"You still haven't told me how you managed that one. Saving me, I mean."

Dalia froze. Suddenly, she wasn't the one in control anymore. Maybe *she* was the one cornered.

"I told you. Your wounds were not as bad as they—"

"Stop. Don't insult me by feeding me that line again."

His smirk fell away, and a much more serious expression took hold. His amused tone darkened. "We both know there's more to it than that. By the Gods, I know I was burned. I remember that much. I remember the pain. No pretty words can take that memory away. And now . . . now there's nothing. Not even a scar to show for it. You really want to insult me by telling me I was imagining it all?"

The stinging realization struck her. She didn't truly know this man at all. Dalia had been so quick to accept him as an answered prayer, that she hadn't taken the time to really question him. Tidesend was burning, and the fault lay firmly on her shoulders for the danger she brought into their midst.

"I'm sorry." Her voice was so soft, almost ashamed of the lie she was telling. "I'm just a girl from a fishing village. I know a few healing remedies, sure. But it's nothing more than that."

"Shame." His voice was taunting. "I really thought you were so much more."

It was a kick in the gut, forcing her breath to hitch as she stood looking at him in distress. A flash of something like pity crossed his face, but he hid it almost as quickly as Dalia recognized it.

A few words and their situations flipped. What little control she clung to was stolen from her grasp. The choice to keep quiet was ripped out from under her. There was too much at stake now. Her net was unraveling. Tidesend was under attack by someone who wanted this man, or her, or both. There was no staying now. No promise could be kept when it all burned to ashes.

"What did you think I was?" Her lower lip quivered. She had been given ten years to prepare for the possibility of someone finding out the truth about her. Still, the prospect of this man knowing she was a monster threatened to bring her to tears.

"I think you're a Crystalline."

Her whole world stilled. She hadn't heard that word spoken in so long. He knew exactly what she was. Not just a monster or abomination, as any other human might have called her. No, he knew her by name. The only people who ever called her that, to her limited knowledge, were elves. The same ones who tortured her, subjected her and the other stolen children to so much in order to make them into weapons. This healing power she possessed came from such torments, that much she could remember.

"How do you know that word?" Dalia drew back, stepping even farther from him.

"I'm going to assume I am correct, considering you know it as well." A sigh escaped his lips and his voice softened. "It's alright. If I wanted to hurt you. I would have done so already."

It was a fair point, but that word — *Crystalline* — struck every warning bell within her. So many things from her childhood had been repressed. Hidden away in corners of her mind she didn't dare venture to, if only to survive. That word belonged there, locked away where it couldn't hurt anyone ever again.

"Would you believe me if I told you that you aren't the first I've met?" Glenn's question caused her shoulders to slacken, though mistrust still clouded her expression. "He told me that he escaped the camps about ten years ago. In a fire."

The room around her tilted and her hands trembled as she drew them close to her chest. Up until now there was a simplicity to her life. Hold onto the promise. Stay in the North. Her sister would come for her. These were her universal truths, no matter how much she resented them. Yet, mere moments were all it took for her life to spin out of control.

He was telling the truth.

This man knew of her fiery past. The night that haunted her was real. Not just some concoction of a frightened child's imagination. It was a reality, and she wasn't the only one to escape.

Glenn started to close the distance between them. Each step a ginger approach as he navigated towards her as though she was a frightened animal. Hands held out before him as if to say he meant no harm.

"He died, the night you found me," Glenn continued. "That night we were attacked by a group called the Wolven Hunt."

"The Hunts have names?"

"Some do." Glenn scoffed. "This one is a particularly sick joke. They go after Stags, like me. So, they fashioned themselves as wolves."

The picture was finally clear. It was everything Mollie's rumors spoke of. Villages that took in White Stags ended up getting destroyed. This man was a member of that resistance, and she had saved him. Now it brought this Wolven Hunt to their doorstep.

"We have to help them," Dalia said quickly, trying to make

her way past him and through the door. His hand caught the crook of her elbow, holding firm. Dalia gawked up at this man she barely knew. "What are you doing? Let me go. If people are hurt, I can help. I have to help."

"Dalia, listen to me." His grip on her arm tightened. "Do you know what they would do to you if they found you? If they knew what you were?"

"I don't care. This is my fault. I can't just let people die!"

"They wouldn't just kill you," he explained calmly, ignoring her outburst. "They would cut you up. Take your heart and fashion it and the power within into a weapon."

Nausea rolled in her gut as disbelief sunk in. Dalia knew they were created to be weapons, that was the purpose of their magic. It was the reason the elves took children to the camps for experimentation. She vaguely remembered how others in the camp would disappear, but it was always a blur. Somehow, this was worse than any nightmare she could have concocted.

They were not made to be weapons themselves. They were just materials. Their very hearts ripped out and perverted to create tools for the elves to continue their subjugation of Belestara.

She yanked herself free of him, covering her mouth with both hands as she barely kept herself from getting sick all over the floor. If these were the memories she'd locked away, she didn't know if she wanted to ever remember. The courage to face whatever else might have been lurking in the shadowy recesses of her mind threatened to flee her entirely.

"Dalia?"

It was not Glenn's voice. It was the soft tremble of a frightened woman.

"Mollie..."

Mollie stood just beyond the door, her hair and clothes bedraggled, wearing an expression that reflected only terror.

Blood ran down over the bridge of her nose, dripping from a cut near her hairline. She stood there a moment, a glassy look in her eyes, before falling to her knees.

Dalia didn't hesitate, rushing out of the shed and skidding down before her friend.

"Mollie, what happened? Are you alright?"

Clearly, she wasn't. Her usually playful friend was a mere puddle on the ground. Tears streamed down her cheeks, and she hardly seemed to notice Dalia was there holding her. Her head hung low; her palms bracing the sandy stones somehow managed to keep her from sprawling out on the ground completely. She was a ghost of the girl Dalia held so dear.

"It's gone." Her voice was a whisper, a hushed, shaky tone Dalia could hardly make out. "It's all gone."

Dalia's heart raced, her hands grew clammy, and the world once again threatened to start spinning around her. It would have been easy to give into panic, but Mollie needed her now, so at least for this second, she held herself together. Dalia willed her breathing to slow and her heart to stop pounding as she asked questions she did not truly want the answers to.

"What do you mean? What happened up there? Who started that fire?"

"It wasn't just stories. Oh Gods, Dalia. Nora's dead." Mollie's voice cracked as she barely managed to get the words out of her mouth. It didn't answer Dalia's questions, but it threatened to break her all the same. Mollie broke out into sobs, her body wracked by them as she collapsed into Dalia's chest.

Someone was screaming. Dalia couldn't make out who as she was frozen, her only friend clutched to her as she slipped away from herself. Dead. Nora couldn't be dead. She often disliked the woman, but she never wished for her to die. Desperately, Dalia tried to feel something other than numb, but there was nothing. Just a vast emptiness inside her threatening to swallow her whole, and that damn screaming.

It wasn't until Glenn's hand grabbed her shoulder and gave a shake that she realized the screaming wasn't coming from around her, but within. A piece of her past leaking out. The shrieking memory of a little girl surrounded by fire, screaming for her sister as everything around her turned to ash.

"It was them, the Wolven Hunt. It must have been. I'm sorry Dalia, but we have to go. It's not safe for either of us here anymore."

Glenn's voice was so calm, his face measured, and he didn't so much as flinch as Mollie reacted to his voice. Violently, she pulled away and scurried back. In her shock, his presence had gone unnoticed, but now terror took hold.

"Who is this?" The question was a shrill accusation which hurt not only Dalia's ears but her heart.

"It's okay. He's a friend," She tried to reassure her.

"Who is he?"

Mollie was desperate. Her sense of adventure leeched out of her, torn away with the loss of all she ever knew. A mirror to the young lost girl Dalia had once been.

"This is Glenn," Dalia explained as quickly as she could, trying to quell the storm rising within her frightened friend. "I found him after the storm about a week ago and I have been helping him. I'm sorry I didn't tell you but . . ."

Realization dawned on Mollie's face and twisted there. "That's why you needed me to cover for you? This is who you were seeing?"

Guilt stung like bile in her throat as she opened her mouth to explain, but Mollie was not in the mood for reason. She didn't really want answers, she just wanted someone to blame.

"You." She snarled at him. "They were looking for you. Our home is gone, because of you!"

Glenn seemed resigned to accept the blame. He stepped back from the woman. The corners of his lips twisted downward. But Dalia couldn't let him take responsibly. This was on her. The Wolves were at their door, but her choices led them there. Not his.

"They aren't after him. They're after me." This place was no longer safe for her. Glenn's secret could still be kept. Marking him as a White Stag would only condemn him further, so once again she made the choice to protect him.

"You? Dalia, why would anyone be after you?"

The words stung. Sure, she spent her life trying to fit in, to go unnoticed. But she thought if anyone knew her at all, it was Mollie. She'd been the one pushing for her to leave. Dalia thought she'd insinuated that she was meant for more than this village. Maybe she hadn't seen through her facade quite as well as she thought. Words would not be enough to explain. Instead, she simply lifted her hand, hovering her palm over the cut on Mollie's forehead. Glenn stood to the side, worrying his lower lip. Ready for the inevitable fallout.

"What are you doing?"

Ignoring the angry question, Dalia closed her eyes, allowing the caged piece of her to blossom once more. The magic came easier this time, rushing through her veins and spilling from her fingertips. Mollie had seen Dalia mend nets hundreds of times. Her job was often to fix what was broken. Now Dalia could show her what she was truly meant for — mending *people*.

A blue glow entered her eyes as she opened them to see the gash stitch itself back together. The exchange between them shut down as Dalia's work ended. Silence stretched in an uncomfortable way and Mollie frantically touched the tips of her fingers to her head, as though trying to make sense of what just happened. Hope swelled in Dalia that she might understand. That their friendship meant something and would be enough.

Her hope shattered when Mollie's hand connected with her cheek. The sting of the slap was one thing, but the word she spat was worse than any physical blow.

"*Monster.*"

"I'm sorry," Dalia muttered, trying desperately to find her voice.

"Get out. Your kind isn't welcome here."

"No," Dalia replied desperately. "No, please. I can help any others who are wounded. Let me do at least that. And then I'll leave. I promise. Just...let me help."

"Help? Nora is dead because of you!" Mollie's voice was unrecognizable as she lifted herself from the ground and stood over her once friend. Fear may have ruled her when she first arrived, but now rage stood in its place. "Get out!"

The girl advanced, hand raised to strike again. Dalia recoiled, closing her eyes, but the sting of another smack never came. Breath was hard to come by, her chest heaving, but she opened her eyes to see Glenn standing between them, Mollie's wrist caught in his grasp.

"That's enough." His voice was firm, but still somewhat gentle, as he navigated the delicate situation. "We'll go."

He let her wrist drop before turning to Dalia. A calloused hand outstretched to her, and now Dalia knew there was no other path. There was no staying. The shackles of her promise burned away, floating like ash on the wind.

This place she and Mollie once shared. Her little haven when she wanted to pretend staying here wasn't slowly destroying her. It was now the place where their friendship died.

Monster. Maybe she really was one.

All she had left was the hand before her. A caged bird might not know how to fly, but at least she didn't have to learn alone.

Her fingers met his, giving Dalia support to stand through her daze. If Mollie said more or Glenn said anything at all, she didn't know. Freedom didn't feel like she dreamt it would. It felt hollow. A void she didn't know how to fill. Tears didn't come no matter how much she willed herself to feel anything. All she could do was just take one step after the next, towards what she had to believe was the path set out for her the night of the storm.

CHAPTER SEVEN

This time, trekking over the rocks went slow. Dalia wasn't alone. Glenn followed and was still recovering from his injuries. Their pace was slow, lest he slip and make matters worse. She didn't know exactly where they were heading, only that they needed to go. She needed to finally leave this place behind.

It really was gone. Tidesend may never have been a home, but it was where she felt safe for ten years, and now it was just gone.

Once they made it to a less treacherous landing, Dalia stopped to finally take it all in. Not too far in the distance she could make out what remained of the little village. Shouts and cries rang through the evening. Proof enough that not everyone had been massacred in the attack. What was destroyed was the place itself.

The house she once shared with Nora was reduced to nothing. Smoke and soot filled the air, and hot embers still faintly burned in the distance. Smoldering and scorched rubble was all that was left. The need to rush back and help rose within her, to use her gift to save as many as she could, but such desires were foolish. Mollie had been the one person to always care for her, no matter the circumstance. A simple display magic rendered all those years of friendship useless. No good would come from her showing her true self to those people. They would see her dead before they allowed her to save them.

The Crystalline were regarded so widely as monsters, because human suffering was indeed on their hands. Faded memory or not, Dalia knew that well enough from the stories she'd been told growing up. The elves' subjugation of Belestara was so complete because of the magical weapons they wielded. No one would believe she wasn't responsible for this. A Crystalline found in their midst and their town burned to ash, it would seem clear as day.

The logical conclusion, true or not, was that she was a weapon to be used against them. A tool of the elves and nothing more.

All she could do was stand there, watching everything she once took for granted destroyed, as familiarity clawed at her heart. It took root and festered there, making her vision blur.

Her focus was on everything and nothing all at once. There and somewhere else at the same time. Her head hung low and her eyes squeezed tight.

Wait for me.

The memory of her sister's voice was clearer than ever. The levy in her mind holding the memories at bay sprung a leak as the sickening smell of burnt flesh filled her nostrils. Just as if she was surrounded by it all herself, not just watching from afar. As if she was just a little girl again.

Everyone was screaming. Tiny feet stumbled and pushed

against the hard ground. Smoke choked the oxygen from the air, causing her to fight for every breath.

"Ammy!"

Her sister. This was her — her fire. Her power. She had finally broken. Finally exploded and fought back.

Dalia needed to find her. Alone she was nothing. With her sister, she was protected.

She screamed her name. Over and over. Not stopping no matter how raw and painful her throat became. Her voice threatened to give out on her at any moment.

The tiny tents around the Keep were ablaze. Children of all ages ran, screamed, cried, all with a single aim. Freedom. Her sister granted them a chance. A risk even the youngest were willing to take.

"Ammy!"

It was the last word she managed before a firm hand clasped over her mouth, another wrapping around her waist and pulling her back into the shadows against a crumbling wall of stone. She wanted to fight, to lash out. The sound of hoofbeats silenced her desire. A Hunt. Reinforcements for the overrun guards.

"Stay quiet." Her captor's voice had been so calm. So soft and familiar that her fighting instinct left her completely. She turned to look at him. Known him and those dark eyes. Now, he was but a misty form in her memory. Someone she tried to forget. A boy who she somehow knew had given everything for her that night. No name came to her, barely a face. Just those familiar eyes and the aching hollowness of loss.

"Dalia?" Glenn's voice was weighed down with concern. He paused not too far away from her. "We need to keep moving."

With a shaky breath, she fell back into herself. It was just a memory, nothing more. How could she have forgotten it? How could she have forgotten that boy? He'd invaded her night-mares and yet, she still couldn't allow herself to remember him. Easier to forget him and all the others stolen from their families along with her. Remembering meant to accept the loss. If she forgot, she didn't have to acknowledge the guilt consuming her heart for making it out when they hadn't.

Now, she stood by another town destroyed and filled with the dead. Would she forget their faces someday, too? Nora's name could become yet another memory she locked away for the sake of survival.

No, she would not allow that. Not again. Dalia would remember them, and she would strive to reclaim those forgot-ten. More than that, she would make their deaths mean some-thing. Especially that boy, who more than likely died the night of the fire. It felt like the only way to keep his eyes from haunting her to the end of her days.

"It's not your fault." Dalia finally looked to him. Glenn moved to her side, a rock in the storm she was weathering. Still a stranger, but the only constant she had left. "This is what the elves do. There's nothing you could've done."

His words were appreciated, but they didn't make the pangs in her chest stop.

"Glenn…"

"Yes?"

"Promise me." Her voice shook with her body, an anger bubbling within her she hadn't even known she was capable of. "Promise me that if I go with you, we can avenge these people. We can make the elves pay for this."

He was silent for a moment before he reached out a hand to clasp her shoulder. The pressure there gave her a gentle anchor back to shore. "That is the one thing I can absolutely promise you."

THE ONLY ROAD out of Tidesend towards the market was one she knew now, but Glenn insisted they make their way through the forest instead. He explained the Hunt couldn't be far, and they would be watching the road. No matter how easy the path, it would just expose them to the looming threat.

So, through the woods they went. Glenn seemed to handle it all just fine, but Dalia was struggling. Rocks and sand she could navigate with ease from years of experience. This underbrush proved to be far more of a challenge. The thicket caught on the hem of her skirt, tearing at the dark brown linen as she trudged forward.

Walking beside Mollie's cart on a well-beaten path had been far more enjoyable. That would never happen again now. It wasn't an easy thing to swallow. Dalia tried desperately to push the moment from her mind. Yet, it played on repeat in her head, and her cheek seemed to sting all over again.

Distraction was the enemy when trying to navigate, and Dalia's mind was all over the place. It jumped from Mollie to the ashes of Tidesend, her sister, the boy in her nightmares, and back again. Round and round it went until something hard connected with the tip of her boot.

Letting out a little surprised squeak, she tumbled forward, bracing herself for impact with the cold ground. It never came. Instead, a warm embrace caught her. Keeping her upright by pulling her to his chest, Glenn smiled down at her.

"You good there?"

Her cheeks burned as she tilted her head back to look up at him. Perhaps it was embarrassment from her clumsiness, or maybe it was their proximity. Either way, she cleared her throat, trying to reign in her soaring emotions. "Yeah, yeah . . . I'm fine."

Quickly she pulled back some, scrambling to put some distance between the two of them once more. An effort which was met with a chuckle.

"Not used to this kind of thing, huh?"

Dalia set about brushing off her skirts. It was a useless task. The fabric was all but ruined at this point. The hem torn and caked in muck. What mattered was keeping her hands busy and quieting her mind. She was an utter mess from the events of the day. The setting sun and this strange man were only confusing her more.

"Not particularly," she admitted. "I didn't do much traversing before today. Not unless it was walks along a shore or cliffside. I do well over rocks and by the shore, but this forest seems set on trying to trip me up. I'm not what you would call experienced in travel."

"No. Not that." His voice rumbled with a laugh as he spoke. "I mean being held by someone."

Her face must have been beet red. Dalia snapped her attention from her tattered skirt to him, the heat in her cheeks reaching the tips of her ears. She opened her mouth to stammer out some sort of response, but he just turned, continuing on as if he hadn't just utterly embarrassed her.

"You're cute when you blush. It makes your freckles stand out," he called back over his shoulder before motioning for her to follow him. "Come on, we have a lot of ground to cover."

Her mouth hung open at the audacity of this man. No one had ever spoken to her like that. Sure, some attempted to flirt in the past, but most deemed her too much of a hassle and moved on to girls interested in dalliances.

"Wait a minute!" Gathering up the ruined fabric of her skirt she stomped forward, trying to keep up with him. "You can't just say that."

"And why not? I hardly said anything offensive. I could make far more forward comments about you."

Her blush only deepened.

"Mr. Cahill," she said. It was the most formal she had ever addressed him, and he nearly burst out into laughter. Practically snorting to keep his amusement contained. "I do not think this is an appropriate time for—"

"It got you to look something other than broken. Even if it was just to yell at me." He didn't look back, but his words were enough. "Which means my goal was achieved."

So not flirting then? Or maybe it was but that wasn't his only goal. He'd been trying to take her mind off all she'd just lost. Maybe she should have been thankful to him. It worked, after all, and he'd made her forget her bleak situation, if even for a second, just as he said.

Her march forward suddenly halted. Glenn had stopped and turned so quickly she almost collided with him again. Dalia managed to stop in time, but now found herself staring up into those pale blue eyes.

Her mind stilled as she stood there, memorizing the lines of his face. The sharpness there so in contrast with the gentle curve of his lips. He drew her out of the recesses of her own mind in such a way that made her long to linger. The want to grow close to him was palpable, and Dalia couldn't know if it was because he was all she had left or something more. The memory of her only friend turning on her as soon as the truth was revealed emblazoned in her mind, while this man, a stranger, accepted her.

Yet, his gaze did not reflect that he was sharing in the same tranquil moment. It was as if he was staring right past her. Suddenly, he reached out grabbing her wrist. It was not the gentle touch she had come to expect from their few moments together. She drew in a breath at his firmness, brow furrowing, until he uttered a single word. Soft but effective enough to make his intentions known.

"Run."

A twang sounded. Glenn tugged hard at her wrist, and she gave way. An arrow impaled itself in the oak not a few steps from them. Without Glenn's insistence, her skull would have been its resting place.

CHAPTER EIGHT

His pace was punishing. Dalia stumbled over almost every step. Her ankles and feet ached, but the constant pull on her wrist wouldn't allow her to stop. They both knew what was at stake, and Glenn's grip on her held like a vice.

Where she struggled, he soared, weaving through the woods as though he had been born to them. A true stag, bounding forward, not pausing even for a second. It was Dalia who allowed herself to look back over her shoulder, to catch a glimpse of what was chasing them.

Horses. Three of them. Maybe four. Hooded figures mounted on each. Cloaked in shadow and fur. An Elven Hunt. Every human child knew what they were, no matter where or how they were raised. All were taught to fear the Hunts. They had one singular purpose, to kill, and they were damn good at it.

"Don't look back!" His voice was strained as he plowed forward, pulling her behind him in tow. "Just keep moving."

She obeyed, whipping her head back around just in time to hear another twang. The arrow caught the sleeve of her chemise, grazing the skin there and drawing crimson blood. Dalia grit her teeth and allowed out only a whimper. She needed every bit of breath left in her lungs to keep moving; none could be spared to scream.

They were lucky to have avoided the road. It was as hard for the horses to move through the underbrush as it was for them. It was probably the only thing that kept them just out of reach. Dalia wished she possessed her sister's abilities. Fire certainly would have suited them nicely in this moment, but as it stood, she could do nothing but run. Her magic was hardly something she could go on the offensive with. While she assumed Glenn could fight given his affiliation, he wasn't armed.

Their only chance was moving forward, to desperately try to lose the Hunt. To find a place they could hide.

The thundering of horses seemed to be everywhere. The sound of pounding hooves bouncing off the trees around them filled every bit of empty space until Dalia felt utterly suffocated by it.

Suddenly, Glenn stopped.

This time, Dalia did crash into him, connecting hard against his back before stumbling back. His grip still on her wrist was the only thing steadying her enough that she managed to stay upright. Lip quivering, the question of why they'd stopped died before it was spoken as she followed his line of sight. Before them was a hooded figure mounted on a white steed. They'd been cut off by one of the Wolves.

The others couldn't have been far behind; standing still meant being surrounded.

Glenn swung her around to place himself between her and the elf. One hand still firm on her wrist, ready to drag her out of nightmare if able. The only chance of getting out of this was by following his lead, so Dalia pressed against him. Her face practically buried against his shoulder blade.

Peeking out, Dalia could just manage to get a look at the elf who cut off their escape. He wore furs and a hood like all the rest, only the bottom half of his face visible. The slight aquiline curve of his nose and a scowl peeked out from the shadows. If the hood's intended effect was to make the members of the Hunt seem fearsome, it did its job with ease. At this distance she could make out the pelt: a gray wolf, its head resting on the elf's shoulder, the body spilling down like a cloak across his back. From what little she'd seen of the other riders; he was adorned in the most elaborate pelt. A signal he was the one leading this band — the one to fear.

It wasn't a bow he took aim at them with, but a dagger.

A slender graceful weapon, with bits of greyish crystal embedded in its silver hilt. Veins of blue rippled down the blade itself. It was the weapon of someone important.

He didn't move from his horse to attack or even throw the dagger. The Wolf just sat there, merely pointing the tip of his blade at them. Somewhere beneath the terror Dalia was somehow functioning through, confusion poked to the surface. Until Glenn tensed before her. One glance at her companion sparked fear in her belly. Even in profile, his face twisted in horror.

Attention snapped back to the elf before her, the air chilled. A faint glow came to life from the hilt of that weapon, and she sensed something familiar. Something just as much a part of her as breath. Magic.

The blade itself seemed to come alight, power whipped from the tip of it in a blue flurry, hurtling towards Glenn. The force of the blow slammed into the front of his knee, causing it to buckle. A painful grunt left his lips as he tried to push himself up from a kneeling position, but the infernal magic was spreading. Icy tendrils crawled around his legs, his waist, rising up towards his shoulders. Sheer panic drove his movements as he attempted to rip the frozen fragments from his skin, the cold spreading at an alarming rate, battling against his struggles.

Dalia cried out, terrified. This was going to kill him. If she did nothing, Glenn would be completely entombed in ice.

Stolen magic. Taken from the heart of a Crystalline and infused with this weapon to grant the elf abilities, just as Glenn had said.

"Stop!" she bellowed, charging between him and the elf.

The elf said nothing in return. He simply dismounted from his horse just as the other three hooded figures caught up to them. They formed a semi-circle around the scene, their horses bracketing them in.

The Wolf before her didn't remove his hood, keeping his visage hidden. He just stalked forward, looking between the two humans before him. With a twist of his wrist, the ice halted. This wasn't over though, far from it. Those frozen tendrils still reached up towards the Stag's neck and chin, holding Glenn down. One wrong move here and their ascent would continue, and from the fear in his eyes, Glenn knew it too.

"Let him go," she managed bravely, voice and body trembling. "Please, he's not the one you should be after."

"Oh no?" The elf's voice was impossibly low, making him all the more frightening. He stepped right past her, as if she was exactly what everyone else seemed to think she was. Nothing. "I've been hunting this Stag for weeks. He is exactly who I am after."

It couldn't end like this. She had not saved his life just to leave him behind to die. He was the one with a promise to keep now. They had to make their lives mean something.

"I said, stop!"

The scream bubbled up from within her, along with the pieces of herself she could no longer cage. Magic roared to life, flaring out. Her blue eyes took on that all too familiar glow as the gash on her arm stitched itself back together. After nearly a decade, her magic refused to be chained down any longer, acting on its own without her bidding.

Taken aback, the elf truly acknowledged her for the first time. The shadow of a face transfixed on her. His weapon lowered.

Fear coursed through her, remembering what Glenn said his kind did with Crystalline. He would want her alive. With her power shouting to life, she doubted he would kill her now.

What she didn't expect was for him to give her his full attention and step right up to her, placing himself within her space uncomfortably. She drew in a strangled breath as a gloved hand outstretched. Fabric encased fingers hovered mere inches from her, as though he might touch her. Yet he stopped. Something confusing churned in her belly as she stood just as frozen as Glenn. Those fingers curled back softly away from her, his intentions impossible to read, as his hand lowered once more.

He turned from her as quickly as his attention had been snagged, barking orders. "Take the Crystalline, leave the Stag. He'll freeze to death anyway."

"What?" Dalia screamed rushing after him, a mounted hand grabbed the back of her collar, like a dog hauling away a puppy by the scruff. "It was supposed to be me in place of him!"

"I made no such deal." The elf drawled as he mounted his

horse once more, regarding her from the shadows within his hood. "You would do well to make deals more carefully."

Dread pooled in the pit of her stomach. Now they were both going to die, and Glenn would be yet another life on her conscience before the end.

"No!" She struggled against the elf who was hoisting her up towards their saddle, when a horn broke through the air. The hand pulling at her stilled as the elves around them tensed. Dalia glanced back to Glenn — the fear on his face gone. Instead, he wore that same easy grin he had revealed to her only hours ago back in the shed. The one that fit his face so well. Her mind raced, trying to piece together what was happening, when the grip on her collar slackened. A metallic smell of copper filled up her nostrils as something warm splashed her face. Time seemed to slow as she descended, as she realized that the hand grasping her collar was no longer attached to its owner. She hit the ground *hard*.

HER EARS RANG as the world around her sped back up again, spiraling out of control. One second Dalia was trying to just get air back into her lungs, and the next she had to stomach the realization that a battle waged around her. Horror dawned with the understanding that the warm sticky liquid dripping down her cheeks was blood.

The tree line erupted, white cloaked individuals peppered in and out of the trunks. The Hunt was outnumbered and caught by surprise. The elf above her howled in pain. The piercing sound filled her senses so thoroughly that all she could do was just lay on the ground, consumed by the terrifying scene.

A moment later she realized there was a hatchet stuck in

the ground next to her. Blood splattered on its blade. An armored foot came down beside it and a slender hand wrapped around its handle. Dalia's gaze traveled along that arm to look upon the knight who rescued her. A woman in silver plated armor flipped umber braids off her face. There was only time to make out her brown skin and strong jaw before the woman whipped around, yanking the axe from the dirt, and throwing it back. The weapon found its hold in the neck of the now one-handed elf with a sickening squelch.

It took everything in Dalia to keep from screaming. This woman may have saved her, but Dalia was not accustomed to death or killing. No matter her nightmares. No matter the burning village they just left behind. No matter that these elves would have murdered Glenn and taken her for a far worse fate. It still twisted her stomach and the world around her threatened to go blurry and fade.

Only one thought bubbled up to the surface of her mind and kept her from giving into darkness. Glenn. He was defenseless, trapped in a tomb of ice.

Scrambling to her hands and knees Dalia forced herself to move, staying low to the ground, just one hand and one knee at a time. A singular need to get back to his side, allowing her to shut out the horrors surrounding her.

With a frantic urgency she made her way across the ground. Away from the female knight who engaged herself with another of the Hunt. Passed the rearing horses. Her only goal was getting to him.

Luckily the elf with the stolen magic seemed to be preoccupied, as all she could see, trapped in the center of it all, was Glenn. Still on his knees, rocking back and forth desperately in an attempt to break the ice's hold on him.

"Dalia!"

His voice was like a beacon, willing her heart to steady and her mind to still and focus. Crawling forward, she scrambled to his side.

"I'll get you out of there," she said, trying desperately to find a crack in the ice she could start chipping away at.

"No." His voice was firm. This wasn't a request; it was a command. "Dalia, you need to run. Get out of here."

"I didn't save you on that beach just for you to die now!" She was desperate. Not so much as stopping to look at his face, she started clawing at the ice, frantically trying to find a way in. The frozen coffin that kept him from her couldn't be impenetrable, no matter how the cold bit and ripped at her fingers. "They're not taking you too!"

Glenn's protests died. They both knew what she had lost. This Hunt destroyed all that she had known for so long. The cage of her promises had broken apart in the process. The last tether to her sister was gone. By the Gods, she would not allow them to take him too.

Her fingers were rendered red and raw by the time she managed to wiggle them into the space on his neck where the enclosure started. From there she just started tearing, ripping away chunk after chunk. Glenn helped where he could, pulling his body this way and that to try and wiggle free.

The air around them seemed to still as a chill ran down her spine. The sight of her breath suddenly foggy told her all she needed to know. The Wolf was about to use his weapon again. Dalia whipped around and shouted back towards the Stags, someone needed to warn them.

"Look out!"

Whether or not they heard her cry, it didn't matter. Before any of the White Stags so much as turned towards her voice, the ice ripped across the ground, plowing a path towards them. Jagged fractals shot up and impaled four of them at once. Blood running freely, crimson down the stalagmites of ice.

The need to be sick consumed her. That power once belonged to one of her brethren. A child gave their life to create such a horrific weapon. That elf was wielding more than just stolen power. He was wielding a heart taken and twisted into something terrible. This was what they were created for. Dalia was being forced to witness the very reason her childhood had been lost to experimentation and torture. No wonder they were called monsters when their hearts were shoved into instruments of devastation.

Hatred was the only word to describe what burned in her now. This elf corrupted the heart of one of her own and was using it to kill. She would have ripped him apart with her own hands if she could have, but her own skills lay in healing, not destruction.

They needed to go. They couldn't fight against a weapon like that.

Glenn was free enough now to struggle to his feet. With her wrist in his grasp, he took off, pulling her along behind him. It was once again a mad dash through the trees.

"I'm sorry." She heard him utter, barely audible, and the screams behind them were enough to tell her why. The Stags who came to save them, they were being decimated. They stood no chance against a Crystalline weapon. They'd become yet more lives to add to the growing list of those who died so that she might live.

Dalia was about to tear her gaze from the carnage when she saw him. The Wolf's attention pulled away from the battle. Somewhere in the dark shroud of his hood, his eyes bore into hers. So like how those dark eyes in her nightmares followed her. Only those eyes, no matter how they haunted her, filled her with a strange comfort. Not the Wolf's eyes. The eyes of the killer before her, sensed only in the shadows of his face, instilled only hatred and fear.

Glenn forced her on, and The Wolf turned from them with a cry of rage, before impaling yet another rebel with the icy magic of his weapon.

Her fault.

Tears stung her eyes as she made herself turn away from the scene. This was all her fault.

PART TWO:
AMONG THE STAGS

CHAPTER NINE

Golden flecks of sunlight filtered through the lush green canopy by the time they finally stopped moving. Throughout the night, Dalia was sure she'd heard someone following them. Daring to look back had not been an option. Not when dread still curled in her heart from the memory of the Wolf staring at her through the battle. Instead, she pushed her body beyond a limit once deemed unachievable. Thoughts of death chasing their heels the only thing to push her on.

Glenn slowed and dropped her hand, leaning against the hard trunk of an oak tree to draw in unsteady breaths. Dalia fell to the ground beside him. Adrenaline had been the only thing keeping her pain at bay and finally the ache started to set in her bones. Her feet screamed in protest. Dampness pooled in her socks, and she was worried it wasn't just sweat. The result of non-callused feet pushing through miles of uneven ground.

Neither of them said anything. They just stayed there, struggling to breathe in unison.

The footsteps following them grew louder. What she hoped was simply a fit of her imagination now caught up with them. Dalia tried to shoot up, her knees buckling beneath her as she did. Glenn, on the other hand, was still.

"Took you long enough to find me."

His calm voice quelled her panic. Following Glenn's casual statement, the green of the trees gave way to the sheen of metal armor, adorned with a half cape — white and gold. The same colors worn by the Stags. Quickly, Dalia realized who those footsteps belonged to. It was the knight who attacked her captor.

The warrior brushed the sweat and blood from her face with a gloved hand as she marched right up to Glenn. If she was as tired as the two of them were, it hardly showed in her composure.

"Where have you been?"

Glenn just adjusted his face back into that half smile Dalia was starting to associate with him. The Stag turned to lean his back against the tree. This woman's demeanor was frightening and commanding to say the least. It was enough to cow Dalia, but Glenn's posture was comfortable if anything.

"Hello to you too, Bethana. I would have expected a warmer welcome from my beloved sister," he chided.

Sister? These two looked nothing alike.

"Don't you dare!" Bethana bellowed. "I just lost a whole brigade trying to find your ass. I don't have time to play your games, Glenn. And I told you not to call me that."

Glenn merely scoffed at her outburst, smirk still in place.

That explained it. It was a more complicated situation than simple blood it seemed.

She was a mountain. Not in size, but presence. Unyielding, she seemed to be made of disparities — cheekbones, square jaw, and heavy brows in direct contrast with feminine curves and long deep braids pulled up into a crown on her head. Perhaps in her early twenties, her womanhood was adorned without shame. A strength, not a hindrance. Dalia wondered if she would ever be able to do the same.

"Where is Emil?"

Bethana's demand shook Dalia to her core. Glenn was merely somber in response, shaking his head.

A ripple of sadness and fury clenched at the warrior's jaw, before she hung her head. The losses of the day weighing heavy.

"That was the Wolven Hunt, wasn't it?" Bethana's question came in a softer tone. One that teetered on fear. "I was hoping those bastards wouldn't catch up to us."

Glenn nodded. "It was, but they haven't. We're still one step ahead of them."

A scoff rattled her. "And how is that?"

"We have her."

Glenn gestured his thumb towards her, and Dalia suddenly felt exposed. Overwhelmed by the feeling of becoming a playing piece in a game she didn't yet understand the rules to.

THE WHITE STAG camp was much larger than she expected it to be. For all the rumors of the resistance that made their way up as far north as Tidesend, Dalia never imagined the scale of the operation. This wasn't just a few bandits coming together. This was an army.

A sprawling white field of tents all grouped together, with so many people bustling about. Blacksmiths, a training ground even. It was so elaborate, so planted and stable. If the stories were able to be believed, she would have expected a ragtag group hardly keeping themselves together. Dalia wondered now if that wasn't more elven propaganda. A way of not allowing their subjects this small bit of hope.

Glenn smirked down at the wonder on her face. "Certainly more exciting than a fishing village. You won't have to dance in the rain to find adventure here."

A new light sparked in her eyes. A burning sort of excitement. For so long she waited for something like this. Purpose for more than what Tidesend allowed her. Though, she couldn't quite bring herself to condemn it as maybe she should. It was too soon a loss.

Their new traveling companion burst between them, stalking past without another word and heading towards one of the tents. Dalia knew now she liked to go by Beth. Despite having a still not fully explained familiarity and perhaps even duty to Glenn, her temper with him ran on a short fuse. The woman spent their whole three-day journey practically interrogating both of them. Criticizing Glenn's every move and choice that led them to those woods.

"Had to go and get Emil killed. You had one job."

Emil. The name of the Crystalline traveling with Glenn before they'd been brought together. The one he'd briefly mentioned to her at the start of this journey. Dalia didn't think it was fair for Beth to blame his death on Glenn. They all witnessed firsthand what a single member of the Wolven Hunt could do when armed with a Crystalline weapon. A human stood no chance against a foe with magic, especially magic that deadly. Glenn couldn't fight against that weapon alone. It might have been easy to blame him, but Beth hadn't been there the night of the storm. She wasn't the one who found him clinging to life by a thread, having clearly fought for Emil and having paid the price dearly.

"I'm sorry," Dalia muttered softly. "She shouldn't treat you like that. You did all you could."

Glenn just waved it off, shoulders lifted in a shrug. "That's just Beth's way. She doesn't like when things don't go as planned. Besides . . ." His voice trailed off a moment. A bit of sadness peeked through the cracks of his easy expression. "Those men who died, they were in her charge. She needs someone to blame, or else she will have to blame herself."

Dalia could understand that. Her cheek burned once more. A faint memory of Mollie's final farewell.

"It still isn't fair. Especially if she's your sister?"

"Ah." He half-chuckled. "Well, that's an even more complicated situation."

Dalia didn't press further.

"You don't deserve such treatment. You fought for Emil. I know you did. I saw what trying to save him cost you."

Her soft words caused him to pause, turning to look at her with the same admiration as the night she'd saved him. A reverence he seemed to show only her. Everyone else received a cool playfulness she was coming to understand as the face he wore like a mask. A shield to hide away beneath. At first, she thought the person she'd gotten to know their first week together had been the act. Now, she was questioning if it wasn't the other way around. Every so often when he looked at her, the shield slipped just a little. Reverting him back to the person who watched her spin in the rain with such a peaceful smile. Dalia found herself praying for those moments and flourishing in them.

"I don't know exactly what I have done to gain such fierce loyalty." His voice was soft, leaning in closer so she might hear him. "But I am thankful for it."

"Thank the Gods," she teased back. "They're the ones who brought you to my shore."

A low chuckle rumbled in his chest, and reaching out, his

thumb caught under her chin. Tilting her head up and back so that she looked directly at him.

"To the Gods then."

Dalia's heart threatened to burst from her chest. Was he going to kiss her? She wasn't so sure it would be extremely out of line if he did. Anticipation fluttered in her chest, but there was nothing. His lips did not met hers, and his hand dropped from her face. Left confused by the exchange, Dalia steadied herself with a breath as Glenn turned from her. His whole demeanor changed back as he shifted his attention forward. Realization hit her that they must have been interrupted, and he really might have intended to kiss her.

Dalia had never been in a position where she'd even wanted that from someone before. It left a confusing coil of tension in her belly. Quickly, Dalia pushed those thoughts from her mind, instead turning her attention to the two who interrupted their moment.

One was Beth, but the person next to her set Dalia to stone. Her chest shook with the weight of her inhale as she examined the person approaching the two of them. They were tall, but not necessarily slender. Curves ran in a gentle cascade down their length. It was more like everything was just stretched a little compared to a human form. Something which made them seem off in an almost ethereal way. That might have been enough to tip off Dalia to what this person was, but the pointed ears peeking out of their short chestnut hair confirmed it.

Her nostrils flared as she flinched back, practically tripping over herself.

An elf.

Glenn caught her, saving Dalia from falling unceremoniously onto her back side.

"It's okay. They're one of us," he explained softly, no judgment in his tone from her fearful reaction.

A second glance at the elf revealed this to be true. Beth stood all too close to them, almost protectively so. Round, golden eyes were filled with what could easily be interpreted as shame, as their new companion drew their lips upwards in an apologetic smile.

"It's quite alright." Their voice was so smooth. A melody on the wind, practiced and even. "This is one of my gentler introductions. Please forgive my companions, my dear. They should have at least warned you."

Every muscle in her body pulled tight. She had met quite a few elves in her life — never one who was understanding. Never one who wanted to treat her like a person and take her feelings into consideration.

"Ah, so it's my fault then." Glenn chuckled before motioning between her and the elf. "Dalia, this is Fionn. Our very own elven traitor."

Fionn wrinkled their nose in his direction, a sheen playing in their golden eyes, a coloration that, to her knowledge, all elves shared. The warrior beside them seemed to tense at the comment. Even if it was made in jest, the need to protect the elf beside her was clear.

"Show them some respect, Glenn. Without their help we—"

"It's quite alright, sweetheart." Fionn touched the knight's elbow and Bethana quieted.

Dalia marveled at the display before her, trying to piece together their relationship. It certainly felt as if there was an intimate connection between them. She may have only known Beth a short while, but Fionn seemed to have a way of calming the storm within her.

"Glenn, may I please borrow your young friend?" Fionn

asked with a kind smile. "I won't bite. Besides, the general was asking for you."

Stiffness took hold of Glenn at the mention of this general. Dalia might have protested at being left alone with an elf if not for his reaction. The tension in his shoulders alone told her she didn't want to interfere with whatever was about to happen between him and their commander.

Glenn gave a curt nod before turning to her, placing his hands firmly on her shoulders.

"You have nothing to fear here." It was a promise Dalia desperately needed to hear. "You can trust anyone within this camp, especially those two."

The elf's smile grew a little, but Beth just rolled her eyes and gave a scoff.

"I'll come back and find you after you're settled in."

Dalia's gaze locked with his. Up until now, he had been her only lifeline since leaving Tidesend. Maybe it was time for her to start building some new bridges. After all, she couldn't depend on him for absolutely everything. No matter how much she enjoyed his company.

"I'll hold you to that."

His hand trailed up, away from her shoulder, fingers ghosting over her neck as they retreated. Not another word passed between them as he turned on his heels and headed off to the heart of the encampment.

Dalia couldn't help the aching in her chest. A newfound intimacy was budding between them in a way she hardly understood. The desire to be close to anyone never reared its head in her heart before, but Glenn just set her at ease. The way he reached out to touch her. The face he showed her that he didn't to everyone else. The idea of feeling special was enough to make her crave more.

Fionn's outstretched arm dragged her from her longing. "Shall we?"

CHAPTER TEN

Despite Glenn's assurances, Dalia still didn't feel fully at ease around this elf. Yet, she couldn't help but stare. The opportunity to study one of their kind never really presented itself to her before. All the elves from her memory appeared as nightmarish monsters. Hoods had obscured the Hunt from her more recently, so she hadn't gotten a feel for them either, aside from sheer terror.

Fionn was, for a lack of a better word, beautiful. It was really the only way to describe them. Soft brown hair sat upon their head in a gentle puff, longer on top and cropped shorter on the sides. Each part in their hair where the length changed was adorned with a dainty braid. High waisted trousers hugged their curves in a way which easily drew the eye, and on top, a white tunic fell loosely about their form. Around their shoulders hung a well-tailored emerald peacoat.

Human clothes.

It was her understanding from all the stories and broken memories that elves tended to wear things which hardly seemed practical. Their clothes were more free flowing, even their warriors and guards wore outfits that seemed to be draped around them. It lacked the functionality and structure of human tailoring, which Fionn seemed to embrace so easily.

It wasn't only those ears and signature golden eyes giving them away for what they were. The very way they moved was fluid. With hands resting in their pockets, they appeared to almost glide across the grassy campground. It left Dalia feeling like a clumsy oaf in their wake. Elves always seemed like perfect predators in this way to her. For a frightened little girl, the guards moved like wraiths: quick, precise, and deadly. But Fionn did not hold themselves like a hunter, nor did they look at Dalia as prey. Instead, their fluidity was casual. In a way that threw her off guard.

"You're staring."

Her cheeks heated up as she mumbled an apology under her breath. One met only with a bright laugh.

"It's fine. I'm used to it. Most humans, especially in the North, don't get to spend much time with elves." A gleam in their eye and another kind smile set Dalia more at ease. "Honestly, I prefer the staring. It's better than anger. Or worse . . . fear."

The shame flashing across their face when they met not just a few moments ago was all too easy to remember. Her own shame crept in knowing that she might have such a reaction based only on the fact they were an elf. Maybe she wasn't to blame. After all, she knew nothing but torment at the hands of Fionn's kind in her early life. What little memories she still clung to were rife with suffering. It was no wonder she locked what she could of them far away from her conscious mind. Only now could she begin to string together the pieces.

But none of those horrors were Fionn's doing.

A point she would do well to remember when the very

sight of their pointed ears made her skin want to crawl. Fionn was not the person who hurt her. And they were trusted by Glenn. It would suit her well to make some kind of effort.

"I'm sorry," Dalia apologized again. "About before. You didn't . . . I mean—"

Fionn stopped in their tracks, pirouetting so quickly to face her that Dalia hardly followed the motion of it all. She was just suddenly presented with those golden eyes staring down at her with an insatiable curiosity.

"Do you always apologize this much?"

Before Dalia could answer the question, the corners of the elf's lips pulled up. A gentle look shining through their curious gaze.

"You, my dear, have nothing to apologize for. If anything, I owe you an apology. Creeping up unannounced was undoubtedly unkind, especially after all you've been through."

Dalia oddly felt, for the first time in a long while, that she could breathe. No one had ever looked at her and just seen her, acknowledging the things from her past and not brushing them off. This was someone who seemed to know. Glenn had gotten close, but this was true recognition.

"I . . ." she said, her voice cracking as she tried to find it. "I barely remember. I was so young."

Fionn waited patiently for Dalia to continue, and when she didn't, they dipped their chin in a quick nod.

"Sometimes, we hide away the darkest parts of ourselves. So as not to snuff out the light."

The words were a balm. Her eyes stung from the tears wanting to fall. Dalia found purpose in Glenn, but in this elf, she found understanding. Something she needed more than Dalia even realized, and from a source she would have never imagined.

A step forward and the elf held out the crook of their arm for her once more.

"Come, we can speak of all of that when you're ready. For now, you must have many questions."

THEY WALKED the rest of the way arm in arm. Fionn lifted the flap of one of the larger tents for her, and Dalia ducked her head slightly to enter their destination. The sight she was met with nearly took her breath away.

In the center was a large wooden table. Solid, heavy, surely expensive. It alone and their clothes were a statement about the elf's sensibilities. What truly caught her eye, though, was the fact that taking up almost every other bit of available space were rows and rows of books. Shelves lined the white fabric borders, filled to the brim. Even more spilled onto the floor or were strewn across the table. A musty almost vanilla scent filled the space intoxicatingly thanks to those pages. So much knowledge housed in one singular place. It wasn't at all what she expected. Not in the middle of a war camp.

"Welcome to my humble sanctuary."

Dalia scoffed. There was nothing humble about it. The amount of money they must have spent on all these books was unthinkable to a girl like her. Each book was cared for as well. Despite the clutter, there was hardly any dust to be seen. So much work had been done to keep them all in good condition, and the pride shone on Fionn's face.

"I've never seen so many books in my whole life," she said, perhaps a little embarrassed now. Taking a few careful steps forward, Dalia scanned the books on the shelf closest to her. Most of them seemed to be in a language she didn't understand. Elvish, most likely. Fionn spoke Common well enough, but it made sense their books would be in their native tongue. "Are they all yours?"

"Yes," they said with a glow of pride.

"Have you read all of them?"

Oddly musical laughter escaped their lips. Fionn moved to grab a tome off the table flipping through the pages as they spoke.

"What would be the point of lugging around all of these if I didn't read them?"

Dalia reddened a little but smiled at the response at her expense. It was impressive, to say the least. Dalia had learned to read from Nora, but books were quite the commodity back at Tidesend. Having one or two was a privilege —a whole library was unheard of.

"I'm a scholar, of sorts. Self-taught . . . mostly," Fionn said. "My studies mainly focus on Belestara's fading magic and its sources. But I'm sure that is a subject that you're well acquainted with."

Her blush now burned a hot red all the way up to the tips of her ears. It would have made sense for her to have some knowledge of the subject. After all, out of the two of them, she was the one who could actually use magic. But using it and understanding it were two very different things. Fionn's smile faltered the second they saw her reaction.

"Oh. My dear, do you not know how your powers work? Where they come from?"

The question was gentle. Not judgmental. And yet, Dalia still felt lacking. She was Crystalline, but the only life she could remember was trying to hide that fact. Not learning about what she truly was.

"I know some," she offered, trying to explain as best she could. "I know the elves who took me...they changed me. I know I can heal people. I know each of us can do something unique. Glenn told me they—" Her voice failed a moment. The memory of an icy dagger and the sacrifice surrounding it burned fresh in her mind like a brand. "The elves can take our hearts to make weapons. But I don't know how. Nor do I remember what was exactly done to us. Only that it must have been horrible."

Dalia tried to dig it out of the hidden recesses of her mind. Tried to fight through the haze to find something useful. Screwing her face together, she concentrated, wishing she remembered more than those mere fragments. Her sister's voice. The fire. The pain. That boy's eyes. They were the only things swirling around in the depths.

"Come here, my dear." Fionn's voice beckoned her back from within the haze of her memories and towards the table, where they laid down the leather-bound book. Dalia joined them and peered down at the worn pages. There was a simple drawing there. A diagram of what appeared to be a crystal, with notations in that same language she couldn't read.

"This is a Luminite. A crystal that, as far as I know, is found only here in Belestara, and even then, it is growing more and more rare to find a cache. Most of them have been depleted. The magic in our world runs through most of nature in what is known as a ley line. But the tangible form of magic in our world is found in these crystals."

Dalia's eyes widened as she took in the drawing. Only a few lines on a paper, but it depicted so much more. This thing. This Luminite was what made her.

Sensing she was ready to hear more, Fionn continued.

"Belestara is not like my people's homeland. The very heart of your island continent is this magic. It's what keeps everything working." They moved to grab some more books from the shelves. Scattering them open on the table, their voice pitched up in excitement as they spoke. "Over time, this magic has eroded away. Many blame this on your Gods' departure from this land long ago. We may never know the truth but now we only see remnants of the magic that once was. Which is causing quite a few problems."

"Like the Withering?" Dalia questioned, her mind flashing back to the refugees in Bluewater Market. They said the crops in the south were turning to ash. That the land was becoming inhospitable.

"Precisely." Fionn's passion for the subject was beginning to show, their gestures starting to get more exaggerated as they practically bounced from one foot to the other. "No one knows exactly who to blame. The humans blame the arrival of the elves. And the elves blame the humans. Each has their own solutions as well. The elves, as you well know, have been trying to bring magic back in an... albeit misguided way."

Dalia tried to wrap her head around everything being said. "I don't understand. Why us? Why take our hearts? If those crystals have magic like you say, can they not simply use them to make their weapons?"

Fionn raised their hands in an almost defensive manner. It was easy to see Dalia was starting to get a little distressed. Deadly ice from that dagger still fresh in her mind. The idea of an elf using the heart of a child to kill made her want to heave what little food still in her stomach right onto their fine table.

"It's not quite that simple. The crystals themselves can be used, yes, but they flicker out, and quickly. There were a people that could use them, use all magic, in fact. But they are long gone now."

"The Gods," Dalia said with confidence this time. "But as you said, they abandoned us."

"Yes. That is what they say."

So, they were real. Dalia had never been overly religious, but she'd also enjoyed stories of the Gods and would pray from time to time. Not as adamantly as others around her, but it still gave her comfort. That the Gods were real and not simply a story was a hard truth to comprehend. Real enough that maybe one of them was the reason she'd been delivered a dying man and set on this path.

"That still doesn't answer how people like me were given powers. How did they get the crystals to work?"

Fionn paused, worrying their bottom lip a little before they continued. "My people are many things, and unfortunately cruel and power hungry are just a few of those."

Dalia shot her gaze towards the books on the table, both not wanting to make Fionn uncomfortable but struggling with discomfort in her own right. In doing so, something out of place caught her eye.

Not a published book, but a handwritten journal. Curiosity pressed her forward, as she reached out to move the book layered on top of it aside. A drawing of a kind of medical device with a needle was labeled meticulously in elvish on the pages. One glance and she practically threw it from her grasp, slamming the book shut and back down on the table. The look in her eyes something wild, something panicked. Her chest heaving against breaths that barely seemed to get her any air.

"Dalia."

Fionn's voice sounded far away. They were speaking, but she barely heard them. All she heard ringing in her ears were screams. Cries for help. She followed those cries down the tunnel opened in her mind, reaching out for whatever fragment of memory was breaking through the surface.

She fought desperately against the leather straps holding her to the table. All Dalia could do was scream. Nothing more than a child, she cried out desperately for her sister. For anyone, really. The elf who was fiddling with instruments beside her didn't seem to care.

He was unphased by the sound of a child screaming in terror. Almost like it was something he heard many times before.

The rest came in blurs. Having a rag shoved in her mouth to quiet her. A comment about how they seemed to get younger and younger. And finally, there it was. The device from the book. A needle of sorts, connected to a vial of what appeared to be a glowing blue liquid.

Her eyes slammed closed as it pierced her skin, unable to watch. All Dalia could remember from that point was darkness and pain.

"Dalia . . ."

She wasn't standing by the table anymore. With her back hard against a nearby shelf, she sat on the floor, knees pulled up to her chest. She didn't even remember backing away, let alone falling to the floor.

"Dalia."

Fionn's voice was gentle but firm. Their hands rested soundly on Dalia's shoulders as they tried to pull her back to reality. It took a moment for it to register. The sight of an elf holding her jolted Dalia back painfully before she realized she wasn't in danger. A look of shame settled over Fionn's face once more.

After a moment, reality started to come back into focus. Her breathing slowly began to even out and she registered the dampness on her cheeks.

"I'm so sorry," Dalia muttered, trying to grab some sort of semblance of control by apologizing, as Fionn smoothed her hair gently.

"Now what did I tell you about always apologizing?" The scolding brought a weak smile to her face. One that didn't chase away the shame from the elf this time. "It's my fault. I should have been more careful. We should have gone into all of this with more caution. I'm known to get overexcited about things and just barrel in."

Dalia wanted to correct them. Say she could handle it, but she wasn't so sure that was true. Memories of a best-forgotten childhood were seeping out. Piece by piece. Maybe she should have been thankful for this look into her past. A glimpse into all the questions that once consumed her. It should have left her feeling fulfilled, but instead, she was merely haunted by something new. Not questions this time but their answers. To be honest, she wasn't sure which one was worse.

"Come now." Fionn stood and offered Dalia a hand. One she gladly took, allowing the elf to help pull her up. Sniffing away tears as she attempted to brush herself off. Frankly, her clothes were still a mess from the woods and battle. "There will be time to talk later. Let's get you a tent and allow you to freshen up for now."

Questions still lingered. Ones she had been too afraid to ask before with Glenn, frightened they might break the odd connection she was starting to form with him. Still, she needed to know. If she was to take on the goals of these Stags, if they could offer her the vengeance and answers she sought, then she needed to know how that would be achieved.

"Fionn, why do you need me? Glenn made it seem like having me here was important for some reason."

"He didn't tell you?"

She shook her head.

Excitement bubbled back up onto the elf's face, its reappearance comforting her. "My dear, we're going to fix the Withering, and we can't do it without you."

CHAPTER ELEVEN

Dalia started to follow Fionn back out when the flap of the tent swung open and Glenn showed himself in. Relief sighed out of her at the sight. Hopefully, this would be the start of the promised break she so desperately needed.

"Please tell me you haven't been overwhelming our new friend." His voice was as smooth as ever, but something in his expression told her he could see the slight desperation in her gaze.

"Oh, most likely," Fionn said. "But she has handled it smashingly."

Dalia disagreed. She was barely hanging on. Between apparently not knowing a thing about herself, to literally having a panic attack on their floor, she could only assume they were just being kind. Still, she was thankful for it.

"Would I be able to steal her away for a bit?"

To her relief, Fionn nodded enthusiastically. "Yes, yes of course. I'm sure you two must be exhausted even without my ramblings." The elf stepped up to her with a bright smile on their face. "Come and find me whenever you're settled in, and then we can talk more."

Dalia thanked them, promising she would — and truly meant it. Fionn had seen more of her than anyone else, and in such a short amount of time. Despite the complication of their race, she really did want to spend more time with them.

For now, she followed after Glenn, walking back out into the hustle of the camp. Fionn was right, she truly was exhausted. So much had happened in only the span of a few days. Her mind was swimming and her muscles still ached from the journey here. Worse, there was an uncomfortable silence between her and Glenn now as they walked side by side. Questions waiting to be asked making the air between them thick with tension.

"Why didn't you tell me?"

"Hm?" Glenn raised a brow as he glanced over at her. "About what?"

She thought it would have been obvious. Dalia heard his conversation in the woods with Beth. Now, after Fionn's statements, she was beginning to understand. He was never going to leave Tidesend without her. He needed her. They all did.

"You needed a Crystalline, didn't you?" Her voice was firm, wanting answers. "Whatever the White Stags have planned to combat the Withering, you need a Crystalline to do it. Emil died, so you needed me. Why didn't you just tell me?"

"No. No, It's not . . ." Glenn sighed. His confident façade slipping in and out as he tried to explain himself. "It's not so simple as that."

Dalia shifted uncomfortably, his anxiety making her fidget as well.

"Do you need a Crystalline? Yes or no?"

His Adam's apple bobbed. Discomfort flashing out behind the swagger he wore so easily.

"Yes. Yes, we do. And . . . it was a large reason why I asked you to leave with me. But, it wasn't the only reason. I swear."

Dalia wanted to just accept his answer, but she couldn't. Too long in her life she'd kept secrets. She did not wish to be surrounded by more.

"Don't you think maybe it was something I should have known? Before deciding to come here?" Dalia demanded, stepping quickly to put herself in his path. Glenn stopped short of her, brows bunching together. How could he be confused? He must have been able to see why this angered her. "How am I supposed to believe you? It certainly seems as if you'd simply lost one weapon and needed to replace it. And lucky for you one just happened to save you. The Gods really were smiling down on you that night."

The hurt caused her voice to crack a little as she questioned him, and Dalia damned herself for being so transparent. Glenn had become so important to her in such a short time. The idea she could have meant nothing to him besides the fact that her magic might help his cause — it sparked a shamefully unbearable ache in her chest.

"No." Glenn's own voice seemed to be equally hurt. The accusation laid heavy between them. "No, I swear. Dalia, I don't blame you for distrusting me, but please at least believe me on this. I wanted you to come with me, for more than simply our cause. And much more than simply what you are, and what you can do."

Dalia waited for him to say more. She needed him to say more, but silence was all that followed. Once again, they dangled on the edge together, and he stopped just short of taking a leap. It was infuriating.

"Then, why didn't you tell me?"

The question this time was firmer. Dalia stood her ground, squaring her shoulders and pushing her hurt down deep. If she could hide away years of longing, then certainly she could choose to ignore the ache in her chest now. She could pretend there wasn't a flutter in her chest every time she looked at him. Pretend that whenever Glenn drew close to tumbling over the edge they played on, Dalia didn't feel as though she might explode. None of that mattered now. What did, was the truth. And she would have it.

"Dalia, you had just lost so much," he said. "I didn't think you were ready to hear all of that. Honestly, I was worried you might decide you no longer wanted to come."

It wasn't a particularly good answer, but at least it rang true. Dalia chewed on her inner cheek to keep herself from yelling. She tried to see it from his perspective, but honestly, she still felt used.

"You could have allowed me to just make my own choices. No, you *should* have."

Glenn shifted from one foot to the other. She fully expected a fight from him. Instead, what she got was a man with his eyes downturned, looking like a scolded puppy.

"You're right. And for that, I'm sorry." Her jaw slackened and he stammered on. "You rescuing me was a blessing. Not just for me, but for all of this." He motioned generally around him, and she knew what he meant. "This cause is all I have, and I was scared you wouldn't come and my failures in protecting Emil would end us. It doesn't make it right. But it is the truth. We need you. *I* need you."

At his final confession, Dalia's defenses came crumbling down. Now was not the time to keep pushing and needling him for answers on what was between them. Not in the middle of the busy camp. Enough attention had been drawn their way as it was. The fact that he said those words, that she was given some sort of real confirmation she was not alone in whatever this was — it was all Dalia needed to keep going. The kick she needed to tell her this was a path she wanted to keep walking down.

"Just tell me you meant what you said. That you will keep your promise."

"I will," Glenn replied. "We'll make their deaths mean something. Our goals align. The elves will answer for their crimes. With your help, I promise we can make that happen."

"Alright." Softly Dalia let go of the fight, giving him the win. "So then, what comes next?"

His smile made her heart swell. The edges of his eyes crinkled a bit with how much it spread across his whole face. He'd never shown her a smile like that before.

Then his hand was in hers, fingers lacing comfortably. They were in this together, just as they had been from the moment she decided to break her oath for him, and it seemed that fact was not going to change. Nor did she think she ever wanted it to.

"Now, let's get you settled in your new home. Welcome to Camp Hart."

THEY WALKED TOGETHER until her feet couldn't take it anymore, hand in hand. Glenn's pride shone as he introduced her to the place he called home.

Home. It seemed like such a loaded word to her. It was not a thing Dalia had ever really known. Surely, she must have had a home with her sister and parents before being stolen away, but those memories were lost to the wind. Not shut away like her years in custody but, blown off to some unknown place. A part of her life that didn't belong to her anymore. Whoever that girl was with a home and a family, she was gone. In her stead stood an unsure young woman, molded by her lack of belonging.

Tidesend was always meant to be a temporary place; Dalia thought her home would finally come when she was reunited with her sister. In letting her promise go, maybe it was time to accept the idea that home could be more than just her lost relation.

This was clearly a home to Glenn, maybe it could be to her as well.

Shown to a little tent of her own to crash for the night, her exhaustion finally hit in full force. The small space once belonged to Emil, Glenn explained, but now stood empty for obvious reasons.

That night, she hadn't the time or the strength to get a good look around her new abode. Instead, she simply dove into the covers of her just-comfortable-enough cot and allowed herself to drift off to a dreamless sleep. A small reprieve from haunting memories battering at the doors in her mind.

As welcome as rest was, waking up felt like death.

Places she didn't even realize she had muscles were sore. Even worse, it felt like her feet were practically ready to fall off.

With a groan, she managed to push herself halfway up. Bracing her hands on the mattress as she took a moment. Copper ringlets shielded her view of anything else but hair. Excessive exercise was never particularly Dalia's thing, per say. Her hikes gave her a baseline of fitness perfectly suitable for her life, but she had not been prepared for anything like this. Now, as the pain lurched through her bones, she was starting to regret her lack of training in regard to her physical prowess. If only so every move, every bend, wasn't met with agony.

The few moments it took for her to swing her feet over the edge of the cot and sit up went far too slowly. Carefully Dalia tried to roll her neck, her shoulders, anything to try and loosen up her joints. The thought crossed her mind to attempt to use her powers to aid in mending her pain, but she worried the attempt might only weaken herself more with the life exchange necessary. After a few attempts at stretching, she started to realize it was futile and just sat there, finally taking in her new living quarters.

The tent was small, but cozy. The stiff fabric encasing everything was white just like the rest of the tents at the camp. There wasn't much to be found within its walls. The cot she sat on, a rug made out of some sort of animal's hide laid out in the center, and directly across from the bed on the opposite side of the tent was a wooden trunk.

Dalia wondered if Emil's belongings were still inside. After all, he hadn't been reported killed in action until the moment she arrived. She doubted there was time to clear everything out for her. It wasn't as though Dalia brought along things of her own to fill it with. That said, it was uncomfortable.

She wondered if she had known him, this Crystalline who came before her. From what she could gather, he escaped the same night as Ammy and her. But that speculation was all she truly knew about him.

Dalia longed for clarity on so many things, but the more she gained, the more she questioned if knowledge was what she really wanted. Maybe forgetting was a blessing.

"Dalia? Are you awake?"

With a little whimper, Dalia confirmed she was. Honestly though, all she wanted was to be able to go back to sleep. So much had happened in the last few days. She would need to sleep a whole week to just be able to process everything.

"I have some breakfast for you." Beth was the one to poke her head into her little space, holding out a plate of food. The smell of it alone gave Dalia the strength to hobble out of bed and take hold of the plate. The last time she'd eaten a real meal must had been a few days ago. With being hunted by elves, the hunger gnawing in her stomach struggled to gain much of her attention. Now with a plate of eggs and glorious-looking breakfast sausage in her hands, satiating that need was at the forefront of her mind.

"Thank you," she muttered happily, managing to waddle back to her cot. Plopping down, she sat cross-legged on the mess of covers. Popping a bite of egg into her mouth, Dalia hummed in satisfaction. Not bothering to utter another word before continuing to stuff her face.

"Don't thank me just yet," Beth warned, a look of amusement dancing on her face. "I'm just fueling you up. We have a big day ahead of us."

"We?"

That caused her to stop inhaling eggs for the moment. Dalia expected to spend her time with Glenn or even Fionn, but not this woman. Sure, she owed Bethana her life, but she couldn't help feeling a little wary around her. She had been nothing but cold and combative since their meeting. It served them well on the battlefield, but the idea of spending her entire day with this woman was daunting. Especially now, knowing her formal title: Commander Bethana Lachlan.

Daughter to General Lachlan, the man who didn't just run this camp but the entirety of the rebellion.

Glenn explained to her the night before, during their walk about the camp, that he and Bethana were not actually siblings. Her father took him in when he was young. There was nothing official, no papers signed or names given, but he'd been raised as a member of their family. Something the two of them did not always see eye to eye on.

The dark-haired woman nodded as confirmation, and Dalia wished her stomach didn't drop at the thought. She just brought her food. Surely, Beth couldn't be as bristly as Dalia imagined.

"I'm going to guess from what little I saw a few days ago, you've never so much as held a blade before."

Once again, Dalia was found wanting, wishing she came into all of this more prepared. It was one thing to dream of adventure, taking part in one was something else entirely. In practice it required more than a courageous heart.

"No."

"Well then, we have a lot of work to do." Beth stepped further into the tent and left some clothes on top of the trunk for her. "Eat up. You'll need it. And then meet me in the training ring."

A LOT of work was an understatement.

Dalia felt completely out of place entering the ring of fight-ers. By now, the news of a new Crystalline in camp had spread among the White Stags. The gazes of almost everyone she passed seared into her as she made her way to the dusty arena. After so long of doing anything she could to go unnoticed, Dalia didn't know whether their stares should unnerve her or if she found it somewhat exhilarating.

For so long her days were ruled by the fear of what might happen if anyone knew what she was. Dalia had listened to the bedtime stories Nora would tell and the tales Mollie brought from the market. Stories of monsters wielding magic and allowing the elves to have their rule go unchecked, and fear coiled within her at each new account. Not from the terrors in the story, but how the world would perceive her if they knew the truth. Worse, when Mollie found out, is that was exactly what Mollie had seen Dalia as: not her friend, but the monster from those stories. Here, things were different. Everyone was looking at her but none of them were frightened. Wary maybe, but in general they looked at her with a sense of hope.

Just as Glenn said, they needed her.

It was a lot to put on her shoulders, but something in her preened at the thought. Clinging to the way their gazes held fast, like she was something to be cherished, not hidden away.

Yet only a few minutes into training with Beth and she was starting to wish she didn't have such an audience.

The clothes left for her were comfortable enough. A simple pair of brown trousers and a white tunic, much easier to move in than her long skirts. Much cleaner too. The boots were a different story.

While they were most likely the proper choice to outfit her, Dalia fought back tears while shoving her blistered and bloodied feet into them. It didn't get much better as she tried to step through the exercises Beth was showing her. The leather hardly had any give to it and despite the thick socks which cushioned her feet, each step and twist pinched at her raw skin.

Dalia had yet to even hold a weapon. Instead, she spent the last half an hour being taught the basics of how to simply hold herself. Something she might have thought would come instinctively for someone. Apparently, she was gravely mistaken. When it came to being a fighter, there was an entirely different set of rules. According to her new teacher, there wasn't a single thing right about the way she stood, let alone the way she walked or moved through basic exercises.

By the end of half an hour, her hair was plastered to the side of face with sweat. Only then did Beth finally relent, telling her to take a break and get a sip of water.

This whole thing was starting to get under her skin. Dalia hadn't realized by leaving with Glenn that she was signing up for a war. She dedicated herself to their cause in retribution for her childhood and the lost childhood of every Crystalline. Not to mention, the idea of having a place to belong was beyond enticing, but Dalia knew what she was above all else — a healer. The idea of being trained to kill sat in the pit of her stomach like a stone. This was not how she should have been using her time to help them. She didn't even know what was needed from her yet.

"Is all of this really necessary?" Dalia plopped down in the dirt with a canteen, looking out at others in the ring going through a much more rigorous program. Soldiers, preparing for a war she'd not even known was coming. "I'm not a warrior."

"Yes, that is extremely obvious."

Dalia clenched her jaw trying not to be too offended before the expression on Beth's dark features became obvious. There was no malice there, it was more somber, a deep concern set in her brow.

"Emil isn't the first Crystalline we've lost," Beth said softly. "And I've lost too many good people to Hunts."

Suddenly, Dalia was starting to understand her. Glenn tried to explain it before by excusing her actions. Bethana wasn't cold like she originally thought. In fact, she cared more than Dalia had given her credit for. What she was seeing wasn't anger, it was grief. Her family was responsible for these people. *She* was responsible for these people. Now, she was responsible for her as well.

"When they attacked us, it seemed . . . personal." Dalia couldn't help but think back to what the elven leader told them. That he had been hunting Glenn for weeks. Given the look on her face and her nod, it seemed Dalia struck a chord.

"They call themselves the Wolven Hunt and decorate themselves in pelts to taunt us." Bethana's expression darkened and her tone was flat. True anger floated in now. "Wolves are the natural predators of stags, and that's what they aim to be. They would pick us off one by one if they could. I'd never seen them before yesterday. I'd heard rumors that the Wolf leading them had a Crystalline weapon but . . . I didn't want to believe it."

Dalia witnessed firsthand what the Wolven Hunt was capable of. A chill ran down her spine at the thought that she almost handed herself over to them. The idea of elves capable of such cruelty, taking her life only to wield some sort of demented version of her power, twisted her stomach. In the moment, sacrificing herself to protect Glenn made sense. In the light of a new day, it was clear how much she had not thought through that plan.

"I know this will be hard for you but—" Beth's voice lowered to barely a whisper. "I don't want to lose any more people that I'm meant to protect."

Drawing in a deep breath, Dalia pushed past her pain. The motivation and understanding she lacked earlier in the ring, now found. She could not just protect others around her. She needed to also take care of herself. Because suddenly, she mattered. As a symbol, as a person. She mattered to these people even if she barely knew them, and it was intoxicating.

"In that case, we should get me as ready as possible."

For the first time since they'd met, Beth smiled.

CHAPTER TWELVE

"And you said you need my . . . blood?"

"Precisely," the elf answered simply, as though the concept was not disturbing in the least.

Once Dalia cleaned up following her training session with Beth, she was directed back to Fionn's tent for the evening. Tidied up a bit, the place was easier to move through and take in. Books were still laid out on the tabletop, but in a much more purposeful manner. It left Dalia to wonder if the cleaning was for her sake. If they had carefully combed through the books and hidden away anything that might once again send her spiraling.

"My dear, tell me," Fionn said leaning forward to rest their elbows on the table casually. "What do you know of your Gods?"

"I know basically what we spoke about before. Supposedly a very long time ago they walked among us. Took care of us. And then, one day, they disappeared." Dalia often wondered why. So many humans still worshiped the Gods, and yet they had forsaken these lands.

Fionn nodded, standing from their seat and moving towards the shelves. It was a wonder they knew where anything was at all. Yet, they seemed to know exactly where to go, careful fingers tapping spines until they finally rested on what they sought.

"I am almost a hundred years old, and this tale predates even me," they chuckled, pulling the book from the shelf.

Dalia knew elves were long-lived. Not immortal as some seemed to think, but certainly their lifespans were much longer than humans. Fionn didn't look older than twenty if she were to judge them by human standards. The idea of them being a century old was daunting for her to wrap her head around.

"Ah, here." Fionn finished flipping through the pages, moving to sit beside her with the book. The spine was labeled: *The Lumiels of Belestara*. The elf cleared their throat, as though they were about to tell some grand tale, before continuing. "Long ago, this island continent was shared by two peoples: the humans and the Lumiels. The beings that you now call Gods."

Dalia rubbed at her sternum, a little uncomfortable at the explanation. It felt blasphemous to talk about the Gods in such a way. Still, if they truly walked among them at some point, then she didn't doubt it to be true. They would have a name. It made sense they were not always simply known as "the Gods."

"The Lumiels alone could tap into the magic of this land. They could pull upon the very ley line of it and make miracles happen."

"Why did they leave?" Her voice was smaller than she intended.

"Most think it was due to the elves. Centuries ago, my

people invaded your lands, claiming them as their own. Quickly becoming the ruling class. The details are not well known, but the Lumiels did not stay long after elven rule was established."

It stung, though she wished it wouldn't. The humans worshipped the Lumiels. They continued to do so still. Yet, they left in humanity's greatest hour of need.

"How do you know all this?" The question felt like a way to deny the truth. A wish that maybe Fionn was mistaken. Praying their Gods had been forced out, instead of simply abandoning them.

"I have devoted most of my life to researching the Lumiels and what magic they left behind." That infectious excitement was taking hold of Fionn once more as they spoke. "I have spent decades trying to understand how the magic of this continent works. How it can be used, harnessed, and how it might be able to save both human and elf alike from the looming threat the Withering poses."

Her chest expanded as she tried to just breathe and take it all in. Fionn aligned with the White Stags because they shared a similar mission. Dalia wanted to pry more, to dig deeper, and know why they were here and not with their own people. An invasion of privacy would have to wait. There were still pieces of this particular puzzle missing she needed to address first.

"Okay, so you need magic to get rid of the Withering. So where does my blood fit into that? I'm only one person. I know I can heal people, but I hardly doubt I have the strength to heal a whole continent."

Fionn waved the thought away. "Oh no no. That is not what I am suggesting. We need Luminites. If I could get my hands on a cache, I believe with careful study the magic held within them could be used."

"You said they were rare."

"I did." Their golden eyes seemed to flash. "But I know where to find one."

In a flurry, they stood from the table once more. Flipping through the book in hand, before stopping by her side with it practically shoved under her nose. It was in Common this time, but Dalia was hardly given a moment to even look at the pages before Fionn spoke again.

"Legend speaks of a hidden city. Lumiterra. The last known home of the Lumiels. A sanctuary of sorts."

The word left their lips like a benediction. Those words carried more weight than anything she ever heard them utter before. Dalia's lips parted, questions forming and dying there, as the elf bounced away from her, continuing on in an almost dizzying pace.

"The last ten years of my life have been spent trying to find it. Trying to find as many of the Lumiel's temples and ruins as I could. And last year, I finally found something that made all of my research and sacrifices worth it."

With an enthusiastic slam, they brought the book down to the table. Leaning forward over the table, their gaze bore into her, bearing sadness with a mix of an almost mad excitement. Something Dalia was starting to connect with the elf before her.

"I met a Crystalline. Emil. He helped me, and with my magical friend by my side, I uncovered something. Your Gods did not just abandon you. They left behind something. Clues. A way to find Lumiterra. Hidden in one of their temples were runes, guarded by a ward which could only be activated by magic. Something we found out through a happy accident. Emil, in his excitement, pricked his finger on the stone these runes were carved into. The magic running in the veins of every Crystalline brought them to life, providing us with this breakthrough. This proves they must still be watching. They know of the Crystalline and set their wards to only be activated by one of your kind. They must have known of your plight and wished to help."

Every breath shook her chest. It seemed too good to be true. There was some magical safe place hidden away from the rest of the world? Her mind rebelled against the thought. It was most likely a trap of some kind. Yet, her heart ached for it to be true. The loss of her own haven was still so fresh. A gaping hole remained in her heart, begging to be filled.

"They wanted to be found?" Dalia wrung her hands as she considered it all. "Do you think they're there? Hiding in Lumiterra?"

"I cannot be certain your Gods still remain," Fionn replied. "What I do know is there is power there. Enough that we might be able to change the fate of our home."

This cause had not been one she'd even known about until only a few days ago. Her whole life had been about hiding. Staying out of trouble was her only goal, so she could keep her promises. Now, their goals merged. In this there was also a chance. If this path took her down a road only Crystalline could walk, there was still the chance Ammy could find her. At the very least, the possibility that this was a path her sister once walked. Waiting was no longer an option, but that didn't mean she should give up on their reunion completely.

That possibility alone was enough for her to jump at the chance to aid in this quest.

Yet, there was more spurring her forward. It was the look in all their eyes. The eyes of every White Stag she passed on her way to the training ring. How they regarded her with such hope. So like the look Glenn gave her that first night, when he reached for her like she was his deliverance.

Dalia had wished for a purpose all her life. Now, she was

finally being given one. It was not the time to turn away and hide. Not anymore.

"What did this clue you found say?"

A smile crossed the elf's face as she continued down this path with them. Their hand dove into their pocket and produced the leather-bound journal Dalia had found last time. Her body stiffened at the sight, but they did not place it before her. Instead, they withdrew a single piece of parchment, passing it on so she might read it herself.

In the cliffs of the north-most shore
A flower blooms in wait
Follow the glow to find the truth
That will lead you to our gate

"The north-most shore — Tidesend." Dalia looked up from the parchment for the first time, with answers. "That was why Glenn and Emil were there. They were looking for the next clue?"

"You are a quick one," Fionn beamed. "They were, and they found it too before they met disaster, so I'm told. I believe it was in a temple not too far from your village, though I can hardly get Glenn away from General Lachlen for a single moment to discuss it with him and start our preparations on finding the next set of runes."

"What is this about a flower?" Her fingers moved along the paper as Fionn's excitement started to seep into her. "And a glow?"

"The temple we found at the start of this was covered in wildflowers," the elf explained. "All of which seemed to come to life and glow in Emil's presence. I'm assuming this was pointing to the next runes having a similar set up, to make them accessible for someone with magic to find."

Someone with magic. Someone like her. Dalia was standing on the precipice, ready to jump into a world far larger than one she could have ever imagined. Tidesend had been a cage. Now that it was dismantled, it felt like the world spilled out too far, reaching out to places she never even dreamed of. Yet, they were all she wanted now. She wanted to be the person the Stags all thought she was. A beacon of hope.

"Do you truly believe finding this place will change things?"

A deep breath rumbled in Fionn's chest. "I believe whatever side finds Lumiterra, whoever controls those crystals, will control what happens next in our world." They paused, a muscle working in their jaw. "If we don't find it, and my people do, they will use those crystals and start all over again. Create more Crystalline, make more weapons, and I . . . I can't allow that to happen."

Her heart clenched. More children would be stolen if the elves found Lumiterra first. Even if this was a fool's errand, even if finding these Luminites didn't stop the Withering — what choice did they have? The elves could never find this haven. Suddenly, her purpose grew heavy with weight.

"Nor can I."

Chapter Thirteen

The next week was difficult, but also better than most she could recall in her life. Dalia spent her mornings in the training ring. Bethana would always wake her up bright and early with a delicious plate of food. Of course, it always came in exchange for physical labor. Her muscles still protested, and she still had her doubts, but it was slowly becoming routine. Something she desperately needed after all the recent, world-shattering changes she was forced to endure.

Her evenings were spent with Fionn. They were busy trying to find their next move and hadn't opened up to her too much about any discoveries since their last conversation. What they did instead, was offer her a small pile of books and a comfy place to study.

"For when you're ready to face more of your past."

A kind sentiment, and while Dalia was still unsure if she wanted to face down those horrors, she knew it was the right thing to do.

The books themselves were rather clinical, to say the least.

Going into far too much detail about how grinding the Luminites to a powder was needed to create a Crystalline. The substance was broken down through an alchemical process to create a drug. From there it could be injected into a human's veins. Statistics of how many human children survived the transformation were even put forward in one account. About seventy-five percent made it through the initial administration of the drug. After that, they needed to be pushed. The magical abilities manifested after a time of distress, so the children would often be tormented to bring it out more quickly. Unfortunately, with a small attrition rate.

It made her stomach twist. None of it could accurately capture the horror she and so many others endured. And yet, there was an odd peace in understanding exactly what happened to her and why.

Sometimes, Fionn would check in and tell her stories of the Lumiels instead. Offsetting reliving her trauma with grand tales of how the Gods could use all the magic nature had to offer not just a single ability each. How their temples felt otherworldly, and they couldn't wait for her to see one. Obviously, they were concerned for her mental state in facing all of this, and Dalia was thankful for it. Attentively listening to the stories reminded her of Tidesend — of something familiar. It was calming in a way. If not heartbreaking in the fact it was now an elf telling her these tales and not Mollie.

Still, she was most thankful for this chance to learn. For so long she had wanted to fill in the gaps. Desiring nothing more than to wipe away the haze over her mind so she could understand what she was and where she belonged. A lack of knowledge and her promise had held her stagnant for so long. Now, no matter how difficult it was, this elf was offering her a chance to never be trapped again.

No more flashes of memories came to her. Only the familiar

dreams, yet, they were starting to change shape. Ammy's pleas still came to her every night. A vision of her sister's kind face with flames licking up from behind her. Their fiery tendrils wrapped around her arms as she reached out for her. Dalia would try to run to her sister's embrace only to have the vision fade, being replaced by a hazy figure. The only thing visible were those deep dark eyes that bore down to her core.

For some reason, her step never faltered at their appearance. Instead, those eyes propelled her forward. Like she was running towards some kind of comfort. She knew they belonged to him. The boy lost in the fire, along with everything else. This boy must have meant something, but she just couldn't remember. His name and the memory of who he was to her were mere steps beyond her reach.

Dalia never managed to make it to him. No matter how she might try, the rustle of her tent flaps and the amazing smell of those sausages Beth always came offering would stir her before his hand ever met her outstretched fingers.

That morning, Bethana noted she was distracted during their sparring, and she was certainly right. The dream played over and over in her head during each step. Each lunge. Each clumsy attempt to follow her instructor's form. Why couldn't she remember him? Why couldn't she remember any of them besides Ammy?

It was her mind's way of protecting itself, Fionn explained one evening. A defense mechanism to keep itself from breaking. Still, it felt like a failing of her own.

That was not the only plague upon her mind either.

Since they first arrived, Glenn was almost nowhere to be found.

This fact weighted on her heavier than she wanted to admit. She didn't understand. The night they arrived here they were almost inseparable, walking hand in hand. Now, he was as unreachable as the ghosts of her memories. Dalia tried asking Beth about it. Surely, she would know him best, since they were raised together. The warrior only scoffed and gave a warning.

"That man is not worth chasing."

Maybe Dalia should have thanked her. He certainly hadn't been entirely upfront with her about his intentions. Yet, that felt like something she could excuse. These people mattered so much to him, and she was a stranger. It was his choice and while it hurt, she understood.

Logic could not prevail over her heart in this. Her and Glenn, they were tied to one another. A string of fate looped between them that night on the shore. This was not something she was ready to simply let go of. Pursuing it might have been the will of her heart, but it was incredibly hard to do when Glenn was simply absent.

Dalia snuggled into her little corner of Fionn's tent, a heavy book with a map of the magical ley lines of Belestara laid out on her knees. She hadn't wanted to read anything more upsetting that evening, so she instead turned her studies to the way magic flowed through all natural things. It was utterly exhilarating. Dalia always thought her power only drew on her, on her own life force. With the ley lines though, it could be possible to do more. After all, it was all connected. Everything. In theory it was fascinating, but how to go about implementing such a thing, Dalia didn't know.

Loud voices echoed as Fionn entered the tent, followed by Glenn. Her breath hitched at the sight of him. Before the pang of longing could hit too hard, Fionn stomped their way uncharacteristically towards the center table. Dalia had never seen them upset or heard them raise their voice before, especially within this tent. This place was their sanctuary, Fionn had told her so with such reverence that she understood how special it was to them. Something dire must have happened.

"You really mean to tell me that you cannot remember the full inscription?" Their voice was strained, the elf barely holding it together.

In juxtaposition, Glenn was as casual as always. Hands rested in his pockets as he sauntered in after them. Smooth. Unphased. The version of him she was coming to recognize as the mask.

"I told you. We were under attack. I didn't have time to look the whole thing over. I told you everything I can recall." He let out a sigh. "The inscription said to go to the wilds due southwest. It must be talking about Tanbury. That's all we really need right? The location?"

"The Tanbury Wilds are massive." Fionn ran a hand through their hair, practically gripping the loose locks on top in frustration. "Without the rest of what was written there—"

"Relax Fionn," Glenn interjected. "I'm sorry I was trying not to die."

"You had only two tasks!" Dalia drew back further into her corner hearing Fionn yell. Even Glenn's face twisted at the foreign sound. "You were to protect Emil. And you were to find the northern temple and to bring back the clue left there. What you're now telling me is my dear friend is dead, and you don't even have the information he died for?"

Glenn's jaw clenched. Whether it was guilt or anger throwing off his usual calm, Dalia could not be sure.

"We have what we need. It may take us a little longer, but we know where to look."

"Time is against us, Glenn." Fionn's tone came back down, but the anger was still there. "The Wolven Hunt were there. That means they saw what you did not. They are one step ahead of us now. Do you understand what will happen if they find Lumiterra before we do? If they find those crystals first?"

"They won't." Glenn's expression darkened, masking slipping, regarding the elf with a fury and a hint of pride.

Fionn deflated, a breath leaving them as their head hung low for a moment. One more breath and they composed themself again, straightening and looking at their companion with something akin to pity in their eyes.

"I'm sorry my friend. I know you tried for Emil. I should not have said those things."

"No. You shouldn't have."

The look he gave the elf was detached. An attempt to hide back into the facade he wore so well rather than show any real emotion regarding the loss they all had suffered. Dalia wished she could say something to make it easier for either of them, but that would have been foolish. She had not known Emil. While she mustered up the courage to look through his belongings, hoping to find a thread leading to some of the secrets of her past, they'd told her little to nothing about the man. Let alone herself. All the wooden trunk contained was spare clothes and oddly a book on botany, specifically how to identify different kinds of flowers. No, the Crystalline was still an elusive stranger to her. Nothing she could say would fix this for either of them.

Without another word, Glenn turned to leave, his gaze catching hers for a moment. Sadness lingered there. The glisten in his blue eyes suggested the emotions he was holding back. Yet again, he allowed her to see more than the others. Only her. It was like a tug on her chest, a need to go chase after him, but she feared she would only make matters worse. At least she knew now, despite their distance, something she couldn't quite name was still there between them.

"I'm sorry, my dear." Fionn sighed once they were alone again. "I did not mean to disturb you like that."

"It's alright." Dalia kept her voice soft, wishing for nothing more than to be a comfort to them as well. "Can I help in some way?"

"You have done more than enough."

The sad smile on the elf's face brought her own to her lips. Emil had been their friend. Their research companion. Dalia did not think she could fill those shoes, nor did she want to aim to replace the Crystalline who came before her. Perhaps, though, she could forge something new with Fionn instead. The fact she even desired a friendship with an elf was shocking to her. But they were one of the kindest people she ever met, and certainly that meant more than the fact that they were an elf.

"We know where we have to go?" Dalia pressed softly.

"Yes," Fionn nodded. "We leave for The Tanbury Wilds in two days' time."

CHAPTER FOURTEEN

An anxious feeling gnawed at her stomach throughout the next day. The taste of security was so new on her tongue, and yet, soon it would be time to venture out again. Dalia understood the reasons. The mission her new friends held so dear was starting to nestle its way into her own heart, but purpose alone did not keep her nerves in check.

The bustle about Camp Hart rumbled more than usual, something she chalked up to preparing for their leave the next morning. Dalia reported to Fionn's tent for her evening studies, only to stop short at the sight of the elf. Their light brown puff of hair tamed down against their scalp and the well-tailored brown vest clinging to their form could only be described as slick. Even their eyes were adorned with charcoal. It was far too elegant an outfit for another night of studying.

"Dalia?" Fionn finished buttoning their vest before reaching for a velvet emerald green coat. Soft golden embroidery ran along the collar and down its long tails in foreign swirls and patterns. The coat itself was of human make but those embellishments must have been added later. Perhaps by Fionn themselves in a rare show of elven pride. "Are you not getting ready for the festivities?"

"For the what?"

Her confusion only brought out Fionn's delightfully musical laughter.

"My dear, do they not celebrate the Festival of Flora in the north?"

Time, it seemed, had truly slipped away from her. The Festival of Flora was a tradition held midway between Spring and Summer. There was usually feasting and dancing, and people liked to dress for the occasion. Dalia had never been too involved in the festival in years past, but she'd celebrated. Her mind had been so preoccupied with her world flipping on its head that the date had completely slipped her mind, let alone what holidays might have been approaching.

"Do we have time for something like this?" she asked timidly. "Last night when you spoke to Glenn, you made it sound like we had no time to waste."

As they stepped towards her, Dalia couldn't help but note the way they walked — graceful as always. Now, in more form-fitting clothing, the fluid movements were only accentuated, making Fionn seem less human than usual. She wondered if that was why they often wore baggier tunics. If only to try to fit in better with their comrades.

"I spoke out of anger last night. Something I regret very much." Guilt once again danced in their gaze as they explained. "The Wolven Hunt is a problem, but they don't have what we do. They don't have you."

They paused, scooping her hands into their own.

"They cannot find what they seek without a Crystalline. That cursed weapon they possess is not enough, it cannot do what you can. It's not whole. We do need to make haste. But, I think we should be allowed one night to celebrate. We don't get many wins around here, so when they come, we make them count." The sincerity in their tone caused some of her earlier anxiety to evaporate. "I would consider having even part of the next clue and you finding us something to celebrate."

Her eyes stung from the tears threatening to spring to life. Dalia had never felt important to someone before. More and more a sense of belonging was settling gently around her in this place.

"I don't really have anything to wear."

Fionn's eyes danced with excitement.

"My dear, that is something I would be honored to help you with."

Fionn's small living tent was far different than the large opulent space which housed their library. It was much tidier and looked similar to the one Dalia rested her head in each night. The only real difference was two chests sitting in the corner instead of one. Beth's things, the elf explained, before adding that she was also the one responsible for keeping everything so clean.

The contents of their trunk were eclectic, to say the least. They pulled out one outfit after another. Some more traditionally feminine and some more masculine. Some were made of linen and recognizable as human in make while others more fluid and elven in design. All of them in exquisite taste.

"Hmmm, we are hardly the same size," Fionn pointed out, rummaging through the fabric. "I think we can make an elven gown work for your gorgeous figure though. With the way they're draped; it may be more flattering on you than it ever was on me."

By the time Fionn was done with her, Dalia hardly recognized the girl in the mirror.

Her wild hair somehow tamed and brought into submission was plaited down her back. Copper curls woven into a thick loose braid speckled with bits of baby's breath Fionn had expertly tucked into her hair.

No matter how strange she looked to her eye, Fionn's approval was palpable. That alone removed the uncomfortableness of having something of elven make on her body.

The dark sapphire fabric clashed with her fair skin in an oddly pleasant way. The dress was draped on her body with little structure, nearly her whole back exposed in a curving arch from where the fabric rippled from her shoulders. According to Fionn, it wasn't the intended way to wear it, but Dalia looked at her body now and was in awe. The flows of silk were hypnotizing in the way they cascaded down her curves, hugging her round belly and hips in celebration of all she was. Dalia never had the resources to dress in something so fine and blot rouge on her lips. The delicate fabrics and makeup allowed a newfound confidence to brew in her chest. "You, my dear, look stunning."

"This is the nicest thing I've ever worn." It was almost embarrassing to admit, but Fionn took it in stride.

"It suits you."

That was hard to imagine. Her, the girl with no past who grew up smelling of fish was now standing in such splendor. A dress this beautiful fit her like she was born to wear it. An elven one at that. It was enough to cause her breath to rattle in her chest.

"Come on now." The elf grabbed her hand and started to

pull her away from the mirror. "We will be late if you keep standing there gawking at yourself."

No matter her doubt, a laugh burst forth and she surged forward. A spring in her step as she followed her newfound friend out into the night.

The party was being held in the nearest town to camp — Lilivale. Dalia had heard of the town in passing. How they would send food and aid to the rebels whenever they needed. So unlike the isolationists of Tidesend, the people of this village wanted to be active participants in the affairs of their world. The entering Stags were greeted with cheers from the townsfolk. Flower crowns bestowed on each of their heads, along with murmured thanks and blessings.

The joy was palpable, floating in the air along with the sweet thick smell of the blooms surrounding them. These people Dalia had only ever seen either training or performing some sort of duty, they all seemed so giddy. For the first time in a week, the sounds ringing in her ears were not of orders being barked or swords clanging against each other. No, this night was filled with the melody of laughter and music.

"Miss."

A child who didn't come up much higher than her hip stopped Dalia in her tracks. Holding out a crown of pink azaleas.

"For me?"

The child nodded so quickly, blonde hair spilling across her chubby cheeks. A giggle burst forth as Dalia knelt for the little one to crown her.

"What's your name?"

"Anna." She smiled a big toothy grin that shot right to Dalia's heart.

"Thank you," Anna whispered as the flowers graced Dalia's copper curls with their softness. "For protecting us."

The child turned to run, leaving an awestruck Dalia in her wake. The people of this town must have known the consequences their actions could bring upon them. Yet, they believed. One glance down the receiving line and Dalia saw the importance of the Stags cause. Of her own cause.

A single twist of fate and that sweet girl could have been just like her. Taken and mutated into something against reason and will. The White Stags were what stood in the way of such cruelty.

One deep breath and Dalia stood to continue on, lead on by harmony and intoxicating joy. A few of the Stags must have been musicians in their lives before the rebellion as a few minstrels in usual White Stag attire intermixed with the townsfolk and played jaunty tunes. And there, at the very center of everything, was a bonfire. Built for nothing more than to be danced around.

After everything, it was strange to see fire at the center of a celebration. Not a threat of devastation, but a symbol of joy and merriment.

Dalia stayed close to Fionn, navigating through the darkened paths towards the blazing center of it all. As always, she felt eyes upon her. Only now she wasn't sure if it was because of what she was or what she was wearing. Still, she didn't shy away from it. She never would again. Keeping her head high and giggling with Fionn as they quickly made their way down cobblestone streets, her heart accepted a simple fact. She was a person to be seen, not hidden away.

The night was a thrilling blur. Dalia stuffed herself beyond her fill of food, but it was all so good that the thought of holding herself back never crossed her mind. Roast pig, honeyed buns, and a type of flowery wine everyone was passing around. Drinking was not something Dalia was accustomed to in the past, so even the single glass of the amber liquid she consumed went straight to her head. Leaving her wonderfully fuzzy.

"Come here you."

Bethana swooped in between her and her companion, lips claiming Fionn's quickly. The Commander was quite the shocking sight. Her normal armor cast aside for a pale pink dress. The milky color complimented the rich brown hues of her skin so perfectly. She wasted no time after kissing them to pull Fionn with her into the dances. The pair laughing as they joined the fray.

Dalia much preferred her spot on the sidelines, nibbling her food as she watched her friends dance. They were so happy, so free. She may not have known the pair long, but the joy she felt seeing those two dance, it grounded her in an unexpected way. Maybe it was the wine, the music, this place, or maybe their happiness was just so infectious. No matter the reason, Dalia couldn't help but feel almost entirely content.

All except for one nagging feeling deep in her gut.

She wished a stupid amount of her time wasn't wasted looking for him as she sat watching the dancers. Glenn had hardly paid her any mind since the first day they arrived, and while there was the lingering hope she clung onto, doubt still crept in. If she was important to him, then he would have made time for her. She needed to take the hint. It was time to just move on and try not to focus so much on one particular Stag, not when others showed her support and friendship.

"You alright there, my dear?" Fionn wandered back after a few songs. Their chest rising and falling as they tried to catch their breath from the excursion.

"I'm fine," Dalia replied, perhaps a little too quickly. "Please, don't stop dancing on my account."

With a shake of their hand, they laughed. "Your account?

No, I need a breather. That girl is going to be the death of me one day."

A smile rested firmly on her face as Fionn sat down beside her. Bethana was still out there. Dalia could see her spinning and twirling with ease. Maybe it shouldn't have been shocking to her that someone who could wield a weapon with such poise would be able to dance with great elegance as well. All the same, the sight of Beth with so many frills and such a care-free smile on her face was truly something to behold.

"She's truly something, isn't she?" Fionn's voice grew softer, more contemplative. "I could live centuries more and never find someone quite like her."

Dalia ripped her gaze away from the dancers, taking in the elf beside her.

"Why did you join the Stags, Fionn?" The alcohol loosened her tongue, and the questions waiting to be asked since their meeting came before she could think better of it. "Why fight against your own people? For her?"

If the question offended them, Fionn didn't show it. They just stared forward, taking in the dancing woman not too far from them as though she was the only person in the whole celebration.

"That's the simple answer."

Of course it was. The fact these two loved each other was easy enough to see. Dalia could have stopped there, just accepted the simple answer, but she pushed forward. "And the complicated one?"

A sorrow swam in Fionn's eyes. The mixture of shame and pure unadulterated sadness now clouding their gaze made Dalia regret asking almost instantly.

"My people, they are not accepting of what they don't understand. It's even worse when you're nobility."

Her throat constricted and her eyes widened. Fionn, they

weren't just any elf. Her fingers closed around the gentle blue fabric hugging her body. This dress, no wonder it was so fine. Fionn was nobility, and this was possibly a remnant of their past.

"I didn't leave to join the Stags," they continued. "I left because I lost someone. My brother. He died due to my own actions and foolishness. A grave mistake I will never be able to atone for. And in leaving, I discovered my true self. I left behind the elf that was and became Fionn, the elf that is."

Dread fell over Dalia as she realized what she was prying into. From what little she knew of elven culture from her recent readings and the stories she'd grown up on, she knew their views were very strict on certain things. Unlike most humans, they put a lot of stock into their bloodlines. It was her understanding most elven marriages were arranged. Dalia could imagine Fionn would be unable to freely to be their authentic self among their own people. Whereas humans were far more fluid in their understanding of gender and love.

"I'm sorry," she muttered quickly. "I shouldn't have asked."

Fionn shook their head. "I would not have offered it if I wasn't comfortable."

It was a small solace, but Dalia still felt she was in the wrong. Fionn did not have to explain themselves. Not to her, not to anyone.

"All that matters is I am here. I am me. And I have her. Why the daughter of a general, raised to hate my kind would be able to see so easily passed such things and choose me, I will never know. But I am eternally grateful." Fionn's gaze still held on the dancing woman, and the smile that crept onto their face was something poets would dream of writing about. It spoke of devotion. A longing. A reason to fight. One so strong it strengthened Dalia's own ideals with just a curve of Fionn's lips and an understanding.

Drawing a deep breath, the elf stood back up, pausing to look back at Dalia. "I am here because I dream of a future where we can all be free. Elves. Humans. All of us. That is why I choose to fight." With that parting thought, the seriousness in their gaze melted away leaving behind the usual happy go lucky elf Dalia was growing to care for. They ran off, once again being engulfed by the dancers and joining their lover.

So many questions swam about her, but one thing she knew for certain. No matter what sadness lurked in Fionn's past, they were not someone to be pitied. In fact, Dalia admired them. Unlike her, they knew exactly who they were and where they belonged. Whether dancing by the fire, nose in their books, or in Beth's arms, they were home. Dalia could only dream of such self-assuredness.

It was getting late. Not to mention a big day was looming beyond dawn. She was starting to question if it would be best simply to call it a night.

Getting up from her seat, Dalia checked herself for any crumbs or dirt, wanting to keep her borrowed dress as pristine as possible. Making one last glance to the dancers, she smiled. Only to find who she had been looking for all night.

Pale blue eyes locked with hers from across the dancing flames, and Dalia was met with a choice. Go back to camp. Or confront him.

CHAPTER FIFTEEN

"I didn't know if I would see you." There was something a little desperate about all of this, and she knew it. Still, she couldn't bring herself to feel ashamed. Glenn had shown a part of himself to her, allowed them to share something. The loss of it made her heart claw at her chest. If he didn't want the same, she could accept that, but this unknowing was torturous. Glenn needed to tell her right here and now it was all in her head. Until those words were spoken, it was real, and Dalia was willing to fight for it.

The lopsided grin presented in response to her greeting was hopefully a good sign.

"You look beautiful."

"Thanks," she managed to mutter. "Fionn let me borrow the dress."

The awkwardness of this moment crept into her chest, causing her to pause, and worry at her lower lip. She waited for him to continue but all that met her was silence. Still, she waited, giving him the chance to say something, anything. End this torment between them, but when he remained quiet and still, she pressed forward.

"I was looking for you. All night. All week even." It was a pitiful admission; one she might regret in a moment. Despite that fact, it poured from her lips as she could no longer hold in the bitterness missing his presence stirred in her. "I was starting to think you might be avoiding me."

Glenn shifted his weight from one foot to the other. His usual cocksure mask seemed to dissolve as his gaze fell from her. It was enough to tie her stomach in knots.

"I'm sorry. It's not that." No matter his words, it didn't sound like the truth. "The general has been keeping me very busy."

General Lachlan. He was such an elusive figure, and yet, his influence loomed over the entire camp. Dalia had yet to meet the man who had raised not only his daughter but the man she'd come to care for as well. Oddly he showed no interest in meeting the camp's new Crystalline. Odder still, he seemed to only ever summon Glenn to constant duties, while practically ignoring his daughter.

Curious, indeed.

"Did you not have any time to spare for me?"

"I knew you were in good hands with Beth and Fionn."

That may have been true, and Dalia had come to long for their company as well, but they were not him. They were not the catalyst which sent her cascading forward in life.

"I didn't come here because of Beth and Fionn." He knew that. It wouldn't come as a shock. She came here, for him. Sure, her own interests entangled well with the cause they were fighting for. But without him, she still would have been in Tidesend, wasting away in the shackles of her safety there. He was the one who threw the doors of her cage wide open, allowing in death and danger, but also hope, and the promise of something more.

"Dalia—"

"Dance with me."

Her voice cut through his concern, and she held out her hand towards him, nodding back to the fire and the others still moving to the music. Her hesitancy thrown to the wind. After all, one of them eventually had to make a move.

Glenn's throat bobbed. The once proud Stag suddenly looked like nothing more than a fawn caught in a hunter's snare. "I don't really dance."

"I remember. That day in the rain you just watched, but I promise you, it's much more fun when you join in."

His eyes softened as he drank her in, scanning from the tips of her offered fingers back to her hopeful face. For a moment, fear gripped her. What if he refused? Just as that question started to crawl up her chest, it retreated as his hand met hers.

"I hope you don't expect me to know the steps."

Her smile was so wide her cheeks hurt. "It's okay. I don't know them either."

Hand in hand, they entered the fray of dancers. Glenn was stiff as he placed a hand on her hip in an attempt to lead. The tremble there didn't go unnoticed, nerves singing off him louder than the music itself as he put his best foot forward.

It wasn't graceful. It wasn't confident. In fact he moved so disjointedly it was almost uncomfortable. But the fact he was trying was so incredibly endearing.

"Hey," she whispered, leaning in close so he could hear her. "It's just us, yeah? Just us and the rain."

An eyebrow cocked upwards in confusion as she pulled back away from him. Dalia wasted no time with answers, instead throwing her arms up into the air and spinning. Eyes closed, head back, whirling just like she had in the downpour back on their little beach.

This time when she opened her eyes, she didn't see him hiding. Instead, his arms were around her, pulling her back to his body before he spun her again. Slowly, they built a rhythm together. Stiffness gave way to a gentle flow. Each step a little more in time with the music than the last.

Confidence had a tendency of giving way to mistakes, and when Glenn spun her again, Dalia's feet tangled up underneath her. Laughter sprung from her as she collided into him, hands bracing against his chest.

This time, he held firm. Her heart pounded as they just stood there, still in a sea of moving bodies. Calluses met her soft cheek, his hand bravely setting itself there among her freckles. The other idly played with the fabric of her dress at her hip.

"I think if your laugh was the last sound I ever heard, I'd die a happy man."

Her lips parted, sucking in a breath. Words wanted to bubble up, but she couldn't find the will to force them out.

The silence between them stretched out, filling the space and stirring butterflies in her belly. What little inches there were left between them shrunk as Glenn leaned in. His nose brushed hers. Dalia's lower lip quivered, anticipating a kiss she'd imagined for weeks now. Only it once again never came. Pale eyes shot away from her face to look behind her as the rigidity they'd been able to shed rushed back into him.

He snapped to attention, removing himself from her space with a painful casualness.

"I'm sorry, I have to go," Glenn muttered, peeling his hands away from her before clasping them behind his back. "Please, enjoy the evening. We have a big day tomorrow."

"Wait—"

He couldn't just leave, but her protest died as he pressed past her.

She stood there frozen, watching him walk away from the festivities, towards a group of men. One of them she did not recognize. Adorned in armor and a cascading cape amongst a sea of formal dress, she could only assume this was him. The general she had heard so much about.

Disappointment caused her shoulders to dip and grabbed at her throat. Embarrassment threatened to choke forward tears when a hand grasped hers.

"Would you like to join us, my dear?"

She turned to see Fionn and Beth both beaming at her. Her very own knights in shining armor. Dalia nodded quickly and followed her two saviors back into the music, allowing joy to flow back in. Tomorrow she could mourn yet another confusing moment with that insufferable man. Tonight, was for dancing.

CHAPTER SIXTEEN

Dalia fell asleep peacefully that night but woke with what felt like a pit in her stomach. One not chased away by the familiar inviting smell of sausages and Beth's encouraging voice. The world around her seemed to move in a haze. Beth's gentle prodding on if she was prepared for their journey was drowned out by a buzzing Dalia wished she could ignore. Likely more attributed to the wine she consumed last night, rather than a bruised heart.

"Hey." A firm hand on her shoulder helped to pull her more forward, more present. "You okay there?"

"Yeah." The answer came out quickly and easily. Years in Tidesend taught her well to mask her feelings. Dalia mastered how to muddle through without complaint. Bethana raising her brow was enough to show she didn't believe her, no matter how good she was at concealing her emotions. Concern shone in her dark eyes, making Dalia fidget with her food uncomfortably.

"What did that asshole do?"

"What?"

Dalia practically dropped her plate at the abrupt question. She knew Beth and Fionn had at least seen some of what transpired in the fire's glow, so the question was not out of line. Still, Bethana taking interest was surprising to her. Perhaps merely a symptom of them spending the evening together.

"I told you he wasn't worth it, didn't I? I was raised with him after all. I know what I'm talking about." Beth plopped down on the bed beside her. A warm smile graced her strong face, heating up her cold edges a bit. "Men are all pigs, honestly. What happened that made him run off like that? He didn't try and make a move on you, did he?"

In response, Dalia just sat there, her eyelids fluttering a few times. Part of her clung desperately to being heartbroken, wanting to curl up and cry and be lost to the deep disappointment of it all. Yet, something about the way Beth framed it now, just made her laugh. The sound like a bell, breaking away the haze which threatened to engulf her.

"Sort of? But that's not the problem." Her red curls shook with her head before she leaned closer to the other woman, lowering her voice to a playful whisper. "The problem is that he won't *fully* make one. He keeps acting like he's going to kiss me but then he never does." Bethana had the good sense to gasp, bringing forth yet another joyous laugh from Dalia.

"The nerve! What a bastard."

The tension broken, the two women ate their breakfast together with smiles on their faces. The sting of last night slowly washed away. It was not until they were almost done with their plates that Beth spoke again.

"So, why did he really leave then?"

Dalia pushed the last remnants of scrambled eggs around with her fork.

"Your father . . . the general, I mean. He showed up and suddenly everything changed between us."

"Ah." Beth heaved a great sigh. "That makes sense then."

Dalia wanted to press. She wanted to understand why they never talked about him, but she worried it wasn't her place. This was Beth's father after all. It should be her choice to speak of him or not.

Luckily for her, Beth was finally ready.

"He's a hard man. A good general, a great one even, but a shit father."

Dalia worried her lip, but Beth's face stayed calm as she continued.

"High expectations are important when running an army, but thrust on a child . . . well." she shrugged. "I am his only child by blood, but when I was ten, he brought home a stray. Someone else to thrust the weight of his massive expectations upon."

A stray. Glenn.

"In a way it was a relief, but, my father has a way of pitting us against each other. Maybe it's why I don't like to think of him as a brother. We weren't raised as siblings, but as competitors. Each vying for my father's approval. Glenn was an intruder in my family, not an addition. Though admittedly, to no fault of his own. The difference between us is that I gave up on pleasing father long ago. I still love this cause. I still love my men, and I will fight for them with all my heart. But I have also learned to choose my happiness over my father's. Glenn instead became his little pet. Sure, he's closer to my father. He gets all the best missions and is part of the inner circle for every meeting, but the cost is he's miserable. No matter how much he tries to hide it with arrogance and casual smiles."

Beth shifted, turning her kind gaze Dalia's way.

"You know he really does care about you." Dalia furrowed

her brow. She never heard this woman utter a single kind word about her adoptive brother before. More often than not, she would take any opportunity she could to throw proverbial daggers his way or warn her to stay away from him. This sudden defense of his actions caught her by surprise.

"He's not the best at showing this kind of stuff. But . . . I've never seen him act the way he does around you," Beth continued with a little smile. "Yeah, he's a stubborn ass and I have no idea what you see in him. But, give him a little time. If that's still something you want to do. I don't think he's used to having someone in particular to care about. Glenn's whole life has been devoted to the White Stags since he came to us. I don't think he's ever had anything left over to try and give someone. Let him unravel from my father's clutches a bit. If you have it in you to wait, I think he'll come around."

Waiting. Why did it always come down to that? At least it was a skill she was particularly good at.

Dalia's fingers flexed around her fork as she listened. For so long, all Dalia ever longed for was a family. It was hard to accept that maybe not all families were something to aspire towards.

Maybe she read this wrong after all, but not in the way she thought. She was right that he shared her budding feelings for him. Where she had been horribly wrong was in what the barrier was between them. It wasn't some fault in her, but in him. Clearly there was a lot of hurt under the surface yet to discover, and she had been impatient, wanting to jump into what she felt because Dalia never experienced anything like it before.

An emotional, maybe even cosmic, connection with someone strong enough to make her desire any sort of physical intimacy. As exciting and rare as it was, she needed to be willing to wait.

"Beth." Dalia looked up from her plate, taking in a woman she was truly lucky to call a friend. "Thank you."

~

It was a good thing she and Beth spoke because it seemed the team heading to the Tanbury Wilds was quite small. Fionn explained it was better this way. The fewer people they brought with them, the less of a chance they would attract the Wolven Hunt. It was logically sound, but it certainly would have been awkward if she hadn't broken out of her little pity party.

Beth allowed her to borrow some leather bracers, but otherwise she was dressed in her usual tunic and trousers. It was clear they were not intending for her to be involved in any sort of fight.

Counting the steeds waiting for them, Dalia realized they were one short. There was one for Beth, two for the men chosen to accompany them, and one for Glenn. Not one in sight for her to ride.

"You're with me." Her chest tightened at the sound of his voice. Somehow, he'd walked up beside her unnoticed. Glenn wore an outfit much like the one she originally found him in. A white tunic and brown trousers hidden beneath a well fitted charcoal coat. This time he was adorned with leather pauldrons, bracers, and the row of daggers on his belt showed he was ready for what lay ahead. It was clear by his minimal armor the difference in fighting style between him and Beth. She was a warrior, clad in metal and ready for the front lines while he struck from the shadows. The only thing he and Beth bore in common appearance wise were the little wooden stag pins they each wore.

"I can ride on my own," Dalia tried to protest softly.

"While I'm sure you could." Glenn fell back into his smirks and cocksure attitude. By now, she recognized the behavior for what it was. It wasn't confidence. It was a shield to hide just how unsure he actually was. "Without you, none of this plan works. So, that makes you precious cargo."

The young woman prepared to protest once more, an attempt cut short by the rhythmic sound of hooves against the dirt. A chestnut mare approached, carrying a far too graceful Fionn. The elf seemed to move in complete unison with their horse. Like everything else about them, it came as a fluid motion seemingly as natural to them as breathing.

"She can ride with me if she wants better conversation," the elf offered with a wink in Dalia's direction.

Glenn tensed, shooting daggers up at the elf with a single glance. "I wasn't aware you were joining us."

"Of course I am. Someone needs to make sure you don't forget half of the message this time."

The anger radiating off Glenn was palpable. She didn't need to see his fingers curling into fists at his sides to know it was best if she stepped in.

"I'll ride with Glenn," she said. "But I'll be glad to have you with us, Fionn. Gods know I have no idea what I'm doing."

"You'll do just fine," they said. "All you need to do, honestly, is be yourself."

The elf trotted off to the front, meeting up with their lover who seemed quite pleased to have them along. Leaving Dalia to turn to Glenn, hoping to distract him from being too upset over Fionn's want to oversee his mission. She knew from the fight she'd witnessed how important this was to him, what he wanted to prove in all this.

The muscle clenching in his jaw was enough to indicate he wasn't in any mood to talk. So, without another word said, she stood back and allowed Glenn to mount their steed. With a swing of his leg, he easily situated himself within the saddle, before reaching down a hand to help her mount as well. Now sitting behind him, Dalia was unsure what to do with her hands. A blush spread across her cheeks as she contemplated the most proper way to go about this.

"Hang on," Glenn warned with a chuckle. A gentle squeeze of his leg and a tut was enough for them to be off. Giving a gasp at the sudden jerk, Dalia was forced to throw her arms around his waist anyway in order to keep her seat.

Well, problem solved.

Now, they had a long awkward journey ahead of them. The simple comforts of Camp Hart left further and further behind with each stride.

THE NEXT FEW days went by in an awkwardly monotonous fashion. The Wilds were a four-day ride from the main camp, and by day three, the ache in her rear and legs actually made her glad she didn't need to command her own horse.

The first day passing through Lilivale had been the most pleasant part of their trip. The townsfolk cleaning up from the night before still took pause to wave as they passed. Little ones chased after them to throw petals left scattered on the ground from the festivities. It was clear these people truly loved the Stags.

A fact Dalia happily clung to, as she spotted Anna's face among the crowd. A simple reminder of why she was doing this. Why facing her past and her fears was worth the risk.

The rest of the trail had been rather dull. The scenery changed so little with each passing hour, nothing on the horizon besides long rows of fields. Beth explained they needed to go this way. The main roads were treacherous for them, and while Dalia understood, it didn't make the endless rows of fields any less boring.

Nor did it give her anything to focus on besides the hard form she was forced to cling to day in and day out. Dalia would have been happy for any distraction. Instead, all she could think of was his strong abdomen beneath her fingers and firm back she would often find her cheek against when exhaustion threatened. Both brought a blush to her cheeks if she concentrated on them for too long.

At some point she and Glenn would need to talk. The urge to hold on to anger for being left so suddenly still gripped at her heart. Yet, any time she caught a glimpse of those pale eyes, or the way his head cocked to the side when he half assed a smile, she would remember her conversation with Beth and her edges would soften.

On their final night of camping before they would reach their destination, Dalia sunk down by the fire with a groan.

"You alright there?" Beth asked with a smile.

A question she answered with a nod and a whimper before turning to the roasted rabbit Glenn managed to kill for their supper.

The evening was the same as the last few days. Fionn chattered and they all listened, drinking in whatever tale the elf told, Bethana occasionally cutting in to correct some detail or another. It was so easy to be lost in the gentle ease of the evening. Enjoying the comfort and company before facing Gods know what in the Wilds. By some twist of fate or merely because the others wanted to turn in early, she realized it was just her and Glenn left seated. Alone.

The fire's glow bounced off his features. The soft orange glow so reminiscent of the festival.

"What happened?"

"Hm?"

"When we were dancing. I thought . . . I thought you might —" Dalia could not quite bring herself to suggest the truth. That he'd almost kissed her. "Why did you leave?"

His whole attention was transfixed on her now. Those blue eyes a well she desperately wanted to drink from.

"I wanted nothing more than to stay with you." The answer was a tug on her heart, pulling her to inch closer to where he was sitting. "It's just . . . I have a lot of expectations I need to fulfill."

It was just as Bethana said.

"From the general?"

He nodded. "Yes, he's like my father. Blood or not. He's given me so much, and I don't want to let him down."

Dalia wasn't so sure what them dancing together had to do with such expectations, but it was something which clearly hung heavy on him. Their general showed up just as he left, Dalia could only assume he had duties in need of his immediate attention. His constant absence spoke to the fact he was overburdened compared to her other companions, even Beth.

"I should have stayed," Glenn admitted. "I shouldn't have been so distant from you lately. Please know my intention was not to abandon you. I—"

Dalia caught his hand in hers, silencing him. "Apology accepted. So long as you don't do it again."

The smile that broke out across his features was so genuine. Not some show or mask. It was pure, unadulterated happiness which took hold of him. The air between them seemed to thin, losing its unbearable edge. A barrier removed; he leaned forward. Crossing the line into her personal space, stopping just short of his face touching hers.

"I should have kissed you. More than once."

Dalia did not give him the chance to opine on the subject further. Closing those final inches between them and brushing her lips against his tentatively. A haphazard caress lasting only moments before she simply smiled, still mere inches from him.

"Yes, you should have."

Not about to make the same mistake twice, his mouth claimed hers. Glenn surged forward to frame her face in his hands, capturing her in a kiss. Desperate but gentle, stealing the very breath from her.

"We will face this together from now on," he whispered against her lips. An oath as his fingers weaved into her hair. "You have my word."

CHAPTER SEVENTEEN

A half a day's ride led the ragtag crew to a point where the forest was far too dense to continue on horse-back. The limbs of the trees seemed to weave and knit themselves together into a barrier of sorts. The thicket was such a barricade it left Dalia to wonder how long it had been since anyone ever set foot within those limits. There was a stillness in the air that sent a shiver down her spine. The rest of the party seemed to sense it too. Everyone, but Fionn.

The elf dismounted and practically bounced from one foot to the other. It wouldn't have shocked Dalia if they suddenly started clapping like a giddy child. It made sense — they devoted their entire life to studying the Lumiels. Now, they were once again so close to something the ancient race left behind.

The prospect might have thrilled Fionn, but for Dalia, it was terrifying. A cold sweat nipped at the nape of her neck, the desire to flee unfurling within her. This was what they came here to do, and yet, she hesitated.

Glenn's hand reached up, a support cutting through all the self-doubt, and leading her to dismount finally. Their evening of kissing by the firelight a fresh balm over her anxieties.

Her heart was a drum so loud Dalia feared the whole forest might hear its thumping. Standing before those trees, the girl she had once been poked towards the surface. The one standing frozen for a decade. Living in stasis, too afraid to take the steps necessary to claim a story of her own.

Whether he heard her traitorous heartbeat or not, Glenn wore a look of concern. Standing beside her, he was a rock to the crashing waves of her mind. A stark contrast to how they started this journey together.

"You can do this." Somehow, the steady calm of his voice almost convinced her. After all, he had been the one to coax those first few steps into the unknown out of her in the first place. Of course, he would ultimately be the one by her side as she once again stood on such a precipice. Only this time, he didn't push. He didn't ask her to follow him towards a future so terrifying to her. This time he was just there. A comfort as she faced this storm on her own accord for the first time.

So much changed in such a short time. For so long, Dalia was the girl trapped in a net of her own expert weaving, but now she was so much more. These people, her friends, they depended on her. They could not do this without her. She would not fail them.

A simple bob of her chin was all Glenn received in acknowledgment before she willed her feet to move.

The darkness of the thicket loomed closer and closer with each tentative step. No matter the fear boiling away in her gut, Dalia couldn't shake the odd sensation she was somehow meant to be here. That need for purpose propelled her feet forward when her nerve might have given out.

Somewhere deep within her chest, a hum resounded. A low vibration reverberated throughout her entire being.

"This way!" Fionn declared, practically skipping forward through the trees, holding a parchment in their hands. "If we're to start anywhere, we should follow the known ley lines."

Beth rolled her eyes, leaving Dalia to wonder if she might scold the scholar. They all knew there was danger in calling attention to themselves. The Wolven Hunt would still be tracking them. They were lucky enough to cover their tracks and keep them from the main camp. That didn't mean the fearsome Hunt wasn't close on their trail, especially if they had indeed seen the last clue. It was within all their best interests to keep Fionn's excitement in check. Raised voices in the middle of the Wilds would only draw attention to themselves. While Beth didn't chastise them, the warrior did give her lover a gentle nudge. Fionn seemed to instantly understand and keep their mouth shut, silently leading their charges.

The group moved in silence for what must have been almost an hour, drawing deeper and deeper into the heart of the Wilds. The further they got, the more the trees attempted to blot out the sun. It took a moment for Dalia's eyes to adjust. The sparse amount of light filtering in through the leaves only allowed the gloom of dusk rather than the brightness of midday.

Following Fionn's lead, they all stuck close to one another. Dalia might have expected the rhythm of her frightened heartbeat to pick up more and more as they traveled through the darkness, but she could feel Glenn tense at her side more with each passing moment, and an odd sort of calm swept over her.

The hum within her only seemed to grow louder and louder, consuming whatever parts of her might have been fearful. The sound wrapping her in an embrace. Comforting. Beckoning. Tugging. They must have been growing closer because Dalia was aflame. She needed to find it. Whatever was calling to her. Certainly, this was a sign Fionn had properly deduced how to follow Glenn's half-clue after all.

The vibration in her turned violent. The gentle hum shifted, morphing into a buzz like a swarm of bees trapped in her ribcage. No one else seemed to notice, they didn't even bat an eye. A fact which only confused and overwhelmed her even more. Her chest threatened to explode if it didn't stop. If she didn't—

"Dalia?"

Her gaze snapped up to Glenn. She had stopped walking. When did that happen? He was the only one with her now. The others kept their steady pace ahead. Glenn alone stood before her; his brow furrowed.

"Are you alright?"

It should have been such a simple question, and yet the answer felt unreachable. A shaky breath. A too long pause, and then finally, Dalia responded. "They're going the wrong way."

Glenn's brows rose. Surprise etched on both of their features, for even Dalia hardly recognized her voice.

"Wait here, let me get Fionn."

Glenn turned, waving for the others' attention, but Dalia did not listen to his request. It was barely even heard over the buzzing. *Come. Find me. It's this way.* This thing inside her was all that mattered anymore. She turned, heading forward with a newfound confidence and sense of direction. Somewhere over the buzz, she thought she heard Glenn cursing and calling her name, but that could not stop her. All she wanted, all she waited for, it wrapped a noose around her heart and pulled with a force she could no longer ignore.

Lost in her haze of destiny, Dalia pressed forward. Deeper and deeper, she pushed. Desperate to follow the call, to make the burning in her chest stop. What little light still struggled to fight its way through the canopy was almost completely snuffed out by the time Dalia suddenly stopped. Unflinching, she just stood there. Her gaze refusing to focus on anything, instead taking in the forest stretching before her as a whole.

Through the mists of her senses, the sensation of someone touching her shoulder broke through. Only for that hand to be snatched away.

"Beth! What do you think you're doing? Let me go!"

"Give them some space, Glenn."

"No! I need to see—"

Glenn's bellows faded. Her lower lips quivered. Her rigid form fighting against her will to tell him she was alright. What was happening to her?

"My dear . . ."

Fionn's gentle tone cutting through didn't elicit so much as a twitch from her. No sign that she registered her name being spoken at all. Yet through the mist, she heard it. She saw around her, even if she couldn't tell them so.

The elf drew forward, moving to stand directly before her.

"Dalia," they tried again, this time firmer.

Everything started to come back into focus. The magic inside her unfurled, illuminating the irises of her eyes, and faintly glowing tracks down her veins. It was speaking to her. The Wilds themselves. Not the trees or plant life, but the magic slumbering beneath. Somehow, it connected with her own.

"What is happening?" Glenn demanded from behind her.

"You tell me," Fionn replied practically rolling their eyes. "You are the one who was at the last location. What was it like?"

"It wasn't like this! We just searched together and found the stone. Nothing like this happened to Emil!"

Fionn ran slender graceful fingers through their puff of hair, humming.

"Well? Fionn!"

"I'm thinking."

Glenn shoved free from Beth, stalking forward to move in front of Fionn. Making himself the one visible, his hands shot out to grasp onto her shoulders. "Dalia . . . Dalia, please listen to me."

Her shining blue eyes moved to his face, before the ability to speak rushed back into her, along with understanding. "It's here."

"Let her go, Glenn. Let her show us," Fionn pleaded softly.

"No! I don't care about your temple. We can't risk losing her to whatever this is!" Trembling, he kept his grip on her firm. Turning his full attention back her. "Hey, don't do this. Okay? Listen to me. I need you to listen. You have to fight this. Whatever this is, you fight it. You have to come back to us, okay? You—" A pause, his voice cracking as he continued. "You have to come back to me."

Last night, a plea of this nature would have seemed impossible. Even after the clandestine kisses they shared, such a desperate and public display was a shock. The vulnerability he displayed alone broke through.

"It's alright, Glenn."

A fluid motion found her hands framing his face. The hint of a smile showing she was not lost to whatever ancient magic awaited them here.

He seemed to freeze. Closing his eyes at her gentle touch, savoring it. The moment was fleeting, and as Dalia dropped her hands and stepped past him, Glenn looked so small, pulling into himself as she left him in her wake.

The others parted for Dalia, allowing her to lead them. It was at the base of an otherwise unassuming oak tree she finally paused her march forward. For a moment it was just silent. The tension between them was so palpable. The mix of emotions swirling into a hurricane around them. Fionn's excitement, Beth's caution, Glenn's fear, and there, at the center of them all, was the eye of the storm: Dalia and her unnatural calm.

Like it was something she knew how to do since she was born, her hand lifted, fingers resting gently on the rough bark before her. From within her ribcage a faint glow started. Blue, dim at first, and then growing. Power chased down her veins like lightning strikes, running down to her outstretched fingers, it connected with the very essence of the tree. A glow radiated forward from the bark to meet hers. Green. And brighter than anything Dalia could produce.

"The ley line." Fionn was breathless, an awe settling over them. "We're seeing it. That's what this is. It's speaking to her. Connecting with her."

A crack boomed through the quiet. A bolt of energy, and Dalia was thrown backwards. Landing on her backside, she skidded to a halt in the grass a few feet back from the tree with a frightened squeak. The lack of her previous glow left her looking utterly human again. Her breath came in ragged puffs as she came back fully into herself. Glenn was at her side before anything could be said, kneeling beside her with the question on all their minds.

"What was that?"

"I don't know." Dalia's voice trembled as she spoke. "I don't know. The tree, it just pulled me to it, and I didn't know how to stop it."

"The ley line," Fionn repeated. Dalia looked up at them to find tears peppering their cheeks, and a smile cracked across their face. "The heart of the magic in this world. You connected to it."

It was just like what she'd read. And just how Fionn explained her powers worked, how all their powers did. The crystal's essence in their blood streams, tethering them to some invisible force. It seemed a good enough explanation, but this was so much more. This was not just proof. This opened the door to so many possibilities. A million more questions bombarded her and begged to be asked. The ground at their feet seemed to have other plans than to allow them to be spoken, as it began to quake.

Dalia's breath caught in her throat, and while she seemed so confident before, it wasn't truly her. It was whatever this magical ley line had done to her. She froze. Glenn's hand on her wrist and his insistent tugging finally gave her the courage to move. Scurrying back on hands and feet, her backside dragging against the dirt as she pulled back away from the tree.

Before her eyes, the tree sprung to life. Roots withdrew from the dirt like the legs of a spider. The oak's trunk lifted. Up. Up. Up. The tree stretched on its joints to reveal what was hidden beneath. Woven between those wooden tendrils was a ruin. Decaying stone and wood rose before them and no one needed to ask. They knew exactly what this was. The Lumiel temple.

"It wasn't like this in the north."

Glenn's voice was a ghost of his former self. He stuck close to Dalia as if he were her shadow. As if being by her side was the only thing keeping her from being snatched away by ancient magic again. "We just searched and searched, following the flowers until we found the right stone. Emil gave it a drop of blood, and then the next piece of the puzzle appeared in the air before us just as it was carved into the stone. This is something else entirely."

He wasn't wrong. The legends of the Lumiels meant so much to their world. People like Fionn devoted their entire lives to those stories. For people like Dalia, they were Gods to believe in. At night, devout humans would utter prayers that the Lumiels might come for them. That they come to rescue the humans from the ravages of elven kind. Just stories. Faith. What she was staring at now, it was proof all those things were in fact real.

Unable to contain themselves any longer, a shout of utter elation burst from Fionn, as they plunged themselves into the ruins before them.

"Fionn!"

Bethana shot forward. Her frustration with her partner's lack of hesitancy evident in the stiffness of her shoulders as she pursued them. Her men followed reluctantly after her.

Dalia huffed a sigh. Well, at least someone was excited rather than completely overwhelmed. She was still trying to wrap her head around what just happened to her. Though, she knew the luxury of time to think things over was not something they really possessed. Not when they were being hunted.

"Come on. If this is anything like the other two clues, they're going to need me in there."

Brushing off her trousers fruitlessly, Dalia got up to her feet, Glenn's hand on her wrist anchoring her to the spot. The grip stopped any intentions she might have had about just rushing in there.

"Promise me. Promise me, you'll be careful."

It was the same vulnerability shown earlier, and it once again stole the breath from her lungs. This concern, this need in his voice, it was everything she was realizing she wanted from him. Dalia held this moment between them, and what he allowed her to see behind his facade, to nestle in her heart to be treasured.

Softly, she pressed her lips to the corner of his in a chaste kiss.

"I promise."

After what happened before, Dalia was half-afraid she would be pushed down within herself again just by stepping foot in those ruins. Nothing of the sort came to pass, thank the Gods. Instead, she was pretty much left to her own devices, while Fionn fussed and fretted around the place as if it was all their dreams come to life. In all honesty, it was.

Glenn stayed close to her, enough to let her know she had his support, but not enough to smother. This place was completely entrancing. The architecture was so different. Smooth and curving, like it was written in cursive, whereas humans tended to build things with only function in mind. This place felt more like she'd stepped into a painting than a building.

The oddity alone was enough to steal her attention, but what was in a darkened corner caused her heart to skip.

A smooth pillar of rock with a carving chiseled into its surface. Everything else within the small space was so fluid, almost unnatural in its unblemished smoothness. But there, in the corner carved into the stone, was a flower. So unpolished and crude in its design that it sat on the rock like a blemish.

Dalia couldn't make out exactly what type of bloom it was. Its petals were long and swooping. Not like a rose or even the tight-layered petals of the plant she herself was named for. Whoever left this here, they had been talented enough to convey a certain type of flower. Dalia was just not knowledgeable enough to know which one.

"It's the same as on the shoreline." Glenn's attention transfixed to the carving as well, his voice quiet, but more focused than he'd been outside. "That is exactly what we found."

He turned to wave over the others, Fionn muttered something about it being fascinating, as they did a further search of the area.

"So, what do I do?"

This was honestly the part Dalia dreaded. She barely knew how her power worked. It seemed impossible she might be able to wake this stone with her blood alone. Then again, she had just raised a ruin from the ground without any prior experience. Maybe this would be easy.

Fionn's hand stretched back, beckoning her forward. With a deep breath and one last glance at the man beside her, Dalia moved to stand beside them. Even with the trust developed between them, she couldn't help but flinch when the elf drew a knife.

"It's okay." Their voice could be so soothing when they wanted it to be. "Remember I said it reacts to blood. We just need a drop."

Blood. So many elves wanted her for her blood. For what lay in her heart. But those elves, they were not Fionn. If the past few weeks taught her anything, it was that. Fionn, with all their eccentricities and kindness in their eyes. Not just kindness, but guilt, like they blamed themselves for what happened to her. A gentle friendship now bonded them. Something Dalia wouldn't trade for anything. With a nervous smile and steady trust, she offered her hand.

Fionn took it with such care. The tip of their blade pricked her finger, and Dalia drew a hiss in through her teeth. But that was all it was. A small poke and a little squeeze, drawing forward a few drops of crimson red to fall onto the petals carved into the stone.

Almost immediately a soft glow started to emanate from around the blossom, causing Dalia to withdraw her hand quickly. Eyes widening as a bluish glow grew until it finally burst forth from the stone to fill the entire room. Runes appeared on the slab before dancing forward into the air, assembling themselves into words. Or at least what looked like words. They were in a language Dalia couldn't read. Her lips parted, about to ask if anyone could translate, when they started to shift. Flickering in and out of existence before finally they settled, appearing in Common. A proclamation for all to see.

You have done well to come this far,
There's only one more bloom left to find.
Where the mountains split our island like a scar,
Within a field of our names lies what you seek,
May all who find Lumiterra be deemed worthy.

It was silent for so long. Dalia read those words over and over again, trying to make sense of what they meant.

Beside her, she heard the sniffling of tears. Fionn was right. Lumiterra was real. Everything they worked for. Everything they sacrificed for. It was real. The word written right before them. No longer a legend but something tangible.

Without a word, Dalia reached out and took Fionn's hand, knowing she was not the only one whose purpose lay in this ruin. Elf and Crystalline stood there, bonded by more than they could have ever imagined. This moment should have been silent. It should have been sacred. Not interrupted by a chill raising the hairs on the back of her neck and a low voice.

"You become a lot easier to track down when you make the forest glow."

CHAPTER EIGHTEEN

With the large, hooded figure blocking the doorway, Dalia suddenly became aware of just how cramped the space inside the ruin was. It was no bigger than the cottage she grew up in at Tidesend, and the Wolf had trapped them all like rats within those ancient stone walls. There was no question this was the same elf who confronted them before. Had the wolf pelt draped on his shoulders not given him away, the chill in the air certainly would have.

Glancing to where the Wolf stood, Dalia bit back a strangled gasp at the sight of two fallen soldiers cloaked in gold and white. Bethana's men. Blood spilled on the entrance of this holy place.

Rage burned in her. Something deep, eating its way forward as it threatened to burst out. The elves desecrated Belestara enough. Ravaged their lands. Chased away their Gods. Not to mention what had been done personally to her

171

and all the other stolen children. Horrors she couldn't even remember — they scared her all the same. Now, here he stood, mocking them.

"How dare you!" Her voice bellowed off the enclosed space, catching even herself by surprise. "You would spill blood in this sacred place?"

Fionn must have been thinking the same. Their whole demeanor stiffened at her side, but their hand stayed firmly in hers, squeezing and holding tight. Their firm grasp begging Dalia silently not to allow her anger to cause her to charge the Wolf. No matter how angry, or brave, or stupid she was, Dalia knew they lost Emil to this elf already, and almost Glenn. They needed to be calculated in their approach if any of them wanted to make it out of this alive.

"And what do you know of it?" His head cocked to the side, the hood still making it almost impossible to see more than the tip of his nose and the amused curve of his lips.

His next words came after a tut. "Oh Dalia. So noble. So ready to jump to defend anything you think is right."

The Wolf hadn't drawn his dagger, but she felt a chill run down her spine all the same. Her name. He knew her name. Had he been one of the elves to torment her as a child?

No, maybe he just overheard one of the Stags. Dalia wanted to believe that was the truth. There could be no prior connection between her and this murderer. She couldn't bear it, especially not one she couldn't even remember. Yet, the way he drew out her name, chewing on each and every syllable. It was enough to tell her she was wrong.

"You know me?"

A scoff cut the tension in the air. "Clearly I'm the only one of us who remembers."

Her mind was reeling. More than ever, the fact specific memories seemed to be just out of her reach plagued her. The

Wolf knew her. And for some gut churning reason, his tone was oddly offended she didn't know him as well.

There was no point in trying to dig through the recesses of her mind. Not simply to appease an elf who would just as soon see all of them dead. With the exception of Fionn, every elf she ever met had done nothing but torment her. This one could be no different. Whoever he had been to her when she was a child, it couldn't have been someone she would want to try and remember. Dalia didn't want to give him the satisfaction.

A rustle to her left sucked the attention of the room right to it. Glenn and Bethana were in the opposite corner from her and Fionn. Both of their faces curled in distress. Glenn took a step forward, reaching to draw his blade. His impatience winning out over Beth's calm wrath.

"I wouldn't do that if I were you." The hint of a blue glow on the silver blade the Wolf drew from his belt practically stopped her heart from beating and stopped Glenn in his tracks. None of them could stand up to a Crystalline weapon, especially not one as destructive as the one he wielded. Dalia's powers were not meant for fighting, leaving them extremely outmatched, despite their numbers.

"We both know I'm just itching for the opportunity to kill you," he added, the sneer on his lips barely visible.

"Then why haven't you?" Fionn leapt into action. Stepping forward, their arm arched across Dalia's midsection as they corralled her behind them. Maneuvering so they stood between the other elf and the Crystalline. The sheer determination on their face hit Dalia like a punch in the gut. There was a defensiveness there. Their sharp gaze focused only on the hooded figure standing between all of them and the door. Out of the two in the relationship, Beth had always been the one to prove to be confrontational. It seemed if pushed hard enough, Fionn's playful nature reached its limits as well.

"Because I've come to make a deal."

As though sensing what was coming, Dalia pressed closer to her friend's back.

"With her." A dark gloved hand gestured in her direction, and she sucked in a breath.

Glenn's voice shot across the room, anger dripping from his tone. "She has nothing to say to you."

"Oh no?" the dark figure teased. "I don't think she needs you to speak for her. She spoke just fine for herself before. She tried to strike a deal then, even if she wasn't the best at it. I'm just giving her what she wanted."

Her eyes screwed shut a moment. Hearing him out was a mistake. Nothing he would offer wouldn't be a trap. It was what his kind did. Still, there was no other option. Besides dying. They couldn't handle this fight. Maybe there was still a way she could help her friends, even if her powers were useless in this scenario.

"What kind of deal?"

Dalia could feel the eyes of her friends burning into her. Burrowing deep with the hot sting of disapproving emotions. Anger. Betrayal. Fear. Guilt surged through her at their stares, but she knew this was their best chance. No matter their opinion on the matter.

The elf's lips twitched a little. Surprise broke through his fearsome stature. Perhaps that she accepted so easily. Still, it lasted merely a second. A short glimpse into what the mysterious figure could possibly be feeling.

"Come with me." He drew up to stand at his full imposing stature. Dagger in one hand, the other extending. "You come with me. I will take you to where this text describes. Together we can seek out Lumiterra. And in return, I will leave these three breathing."

Such a simple request, but one that would surely damn her.

Going with him could only mean subjugation. They would use her for all she was worth, then take her heart and continue to drain her even in death, further desecrating whatever was left of her memory. Just as he was doing to the poor child whose heart resided in the dagger he wielded.

"Oh, come on," he pressed. "You practically turned yourself over before to save your precious Stag. As I said, I'm just giving you what you asked for."

Dalia's gaze shot to Glenn. His face practically drained of all color, and his hands clenched into tight fights at his sides. They both knew this elf was right. If giving herself over meant she could protect Glenn and the rest of the Stags, she would do it. Their lives were intertwined now. No matter her feelings. No matter the bumps in the road. Her own life force woven into his was what kept him alive, and she had chosen to give a piece of herself to allow him to go on. She would not allow the time given to be cut short now.

The Wolf's hand was still there. So confidently outstretched. Knowing she was beat. Knowing she would take it.

"No!"

The voice didn't belong to who she expected. Dalia thought it would be Glenn to lose his nerve, so when Fionn was the one yelling, shock shook through her. A shock shared by the Wolf, whose attention snapped to the scholar at her side.

Fionn was quick. Elves may not have been able to tap into magic, but they were built more agile and swift than humans. The palm of their hand collided hard with Dalia's chest, shoving her backward to land unceremoniously on the ground in a thud. The choice stripped from her hands, they made one of their own.

In the blink of an eye, Fionn drew their short sword, but even that wasn't fast enough. The outstretched and inviting hand retreated and replaced its beckoning with a dagger. A flash of blue, and the air shifted. Dalia's breath grew visible and Fionn's feet were frozen solid to the stone floor. Ice crept up towards their knees and held firm. Confusion spread across their features as they struggled, tugging and pulling in any attempt to free themselves from the icy bonds. But those frozen shackles wouldn't release.

Dalia watched in horror as the Wolf stalked forward. The ornate blade of his cursed dagger still held towards Fionn. A warning for anyone else who might dare to come forward unless they wanted to suffer the same fate.

"Was that really necessary?" he drawled, the tip of his blade mere inches from Fionn's porcelain neck. "All of this could have been ended without further incident."

He could have killed Fionn. Ended their life with a mere swipe of his wrist, but he instead gave Dalia another chance. His free hand extended towards her position on the ground. Once again beckoning. She could accept his invitation and end this. But yet again, it was Fionn who acted.

"You are not taking her," Fionn said, an uncharacteristic growl in their voice.

Their hand dipped into their pocket and whipped out a spherical object, rolling it across the stone ground. The mysterious ball stopped when it hit the Wolf's boot. A great pop reverberated off every stone in the ruin followed by a flash of light and a high-pitched ringing that filled her head so completely it was hardly bearable. Dalia's eyes slammed shut, wrinkles forming up her nose and between her eyebrows from the force. Palms pressed against her ears in a desperate attempt to stop the ringing and try and reorient herself.

"Now!"

Beth's voice was an echo. Fighting against all her instincts to just shut down to the sensory overload, Dalia opened her eyes. She could not see her friends, still blinded by the infernal flash. But in the emptiness she could hear them scrambling. It took her only a few seconds and the weight of a hand in hers to know this was a maneuver they planned for. Dalia was not privy to all the training and plans of the White Stags; however, it seemed there were plenty of tricks up these rebel's sleeves. When backed into a corner, they could still act. Fionn's alchemy coming into play as more than just science but a weapon.

There was no time to question who pulled her along, so Dalia chose to trust and follow them. An odd sense of remembrance filled her. A hand in hers. Her vision obscured. In the memory, a sharp acrid smell caused her eyes to water. *Burning. Fire.* It always came back to that night. Dalia beat against her mind to remember more, crawling through what she might remember from her dreams, but now was not the time. Emerging from the ruins and into the forest, she could finally make out who was pulling her along. Not the boy from her dreams, but Glenn.

She glanced back over her shoulder. Fionn and Beth were still in there.

"They can take care of themselves. You're the one he wants. We need to move. Now!"

Dalia didn't argue. The Wolf made it very clear what he wanted. He had been willing to walk away from this fight so long as she went with him. Surely, he would come after them instead of wasting too much of his time on the other two. She could only pray, whatever short time they still dealt with him, would leave her friends unharmed.

"It seems we do this often," Glenn teased back at her, cutting through the growing feeling of dread, and bringing some levity to her heart in the way only he seemed to know how. "I'm starting to enjoy getting chased with you."

Her heart fluttered in her chest, and not just from the physical exertion. Whether this was just the playful mask he wore or something more sincere, she didn't care. All she wanted was for this to be it. The two of them, running from a world which wanted them dead. His fingers loosened and allowed her hand to slip into place. Their fingers entwined this time as they ran. He didn't need to pull her along. She would have followed him wherever he led.

Rays of sunlight peeked through the tree trunks not far from them — the edges of the Wilds. They were so close. They just needed to keep pushing and soon they would have the horses to carry them.

A twang sounded somewhere in the shadows to her left, and Dalia whirled just in time to see the arrow. Her breath stuck in her throat as it sailed by her, the edge of the arrowhead barely grazing her cheek, just enough to draw a line of warm red blood. If she thought they missed, her relief was short lived, as the arrow struck home, lodging itself in the back of Glenn's left shoulder.

A strangled sound tried to escape as the man bit down on his teeth. He fought forward, struggling to keep them going, yet he stumbled, falling to his knees and bringing Dalia down with him. Letting go of his hand, she braced herself using her elbows to protect her face as she hit the leafy ground. Fighting back onto her hands and knees, she scanned the tree line desperately from where the shot came from.

How stupid. Of course the Wolf wasn't alone. The rest of the Hunt was surely hidden somewhere within the Wilds. They weren't about to let them leave so easily. Not with her in tow.

That shot was incredible. Someone with lesser skill might have hit her by accident. Judging by the sheer impossibility of the trajectory and the last time they ran into the Hunt, this group either contained an archer with an enormous amount of skill, or they were in possession of a second Crystalline weapon.

The thought shot equal horror and rage through her.

"Stay down," Dalia said, kneeling over Glenn. They wouldn't kill her, but he was as good as dead if the hidden archer got off another shot. They needed a plan or the Stags were never getting out of this place alive.

Hovering a hand over his wound, she could sense the arrow missed any vital organs. "Sorry about this," she muttered, and then, before he could protest, she ripped the arrow free with sharp tug.

Glenn let out a surprised holler, but she was already at work. Eyes aglow, fingers working over him, as she knit back together the torn flesh. The world spun a little after nausea ripping up from her stomach to her chest, but it was a necessary price. They were getting out of this together or not at all.

"A valiant effort."

She stood up straight with a start at the sound of the deep voice before turning to see the dark hooded figure. He had followed them. Distracted by Glenn's wound, Dalia had not even heard him approach. Her stomach twisted into knots. Fionn. Beth. They were nowhere to be seen. An image of their bodies lying broken and frozen to the stone floor flashed across her mind. *No.* Such thoughts needed to be pushed down away from the realm of possibility, even as her body trembled at the prospect.

"Valiant, but futile, considering my archer can still easily kill him." As if by cue, a second dark figure stepped out from behind a tree trunk. Arrow notched and ready to be fired again. Glenn knew better than to stand, though she could feel him lean back against her leg. A silent reminder he wouldn't let them take her.

"My friends?"

"Will live to see another day. Consider it a gift."

Dalia scoffed. "A gift? Why would you—"

"Maybe one day you will remember."

Dalia was still not sure she wanted to remember him. Not all memories were worth having. Still, maybe if she could remember, it would help. She would know why this elf was hunting them and why he was so fixated on her.

The Wolf started to close the gap between them. One step. Two. Three. Each one a painful second drawn out in anticipation of what might happen next. The Wolf made no move to touch her as he had last time, he just stood there, towering over her.

The shadows of his hood shrouding his face made staring up at him akin to looking into a darkened room. Curiosity getting the better of her, Dalia tried to tilt her head to see if she could make out any more of his mysterious face. If she could piece together just who this person was . . .

One side of his lips curled, amused by her attempt. "This little game is getting us nowhere." His voice was smooth and calm. The antithesis of how she felt inside: all anxious fear and anger. She was in turmoil, while he was a calming wave looking to lull her into a sense of security only to ensnare her.

"I quite agree," she snapped back, finding courage in knowing who she stood over. Who she needed to protect. "But I'm not going anywhere with you. Not ever." Even considering it before had been foolish. After all her friends put on the line for her, Dalia hated how she'd almost thrown it all in their faces.

"A pity," he said, his quiet tone suggesting he truly meant it.

Now he did reach out, a gloved finger caught under her chin, forcing her gaze upwards in a surprisingly gentle manner. The urge to recoil slithered through her veins, and Glenn tensed beside her. Dalia held firm, staring into the shadow that was his face with newfound strength. For her friends, she would not budge. For them, she would face down all manner of darkness.

"We both know where you're going next." His voice was barely above a whisper. "We both saw the clue the stone revealed. There is a town on the path to the mountains — Whitehill. I will be waiting there. You have till you reach the mountain pass to change your mind. If you come to me alone, I will spare your friends. If you go for the next stone, I will slaughter every White Stag I can get my hands on."

His finger dropped and Dalia almost faltered. Almost showed the terror she bottled away. Her stance swayed, breath uneven.

He walked past them, moving to stand side by side with the archer, before turning over his shoulder to add.

"This is the last time I can let you leave alive, Dalia. If you do not take my offer, I will not be able to be so generous again."

His voice dipped sincerely, frightened, even. She didn't understand. A chilling implication dripped from his words. Her mind jumped back to their first encounter. That was how she and Glenn escaped so easily. Not because they were clever. Not because Beth was fierce. The Hunt simply let them go.

The horrifying realization washed over her.

There couldn't be a next time. She needed to be brave. She needed to end this. Before this elf — who she couldn't remember — took more from her than he already had. Remembering him would not be a blessing, but a curse. The bits and pieces she could bring forward of her past spoke volumes on what she might remember of him. This was just a sick game. There was no other reason for him to speak so gently to her.

It awoke something deep in her belly. An anger for everything ripped from her childhood. For the years she lost. For her sister. A sister she waited a decade for. Even her long vigil's purpose was stolen away with the destruction of Tidesend. They took everything from her, and now this elf still wanted to toy with her.

Dalia let out a cry and gave into every bit of the righteous anger brewing within her.

She snatched a dagger on Glenn's belt and rushed the Wolf. He didn't so much as move, letting her come and have her attempt. She could hear Glenn yelling her name, telling her to stop, to let him go. It wasn't enough to break through to her senses. She needed this, and the Wolf seemed more than willing to let her try. It was the archer who interfered.

They moved like water. In a fluid motion Dalia could barely see, they slunk between her and her target. Dipping low they whipped around and struck at her knees with the upper limb of the bow. Dalia ungracefully fell to the ground, feeling pathetic as she collided with the dirt. A few weeks' worth of training was never going to be enough for her to even approach a trained elven hunter.

A healer, not a killer.

From her stomach she looked up at the lithe elf before her, whose bow was once again trained on her. Their hood fell back, allowing almost white-blonde hair to spill forth. One look at their features set Dalia's eyes wide. A quick reassessment of the shape of the body before her and its curves gave some confirmation. Dalia thought female elves were not allowed to be warriors. Their strict cultural control on what each gender was allowed to do was far different than humans. A female's presence within a Hunt was a shock to be sure.

The golden eyes staring back at her held no answer to her questions. Only a cold disdain which suggested if she was the one making the orders, Dalia would have been dead by now.

"That's enough, Evanee."

The huntress scoffed at the Wolf's command causing him to press again, his voice as low and calm as it had been when he spoke with Dalia just before.

"That's enough."

A sneer pulled at red-kissed lips, and she lowered her bow, couching down next to where Dalia was still lying on the ground. Up closer, the elf maiden's beauty was even more striking. Yet, the pleasing curves of her face and round cheeks twisted, conveying nothing but coldness. It was not hatred Dalia saw when this huntress looked at her. It was indifference.

"I need to make sure you stay down this time, little weapon," she practically purred. "We can't have you trying that again."

Chest heaving, Dalia stayed put, dropping her gaze to the dirt, not wanting to see whatever was coming next. With a swift motion and a yell she knew distinctively was from Glenn, the elf brought her boot crashing down hard on her head, and then there was darkness.

CHAPTER NINETEEN

Everything was burning. She was back there, the night when she was just a child. Keep Oharn was ablaze. Flames ripped through the tents around the large stone tower, devouring everything in sight. Screams pierced through the blaze, so shrill and loud it was all she could hear.

Anytime she remembered before, the memories would stop there. A mist, a blur. The fire, the screams, the eyes of the boy who grabbed Dalia and delivered her to freedom. At night she would batter against the walls of her mind to try and see more clearly but it was forever in the shadows.

Not now.

Now it was all illuminated. Those flames lighting the dark and fleshing out all her fear had tried to obscure every night before.

Her shoes were practically worn through, and the stony ground stabbed the soles of her feet with every step, but still she ran screaming a name. "Ammy!" A desperate plea from a frightened child. She screamed her sister's name as if it was the only thing she knew how to say.

All around were nothing but horrors. People burning, guards and stolen children alike. It was a mad dash. The moment so many of them waited for. A chance to leave this place, to escape into the woods and never look back.

"Amaryllis!"

Her sister's full name. Lost to the mist of her memories until now came thundering back to her.

A hand clasped over her mouth, silencing her, as she was dragged into an alcove. Dalia struggled against the arms engulfing her small frame, certain if she didn't break free this would be her end. Her future would be nothing but being thrown back into a cage to have the heart ripped from her chest. Used for whatever twisted purpose the elves desired.

The girl thrashed against those arms until she heard his voice.

"Shh, stay quiet. I've got you, little flower."

Her struggle ceased, and she turned to look up at him. Not a mist anymore. Not a blur with dark eyes haunting her dreams, but a boy. Older than she was. A tall, malnourished preteen with black shaggy hair. She remembered him.

Drystan. *His name*. She remembered. Drystan Fletcher.

A boy taken from his family, like the rest of them. Who, like the rest of them, underwent the experiments. But unlike the rest of them, he never developed any powers. He was just a boy. One who's dark eyes bore such a kindness in them the atrocities of this place were never able to snuff out.

One she had wanted to protect.

He pressed a finger to his lips to remind her to stay silent, before motioning for her to follow. Dalia's heart jumped into her throat, but she trusted him, maybe more than anyone else in this horrid place. Maybe even more than Ammy. Where her sister was simmering rage and sharp scolding in the name of survival, Drystan was something else. Something softer, a comfort. He was her friend. The only one she'd ever known. Following him was the only choice. Her power would do her no good in a fight, and despite Drystan's lanky size he was certainly no match for the guards on his own. He was just a child, like she was. Regardless, he was known to take a beating in the place of others more than once.

One of those occasions was for her. No doubt the guards were trying to get her power to finally come to the surface. They often delivered beatings to the children who had just underwent the Crystalline process. Sometimes even taking bets on how long it would take to force the magic out of them. Drystan protected her then. Covered her body with his own, an act which only enraged her tormentors. They left him ultimately bruised and bloody, unable to open one of his eyes. It was then, cradling her friend's head in her lap when her power first sang to her, begging to be set free. Promising to help him.

Only two days had passed since Dalia had discovered her healing abilities, and now something had set Ammy off enough that her fire was tearing through the whole Keep.

She stayed low, following after Drystan. Sticking to the shadows as she tried to push out the sounds of her peers screaming. An impossible feat. Even with his calming presence nearby, the urge to panic and bolt was almost all consuming. Most likely, they were going to die. Just like so many of the others.

Then, a beacon of hope. The entrance of the Keep was not far. Dalia could see it just beyond their current hiding spot. The woods were their best bet. They might try and hunt them down, but out there was a real shot. In the darkness and labyrinth of trees they could be lost, leaving all of this behind. Drystan knew it too. She could see it in his focused gaze, waiting for the right time to try and make a dash for the chance to be free.

"No."

Even in a hush, she could hear his dread. Snapping back to the gate, Dalia saw what sucked the hope right out of her companion. The large crank mechanism started to move; they were closing the gates. If the two of them didn't make it out before that happened, their chance of escape would evaporate. They both knew it, but it was Drystan who mustered the strength and courage to make the choice for them.

"Run! Now!"

Dalia bade her feet to cooperate. Trying to forget the pain shooting through them as she let him drag her along. Little legs hardly able to keep up with his long strides. They were not just running to survive this night, but for a chance at life to begin with. A chance for more than the life shackled to them. It was everything.

Dalia pushed past every limit screaming within her, silently praying Ammy already made it out and wasn't still searching for her. The flames licked at her legs, but Dalia grit her teeth against the pain and just focused on the need to keep moving. It was all she needed to do now. *Just keep moving.*

The gap behind those two heavy wooden doors was growing smaller and smaller. Her heart sank. They were never going to make it. They were never meant to leave this place.

Where her heart faltered, Drystan only pushed harder.

His hand left her wrist, the loss causing the girl to stumble. Instead of meeting the dirt, his arms steadied her.

"On my back. Quick!"

Dalia obeyed, scrambling onto him and clinging to his neck. Drystan pushed to his full height and ran, piggybacking her along with him. Unwilling to leave his friend behind.

They were going to make it. The sliver of freedom just out of reach.

At the last moment Drystan paused, looking over his shoulder.

They both saw the horses approaching. Both knew what nightmares those hooded figures meant. They were not just mere reinforcements for the guards. No, the Crystalline were far too dangerous to let escape, so they'd called upon their most merciless of bands. A Hunt was within the camp. Running from such a threat would do them no good. They would cut them down without prejudice. Even out in the woods, there was little chance of survival if those killers were after them.

It was better to face death now. It was always inevitable for any humans who entered Keep Oharn. Why drag the horrors of this night out?

Dalia shut her eyes, clinging to the young man who held her, and accepted their fate. One Drystan did not allow to come to pass.

"I'm sorry."

The sensation of falling ripped her eyelids back open. He practically ripped her from his back before turning to shove her through the closing gate. Stumbling backwards, her hands outstretched towards him, desperately. Through her distress, he just smiled. There was peace etched on his face as Dalia was allowed a chance. One bought in exchange with his own life. Then the wooden gates closed and her back collided hard with the stone path.

Outside. She was outside the Keep.

The elation was short lived as it dawned on her that, now, she was utterly alone.

"No!" The girl scrambled to her feet, throwing herself at

the heavy wood separating the two of them. Tiny fists pounded on the barrier between them as she sobbed. "Drystan!"

"You need to go, little flower. Find your sister. She started this for you. You need to find her." His voice was muffled by the wood, but he seemed, oddly, calm. "Dalia, I need to draw them off. Or no one is going to have a chance. Now go."

It took every last ounce of strength in her small body to peel herself away. Sobs raked through her as she stepped back.

"I'll find you!" Dalia promised. "You hear me, Drystan? I'll find you."

Not knowing if it was a promise even possible to keep, she branded it to her heart all the same, before turning and taking off into the woods.

All of it was finally clear now, pieces filling in places where they needed to. The life she knew at Keep Oharn, the torment and trials she and the others endured in order to become the building blocks for magical weapons. Some of it was still foggy, but it was there. All of it. Laid in place by this last bit of the puzzle — the reason why those eyes haunted her for so long.

Those eyes did not belong to a monster, but a friend.

A friend she promised to find again, but age and wisdom brought clarity. Drystan died for her that night. Her promises all had been laid bare — all broken.

CHAPTER TWENTY

er whole body ached, despite the softness of the bed Dalia found herself waking up in. What she awoke from should have been yet another nightmare, but she felt so fulfilled. A piece missing from her soul for so long was slowly forming itself back in place. Utterly lost in the sense of peace she felt from this newfound wholeness, it took a moment for her to register what happened before her memories started flooding back.

Where was she? The Tanbury Wilds certainly didn't have a bunch of pillows to soothe her throbbing head.

Shooting up to a sitting position, a sharp pain twinged in her skull. With a hiss, Dalia gingerly touched the side of her head. No doubt where the elven huntress brought down her boot.

"Hey, take it easy. You're okay. You're safe now."

You're safe now

The same words she had uttered on the shore of Tidesend.

The very words which upheaved her entire life and threw her onto this path.

Things started to come into focus. The blur of the morning light gave way to a familiar tent. The softness of the blankets and pillows started to form the memory of a cot she knew all too well. And finally, that voice gave way to a sight which made her heart thump wildly in her chest.

Glenn.

He was sitting vigil at her bedside. Dalia had no recollection of how she'd gotten back to the camp. So many questions, but only one really mattered.

"Fionn? Bethana? Are they . . ." Dalia couldn't finish the thought out loud, terrified her number of newfound friends found itself drastically cut short. But Glenn just placed a soft hand on her shoulder.

"They're fine. Bethana's broken up about her men, but the Wolf was telling the truth. He froze their feet to the floor, but left them unharmed."

His brow furrowed as he spoke. No doubt the same question running through his head. Why? Surely, he would have known what an asset Fionn was to the White Stags. Fionn was a scientist. An expert on the Luminites. Not to mention, they were a traitor in the eyes of elven kind. It was hard to imagine that imposing figure truly leaving them untouched. Yet here they were.

The Wolf told her it was for her. A gift. The idea made her stomach revolt, churning bile. She wanted no gifts from him. Nor did she want his interest in obtaining her for what lay in her heart and coursed through her veins.

Despite all her memories returning, Dalia could not remember one of the elves at the Keep taking any particular fascination in her. It was possible she simply didn't notice. She was only a child then, and all she could remember from her captors was pain and hatred. The only emotions she could muster for the obscured elf now. His offers and gifts were meaningless. Mere ploys to ensnare her for the magic the crystals granted her, and her ability to open the path to Lumiterra. He would have been just as keen to claim her if she were any other Crystalline. No matter his games, there was nothing personal between them. There couldn't be.

The anger rolling in her belly soothed as Glenn's hand moved, cupping her cheek instead of her shoulder.

"I'm so sorry, Dalia." The quiver in his voice was unmistakable.

"For what?" Her voice was barely a whisper, and not from the pain or just getting oriented. Something about his face broke down. The edges of his casual mask cracked. Those brown curls of his that never seemed to stay in place tumbled unceremoniously across his forehead. The dark circles under his eyes were enough of an indication that he hadn't slept, giving more credence to the idea he really had remained at her bedside. Those cracks were growing until they all but shattered his well-maintained mask. The gleam of tears threatening in his eyes. The man who sat before her now seemed almost frightened. Not the cocksure Stag she grew so accustomed to.

"I knew the risks in taking you there," Glenn said. "I was there when Emil was lost. I knew what could happen."

His hand drew back from her cheek, leaving behind a deep longing. Dalia might even have protested if not for his hands wringing in his lap.

"I should have taken more care. I should have known there could be archers hidden. I should have—"

Dalia did not care what he should have done. These things he was beating himself up over — she didn't care one bit. All she heard in his self-berating was how much this man truly cared for her, matching her own feelings for the person who fate allowed to change her life.

The caution which ruled her for so much of her life fled as she leaned forward and silenced him. His lips soft against her own in nothing more than a short-lived chaste kiss. Far less then they shared by the firelight. Even still, it felt as though butterflies took flight in her stomach.

Glenn was practically unmoving, and when Dalia started to pull back, his fingers wrapped around her upper arms. Squeezing as he assisted her to move back and hold her at arm's length. His face a mixture of confusion and an odd vulnerability. It was so different from the night at their little campsite. Now, he was hesitant, lower lip trembling. There was so much to be said, and yet neither spoke. Instead, Dalia just smiled. With that one smile, the man before her finally let his guilt go. Shoulders slumping as he released a long breath.

He looked at her like he had on the beach. Like she was something to be revered. Not a weapon, but something precious. It seemed he meant to worship her as such, his lips meeting hers again. This time with a frenzy.

Dalia let out a small gasp before trying to meet his intensity, leaning into his hard chest as his fingers dove into her voluminous cooper curls. Every touch, every move, set her alight. Stoking a desire in her she never once considered before. Dalia never found something lacking in her life despite never having a moment of intimacy such as this, but now it threatened to consume her.

If either of them possessed less self-control, it might have. The two might have been lost to desire, but his kisses slowed. His lips lazily drifted from hers down to the line of her jaw, and then lower still towards her neck.

That is where he halted, burying his face in the crook there as Dalia bowed her head. Nestling her face into his soft matt of curls, something hummed within her. A warmth blossoming and spreading in a similar way to her power. If she could go on having moments like this with Glenn, she could finally imagine a life where she was content. Not just surviving, but living.

"Can I stay here with you?" His question was so small as he pulled back just enough to look at her face, their noses still close enough to touch. "I mean . . . just to sleep, nothing else. I don't want to leave you but . . . you can tell me to go if you wish to be alone. I know you're still recovering."

Words failed, but her smile did not. Dalia nodded before rubbing her nose playfully against his. A huff of a laugh was his only reaction before gently leaning forward and pecking her lips once more in a featherlight kiss.

WHATEVER ROOTED in Dalia's heart back at Tidesend now well and truly blossomed. Their bodies were still entangled with one another after spending the night simply sleeping within each other's arms. It was something so innocent, and yet incredibly intimate all the same.

Glenn idly played with his fingertips in her palm. Each ghost of a touch went off like a spark. So many times she had told herself she never wanted something like this. Never needed it. Honestly, Dalia probably would have been happy having never experienced a romantic attachment. Until her budding emotions for Glenn began to form, then she suddenly longed for it, but only with him. Only with the man the Gods had sent her. Physical attraction was not what ruled her in this, it was their connection and her unruly emotions.

Dalia had believed she needed nothing else besides keeping those promises made so long ago.

Now, she knew different. Now with her body so perfect beside his, she was instead beginning to wonder why she allowed herself to go so long without. Why she allowed herself to believe she was not allowed to want or dream.

The bitter taste of guilt was still there, lingering in the back of her throat. The night those promises were made was so clear to her now. The memories singing where once only a muted haze resided. But she had allowed herself this. Allowed herself to live. *To want.* One thing she knew so fiercely as they lay there — she did not regret leaving.

"I remember," Dalia finally said, breaking their silence and shifting so her gaze could meet his. His eyebrow arched a little in question.

"What do you remember?"

"Everything."

It felt like relief leaving her lungs. Stuck there for far too long. For so long those memories weighed on her. Ghosts haunted and teased in the night. Now they were just there, existing as part of her as though they never left.

With a small sigh, she sat up on the cot beside him, wondering if he was mourning the loss of their closeness just as she was. A thought answered quickly enough when he reached up and playfully tried to pull her back down beside him.

"Get back down here. It's cold without you."

"Hush. This is important."

Glenn chuckled, but said nothing more on the subject, instead nodding for her to continue.

"For so long I felt like I was living in the dark. I knew next to nothing of myself and needed you and everyone else here to tell me who and what I was, but now . . . I remember. I guess a good shot to the head was exactly what I needed."

A snort of a laugh was shared between them. They both

knew how monumental this was, what it meant to her. Dalia would have to share this information with Fionn as well. There might be something within her memories that could help their research or point them on the right track. But this moment was separate. She wanted it to be Glenn she opened up to first. Who she trusted with the pieces of herself she was just starting to get reacquainted with.

"Do you know how Crystalline get their powers?" Dalia asked.

"Fionn said it was something to do with the crystals and having a piece of them put in your bloodstream."

A kind way of putting the torture they survived. Dalia did nothing to correct him on that front, choosing instead to simply wrinkle her nose in disgust at the memory, pushing it aside for another one.

"Something like that," she said. "The changes are not immediate. They manifest over time, and usually require some sort of traumatic event to actually be pulled to the surface."

Her voice wavered, and his hand found hers. "The guards turned it into a kind of game. Trying to see who could terrorize each of us the most to get us to use the powers we'd been given. I think they might have even put money on it."

A rage flashed in Glenn's eyes, leaving an odd comfort in her chest. He never made his hatred for the elves hidden from anyone. Not even Fionn. While Dalia wished he could see what she did in her newfound friend, sometimes it was good to remember the atrocities their kind were capable of. To know she wasn't alone in her hatred.

"There was a boy there, Drystan." Having her ghost's name on her lips felt so strange. A name alone gave him form, shape, and a legacy besides being someone who haunted her sleep. "He'd gone through the process like all of us, but for some reason, it didn't work on him."

"Why?"

"I don't know," Dalia answered with a shrug. "But after a few months the guards gave up on him. Something you would think he would count as a blessing. But not him. He would throw himself in front of the rest of us. Try to protect us. I never understood why."

"Because he was a good man."

It was such a simple answer to give. It may have been the only one needed. Yet, Dalia still longed to know more. She knew those answers could never come now, but how she wished she could talk to him. Ask him why. She just wanted to understand why she still endured, and he was gone.

"One day after my . . . exposure. The guards set their sights on me. I was only seven." Glenn's fingers tightened around hers. "He intervened. The guards were furious, having enough of his meddling, and gave him quite the beating." Dalia tilted her head back, closing her eyes as though she could see it. As though she could feel the moment her power first awakened. "I remember sitting with him and just wanting so badly to take away his pain. The pain should have been mine, not his. And that was that. My wish had somehow been granted and I healed him."

Eyes open once more, her focus returned from the lost boy of her past to the man beside her.

"I know what was done to me was monstrous but . . ." Dalia chewed her lip, nervously putting a string of thoughts together. "What I can do. It really does feel like a gift. One I want to use to help people."

He shifted so he was sitting beside her, his palm finding the spot on her cheek where it fit so perfectly.

"You were never a monster.' His voice a whisper reaching to her very soul. "Not to me."

All she could do was stare at him. The deep blue of her eyes met the icy blue of his and held there. Until Glenn broke the silence between them.

"What happened to your friend?"

A shudder of a breath tore through her. Tears stinging her eyes as she fought them back.

"He died."

His thumb ran across her skin in comfort as he opened for her. Allowing her more of himself in return for all she shared.

"When I was younger, an Elven Hunt destroyed my village. The White Stags came, but not in time to save most of the people there. I was one of the only survivors," Glenn explained. "The general found me, took me in. Tried to give me a family, and in exchange, I made his cause my own. No . . . no, that's not quite right."

He shook his head, mulling over his next words.

"I knew from the moment I saw my village burning what I needed to do. I knew vengeance was the only path left to take. The general just was able to harness that. To make sure to put a lost boy on the right path. I only wish . . ."

Dalia let his voice fall off a moment, allowing him the silence to find what he wanted to say. And when he didn't continue on his own, she gave him the gentle nudge he needed.

"What do you wish?"

Sadness echoed in his slackened features and glazed eyes.

"I wish Beth accepted me as her father did. We did try to be siblings. But something always seemed to get in the way. Competition or jealousy, I don't know. But all I wanted was a sister. To replace . . ."

His voice failed him again. This time, Dalia knew exactly what he meant to say.

"You lost a sister."

"I did. She died. The Hunt killed her. I tried everything to protect her but, it wasn't enough. Sometimes I curse the Gods that I was the one allowed to live and not her."

A gentle confession. One she suspected was brewing under the surface for a long time. Always there in the silent moments between them back at Tidesend whenever her promises were mentioned. His sympathy was always so apparent. His unspoken discomfort at how she clung onto those words spoken when she was a child.

Acceptance fell over her in a wave. The words she denied for so long finally breaking forth.

"I've felt the same. And yet, I waited. Hiding away the truth." Her lip quivered. "Ammy didn't survive. She couldn't have. I think . . . I think my sister is gone too."

Escaping from Keep Oharn would have only been the beginning. The odds of frightened children making it out alive, fire or not, were slim to none. From there it would take the miracle of going undiscovered. It had taken her months and months to arrive at Tidesend, barely hanging on by a thread. Dalia was the one in a million to make it. The others, whose faces she finally could see again, were most likely gone. All of them. Amaryllis included. No wonder she scrubbed them from her memory. Simply not wanting to accept the reality that she was alone. No one was coming for her.

"Dalia—"

"No, you don't have to say anything." Worried he might try to convince her to hold on to hope, she shook her head. She was done with waiting. "For ten years, I stayed. I did every-thing she asked of me. Not once questioning if it was the right thing to do for myself. Until I saw you."

Tears spilled onto her cheeks. Yet somehow it wasn't sadness pushing them forward, but hope.

"I knew then, I was worth more. I may have held up my

end of the promise I made to her, but she could never hold up hers. No matter how much I wished she could."

His other hand moved now, stroking her hair down comfortingly. What hung between them was more than a mutual sorrow. It was understanding. More than that, for Dalia, it was a long-awaited freedom.

Glenn leaned forward, his lips gently caressing the salty trails her tears left behind.

"We'll make them pay for what they've taken from us," he promised once again.

Revenge. Dalia had never even allowed her mind to toy with the idea until Tidesend was stolen from her. A blasphemous thought when so much energy needed to be used just to stay alive. Just to stay hidden. From his lips, it sounded so sweet. A release they both so utterly deserved. So much was ripped away by the elves. It was time they took something back.

CHAPTER TWENTY-ONE

It was a good thing she had been unconscious when they returned. Apparently, Glenn rode with her all the way back, barely stopping as she was in and out of consciousness. The others arrived after them, and no one besides Glenn knew she had awoken. So no one came snooping around in her tent. No one saw the two of them untangling themselves to get up and face the day. No one interrupted a moment Dalia was sure she would treasure in her heart forever.

They decided Glenn should leave first. Everyone knew he was at her side, so it wouldn't cause any sort of walk of shame to see him exiting her tent alone, even if they hadn't done anything besides sleep next to one another. Besides, he needed to go meet with General Lachlan and give a full report on what came to pass in the Tanbury Wilds.

Seeing Glenn disappear beneath the flap of her tent into the new light of morning caused a oddly pleasant squeezing sensation in her chest. She could not say what she felt for Glenn was love. Just that it was something. Which was more than she could have said for anyone before him. It was enough for now.

Dalia was not expected to get up anytime soon. After a head injury, she really should have still been resting. Once she was alone, a sigh escaped her lips as she fell back into her soft sheets and pillows, soaking in the blissful calm of the night before.

"I could gut Glenn!"

Dalia shot up, eyes wide, staring at the flaps of her tent suddenly being flung open by a very displeased elf. Heat burned in Dalia's cheeks. They couldn't possibly know about her and Glenn sharing a bed! She would simply die of embarrassment.

"That man was supposed to tell me the second you were awake. But no. I had to find out, in passing, as he went off to see the general," Fionn huffed, and Dalia felt a sense of relief course through every fiber of her being. Thank the Gods. She was not about to be having an uncomfortable conversation.

"Are you alright?" Fionn crossed the small area of her quarters in long strides, coming to kneel at her bedside, bright golden eyes flashing with concern.

"I'm fine," Dalia replied, wearing a smile if for nothing else than to calm the elf's nerves. "Truly. My head has certainly felt better, but I'll be alright."

Their shoulders slumped as the tension fled their body. Dalia would never forget her first line of defense against the Wolven Hunt. How Fionn stood between her and the Wolf. Damn the consequences. It only solidified what she already came to know. Not all elves were monsters. Well, at the very least, one wasn't. It was enough for her to trust this elf with everything.

"Fionn." Her voice was soft, a shudder of a word. "I remember."

FOR THE SECOND TIME, Dalia recounted the night of her flight. Laying her memories bare, she answered as many questions as she could handle. She even so much as confirmed that the devices used on them were exactly as Fionn predicted. Dalia expected to see the sadness shining in their golden eyes. No one with a beating heart could hear about the cruelties done to her and those other children and not experience some kind of emotional reaction. What she did not expect was the clenching of their fists, or the way their head hung, almost as if they were personally ashamed.

It tugged at her heart. Fionn could not be held responsible for the entirety of elven kind.

"It wasn't your doing," Dalia said, trying to offer comfort.

Fionn's lips parted, hanging open wordlessly a moment, before shaking their head. "Don't do that. I should be the one comforting you. Not the other way around."

They were right. These were Dalia's memories. Her trauma. Still, she couldn't help it. Dalia always wanted to make people feel happy, to feel better. She didn't know if the powers each Crystalline received reflected who they were as people, but the fact that she ended up being given the gift of healing, well, it just fit. Even more, now that she finally allowed herself to embrace her magic.

"Hey, we're friends. We comfort each other." Fionn seemed to come to life as Dalia labeled them as such. Sure, it had been brewing for some time now: when they studied together, when Fionn dressed her for the festival, when they opened up to her by the fire, dancing by her side, and when they clasped hands in the temple. Both knew what was building between them. A friendship Dalia never thought possible: one between an elf and a Crystalline.

Fionn's eyes glistened, a tight smile pulling at their lips. "You are absolutely right, my dear."

They hadn't stayed much longer, explaining they needed to get back to their work and sort out what steps to take next. Not something Dalia wanted to think about at the moment. The prospect of the Wolf waiting for them and all that entailed was like a snare around her heart. Ready to crush her newfound bliss. Something Dalia was not at all ready for yet, so she was glad to leave the work up to the elf for now.

Still, the idea of laying alone all day was hardly how she wanted to spend her time. After a few more moments stretched like an eternity, Dalia sighed and gave up on trying to go back to sleep. Instead, she chose to take a stroll around Camp Hart. Most of her time had been spent in the training ring or Fionn's library, so it was nice to just get to walk out among these people who came to accept her.

The faces around her were not some fabled resistance anymore. They were people she wanted to protect. A place she longed so much to call a word she never truly known. *Home.*

Dalia paused her wandering when she caught sight of the Stag she wanted to call hers out of the corner of her eye. Glenn was just leaving the general's canopy. He must have been giving his report on their mission, and yet, his face hung in a way which told her the conversation must not have gone well. Of course it hadn't. Knowing the Wolf was out there waiting for them would make anyone look sour.

"Hey." A soft smile raised the sides of her lips as she called out her gentle greeting.

A start ran through his slender frame, surprise filling his eyes. He must not have seen her approaching, too wrapped up in going over whatever the two discussed. The look on his face was unexpected. Fear danced in his pale eyes as he stood still as a statue. An odd sight to be sure. Dalia pricked up an eyebrow in confusion. They were in the safety of the camp now. There shouldn't have been anything to fear.

He moved quickly, snapping out of the stupor which held him a moment ago.

"Hey." His response was tight. His hand caught on her upper arm as he strode towards her. "You shouldn't be over this way."

Her head twitched to him, eyes narrowing in confusion. The question of why died on her lips before it could be born. The voice spoken, in her stead, caused Glenn's entire body to tense.

"So, this must be her then."

For a moment, her gaze just stayed on Glenn. He was so still. His grip on her arm tightened uncomfortably. Taking a deep breath, Dalia finally shifted her gaze to look past him to the man who caused this reaction. His height was not incredibly imposing, but the way he carried himself demanded respect. No armor adorned his frame this time, just a simple pair of breeches and a white tunic. On his right shoulder flowed a half cape in the white and gold of the White Stags. The best way to describe him was sharp. His features, his steely gaze, the way he walked. Where his daughter bore a courageous gentleness in her face, his was a cold wall. From his beard to his close-cropped, dark hair, everything about him held an edge to it.

They locked eyes, and Dalia felt something flutter unpleasantly in her belly, as anxiety crept up into her chest.

"Glenn has told me so much about you. It's about time we met."

The older man stepped forward and held out his hand for her to shake. Despite the smile now plastered on those cutting features, everything in her was screaming to be careful. The way he looked at her did not echo the way the others around camp did. No, a look of disgust flashed by. Just a glimpse of it, now swept away by his pleasantries. Yet, she saw it all the same, and Glenn's sudden change in demeanor told her all she needed to know.

He'd morphed from the man she was so coming to admire to a cowering little boy in the general's presence.

With a thick swallow, Glenn released her arm and stood aside. His gaze kept down as he allowed this meeting to happen.

Dalia suppressed the shudder wanting so desperately to run through her, before forcing her lips to curl up and taking his hand.

"Our general, I presume."

"Yes, General Lachlan, and you're the Crystalline."

The Crystalline. It felt like he punched her rather than shook her hand. No name. Just what she was. It made her want to recoil into herself. He may not have been seething like Mollie was when she called her a monster, but the phantom sting on her cheek was still there all the same.

Words did not come. Somehow, she managed to force herself to nod, at least offering some acknowledgment. Dalia pulled her hand back from him, flexing the fingers at her side as if she just touched something hot.

If the man noticed her discomfort, he did nothing to show it. Instead, he turned and waved his hand for them to follow. "Come, Glenn was just telling me about the Wilds. I would like to hear your interpretation as well."

"I don't think that will be necessary," Glenn interjected.

"Nonsense. Let the girl speak and share what she knows."

She shifted her weight, eying Glenn a moment. His head hung, resigned to obey the instruction he was given.

Swallowing her pride, Dalia stepped after General Lachlan, not wanting to hear what she knew was about to come from his lips. This man who she trusted so completely, the reason why his treatment of her would at times waver was becoming so clear. The general who he worked so closely with, who he called father. It was this very man who would not even allow her the dignity of a name.

THE CANOPY of the war tent was easy to spot from almost anywhere in the camp. It was far larger than any of the other dwellings. Even Fionn's makeshift library failed to rival it. Often, Dalia caught herself glancing its way, mostly to see Glenn disappearing beneath its flaps. A longing to know what was going on inside its fabric walls always tugged at her. Now, she finally had the chance to get the glimpse she so desperately wanted. Only now, it was the last place she wished to be.

A giant wooden table sat in the middle dwarfing the size of the one in the library. This one was not haphazardly covered by books either. Instead, it seemed meticulously organized. In the center of it all was a map. It stretched over the table's wooden surface with carefully-placed figures, most likely signifying troops of some kind. Dalia held little knowledge of what was brewing within the human resistance outside of the small part she was playing. The figures meant nothing to her in terms of factions or numbers. What they did show her was war truly was coming. It was no longer just gossip at the market. It was there. Tangible. Inevitable.

"I hear you've worked out just fine in replacing our last one."

Her fingers curled into fists at her sides.

"You mean Emil?"

It was a challenge. A push for him to say his name. The name of the man who gave his life for the cause this man was leading. It wasn't enough. He simply scoffed, eyes glued to the few bits of paper he now idly moved around on the table, barely paying her any mind — let alone respect — to the fallen Crystalline.

"Glenn tells me you're a healer."

"Yes sir." A curt quick answer was all she gave. All she had the stomach for.

"No means of offensive magic, at all?"

"No sir."

"A shame."

Dalia shot a glance at Glenn, anger dancing on the tip of her tongue. She wanted — no, needed — an explanation. Furious questions buzzed around her head, banging around her skull in an effort to be free. But the sight of Glenn kept her silent. He was not the man she had started falling for. The cocky rogue with a vulnerability he only showed a select few. No. The man beside her now was a coward, standing there with his gaze transfixed on the ground like a child being scolded. He'd not once spoken up in defense of her. Not so much as moved an inch. Inside this war tent, Dalia was on her own.

"I'm sure I need not tell you just how important it is we get to the Luminite cache before the Wolven Hunt does."

No, she understood better than most. Dalia knew all too well the weight she carried. This may have been Glenn's mission, but without her it could not continue. Without her the hopes of the White Stags all burned to ash.

"Do you know how a Crystalline is turned into a weapon?"

His question startled her, heart clenching in her chest. Dalia set her jaw and drew up some courage. She would stand on her own if Glenn refused to stand beside her.

"Only that it involves our hearts being ripped from our chests," she spit back indelicately.

"Something like that," the older man drawled, turning from them and walking to the back wall of his tent. There, on a weapon rack all its own, was a longsword. More ornate than the weapons she witnessed any White Stags wielding on the training yards. Its hilt bore streaks of orange inlaid within the metal. As General Lachlan lifted the sword from its resting place, she caught a glimpse of something that arrested her heart. Veins of striking blue, glinting in and out along the steel of the blade, much like the dagger used against them twice now, or like her own hands and eyes when she used her power.

This was a Crystalline weapon.

"Deathbringer," the general introduced, speaking the weapon's name. A dignity given to a sword but not her.

A shudder crawled up her spine, shaking to her very core. One of her brethren was slaughtered and their body desecrated to create that accursed thing. This sword held power at the expense of a child's life.

"From what our elf tells me, the Luminite Crystals are dormant until combined with living matter."

A scream clawed at her throat, threatening to tear free. Our elf. Fionn was a respected member of the White Stags. It was their science which propelled the rebellion this far. More than that, Fionn was his daughter's partner.

With her, she almost understood. She was a stranger to this man. A new face. Maybe she could excuse the lack of recognition. But Fionn? Hearing them reduced to their race made her wish she was braver. That she wasn't just standing there silently as her insides crawled. She wished she could muster the courage and strength enough to teach this man a lesson.

He continued and she stood firm. "I suppose that's why the elves had to create people like you. They couldn't harness magic without your hearts, as you said."

He stepped up to her now. The sword held between them, the blade resting flat on his palms. Dalia didn't so much as glance down at it. Her lip trembled, but she kept her ground, meeting his strong challenging gaze with her own. A sharp contrast to Glenn, whose head was still slightly bowed.

"The shards of the Luminites mixed with the blood and tissue of the Crystalline are then mixed with molten metal and forged into something like this. A weapon with a connection to the magic of our world."

"Funny." Finding her tongue, Dalia finally spoke. "You make it sound so simple. Leaving out the torture and the murder bit."

A chuckle rattled through his chest. "You're not wrong, girl."

He turned away, heading to return the weapon to its place of honor, and Dalia felt like she could breathe again. She drank in the distance now created between them as though it was a sip of water to cool her nerves.

"It is a shame the elves saw fit to simply end the lives of their experiments. A good soldier is worth more than a good weapon on the battlefield any day. And these magic weapons don't last forever. The crystal shards stop working after a while without the host body. Though, the logic is sound. Soldiers have minds of their own. A sword won't stab you in the back without someone wielding it."

It explained why the elves kept their program going for so long. They needed more and more Crystalline to be able to make more and more weapons, especially when the old ones were starting to snuff out. The information might have been valuable, but the insensitive way it was put only made her want to run from this tent and retch even more.

The man finished taking in his sword before spinning to look at the pair once more.

"Glenn tells me the Wolven Hunt's leader seems particularly interested in you."

Dalia couldn't deny it. Even if she knew no explanation why besides the obvious one of what she was and the fact that he claimed to have known her. "Yes. He let us go with the understanding I might choose to go with him."

"And would you?"

Her nostrils flared at the insinuation. Dalia chewed on the question for a moment, angry to have been asked it in the first place.

"No."

The idea was preposterous. She would never abandon the White Stags to go back to the people who tortured her as a child. No matter what this man thought of her, no one in their right mind would do such a thing.

"Good." The way he said it made her skin crawl. "Glenn."

"Sir."

The curly head beside her finally snapped up, ready and at attention. It made her jaw clench and her mouth sour. She knew he was like a son to Lachlan. But never had she imagined her Glenn, so full of life and headstrong, would be so cowed by someone. Especially someone who treated her this way.

"It seems then we have the perfect bait to put an end to a thorn in our side once and for all. I trust you will not get this asset killed like the last one."

CHAPTER TWENTY-TWO

The word still rang in her head as they silently crossed the campground together. *Asset.* That's what he called her. Like she was no better than the sword he seemed to treasure so much.

No, she was worse, for that sword bore a name. Deathbringer. It wasn't just her. It was Emil too. They were weapons. All of them. Not children ripped from their families and forced through unspeakable things. The dreams she felt just moments ago of finding belonging here became leaves on the wind. Ripped away from her by a breeze she couldn't possibly control.

This could not be the man who led them.

This could not be Beth's father. Glenn's father.

That thought burned since their introduction. Only now with her and Glenn alone, walking so awkwardly together, did she feel like she could address any of it.

"What was that?"

It was the only question she could even think to ask, and it stopped Glenn in his tracks.

He paused for a moment, staring ahead. When he turned to her there was no easy smirk. Not even the vulnerability she came to treasure so much. There was just a look of utter defeat. One that stuck her to her spot beside him, willing to hear him out.

"I tried to keep you away from him."

She couldn't believe that was Glenn's solution to this mess. He just intended to keep them separated, as if simple distance solved everything. It didn't address any of the actual problems at hand. Dalia's mouth ran dry, trying to accept his words. She didn't know what she expected, but at least an apology might have been nice.

Dalia scoffed, her gaze shifting around as she tried to find the right words to describe the immense hurt gnawing in her chest. "I can't believe you said nothing," she spat, letting her emotions flow instead of bottling them up for his sake. "Did you hear what he called me?"

"Dalia." Her name was a sigh on his lips. "I told you. He is my general. More than that, he's my father. Without him, I would have nothing."

Such a sentiment didn't make this better. If anything, it made it so much worse. Glenn seemed to know it too. Not doing much more to protest against her, instead just allowing her to let him have it.

"Does that excuse what just happened? He wouldn't even speak my name. He wouldn't even speak Fionn's name! *Fionn!* You know, the love of his own daughter's life. How can any of you follow him?"

His silence spoke volumes. Dalia was so quick to trust this man, believing so much in the fate of their meeting and what it might mean. She clung to every sign, the way he made her heart flutter. This morning she might have said she was beginning to fall for him. That their special moments outweighed any of the hurdles to get to this point. Now, she was beginning to question her judgment. So desperate to have any sort of attachment, she formed one with someone she didn't truly understand. What a stupid girl she was.

"You'd better come up with a plan to keep me safe, I guess. Don't want to risk your general's asset."

The words were pure venom. As she turned to storm off, a hand caught her wrist, stopping her in her tracks. She paused, looking at the face of the man she wanted so frustratingly to keep clinging on to. His casual mask had started to show the cracks of desperation.

"You know I don't think of you like that." His voice was so soft, barely a whisper. A promise for only her to hear. That clandestine fact was enough for her to snap her wrist back out of his clutch.

This whole time since they arrived, she'd done nothing but chase after him and vie for his affections. She'd tried to be understanding of the changes set in him. The soft intimacy they found mere hours ago had truly been something special. But it, like the rest of her treasured time with him, was private. Dalia thought it to be as Beth suggested. Glenn was just not someone who found it easy to be open with his emotions. There may have been some truth there, but after their little meeting with the general, it became increasingly clear she was part of the problem. Or more precisely, she was something he might want to keep a secret.

"Then act like it," Dalia demanded. An order he was going to need to follow through, or she knew she would have to walk away from whatever this was between them while her pride was still intact. "I don't want someone who only defends me in certain company. If you're not proud to be with me, then maybe we shouldn't do this at all."

Dalia was surprised by how firm she managed to be, and clearly so was Glenn. A muscle worked in his jaw as he seemed to take in all she said to him. An answer would have to wait, for she was not ready to hear it. Turning to go once more, she left him standing there, in the courtyard just beyond the general's canopy. This time if he wanted to fix things, he would have to be the one to do the work.

DALIA THOUGHT AVOIDING Glenn would be easy. After all, before it seemed like she never saw the man, despite him being the only person in the camp she originally wanted to spend time with. Now that she wanted to put some space between them and think things through, it was like she couldn't shake him.

Glenn was there when she wandered through Fionn's library to hide within the books. She wanted to look through some of the history of the Lumiels, given all they'd seen in the Wilds. Fionn had been delighted in her interest, and Dalia thought it might be a good time to ask them their opinion on General Lachlan. That opportunity faded away when Glenn entered the tent with an excuse of his own, claiming he needed to speak to Fionn about what their next steps might be. It may have been true. It was what the general had ordered him to do. Still, Dalia couldn't help but wonder if it truly was his purpose or if he was just trying to find a way to be near her.

Trying not to think too much about it or meet his eye, she simply left. The next two days meandered on about the same. Dalia tried to busy herself with something — anything — and somehow he was always there.

"Why is my brother following you around like a scolded puppy?" Beth asked as Dalia entered the ring for their regular training session.

"I thought you didn't like calling him that."

"I don't. Usually. But Gods, when he looks so depressed it's hard not to take pity on the guy."

Dalia didn't turn to look. She didn't want to. The last thing he deserved right now was her pity. Instead, she struggled with wrapping her hands. Pulling the cloth taunt over her knuckles with gritted teeth.

Beth eyed her a moment, before raising her brows in some odd understanding.

"Oh. You met my father didn't you?"

Dalia's lips pulled tight.

Beth knew too, she must have. She knew how narrow her father's view of the world and personhood was, and yet, she hadn't warned her. No one had. She'd said long ago she stopped trying to please the man, but that was hardly a warning for what Dalia faced in that war tent.

With a sigh, Beth moved past her, dropping a few wooden practice swords into a pile unceremoniously.

"I'm sorry. He's a piece of work."

"Then why do you follow him?" Dalia snapped before she could stop herself. "Why do any of you follow him?"

Bethana turned, crossing her arms over her chest and cocking her head slightly. No anger furrowed her brows, only softness reflected upon her face. A look that, compassionate though it was, threatened to render Dalia bare.

"He's my father."

Dalia shifted, pushing down the urge to snap again, but Beth raised a hand. A parlay and sign she was not finished.

"But that is not enough, nor should it ever be. I follow him because he's the only chance we have. Yes, my father is a bigot.

Yes, he's made my life hell at times and made the person I love to feel less than and I hate him for it. But I also know that without him, without his White Stags, we would have no chance at freedom. There's just . . . no one else."

She wasn't wrong. Humankind was broken so thoroughly. Elves had ruled them for centuries and no one stood up. No one claimed back their lands or fought for their rights to govern themselves. No one prevented the elven kind from stealing children in the night to do heinous things to.

General Lachlan, for all his gut-wrenching beliefs, represented something humans desperately needed. *Hope.*

"I know Glenn didn't keep you from our father to hide the way he is from you," Beth continued. "No matter how misguided, I think he was simply attempting to spare you pain."

Dalia worried at her lower lip. Was that what it was? All of this happened because Glenn was trying to protect her?

"Ten rounds with the sparing dummy." Beth nodded to the corner of the training area where the silly hay men were set up for trainees to beat the crap out of. "Take out your frustrations there. And Dalia, please put Glenn out of his misery soon. I don't care if you yell at him, forgive him, whatever you need. But he's becoming unbearable."

A laugh snorted its way forth unbidden. Picking up her wooden training sword, she rolled her eyes and started to run through her regular routine of exercises. Maybe it should have felt good to let off the steam but two rounds in and Dalia was groaning.

Silently she cursed herself for spending the better part of a decade practically doing nothing. Bethana had been quick to interject any sort of negative self-talk whenever it bubbled forth and to tell her to not pay others any mind while pointing out trainees of all sizes around camp. She'd made it clear

Dalia's curves and love of food were not why she was struggling now, but that this amount of physical exercise would give anyone a problem. No person would just suddenly be battle ready. Her morning walks and climbs here and there had certainly not prepared her to wield a sword, and each day seemed like a new trial in futility.

"Your blows won't have enough force that way."

His voice cut through her training, producing an eye roll and a sigh. So much for trying to use the training to get through her anger. He couldn't mean to do this now. Not when she was sweaty, struggling, and feeling like an absolute buffoon.

"What?" Dalia lowered her wooden blade and looked up at Glenn, exasperated. He was sitting on the fence which surrounded the arena, leaving Dalia with the hounding question of how long he had been watching and if he'd heard her conversation with Beth. Leaning forward, that all too familiar mask of a smirk met her. Dalia wished she could crack it open. Spill forth the vulnerability she knew he hid there and devour whatever other secrets lingered behind the causal curve of his lips.

"You're swinging from your shoulder," he continued, hopping down from the fence and picking up a training blade of his own. "That's just going to tire out your arms faster and make your strikes weaker. You need it to come from your core."

Her core. Beth certainly reminded her of that a few times, but admittedly, her focus had never been the best in this ring.

"Show me then," she huffed. "Enlighten me on what I'm doing that's so wrong."

He snorted a chuckle and fell in beside her, holding his sword out in front of him, the tip barely an inch from the training dummy. Dalia knew enough to know he was checking his distance.

"This is what you're doing," Glenn explained, before stepping into a strike to the upper right of the dummy, leaning into it with his shoulder just as he described. "That's not going to get you anywhere. Now this," he said before stepping again. This time, twisting from his waist as he delivered the blow. The dummy shuddered from the strike, proving his point. "See the difference?"

She did. Now whether she could replicate it was an entirely different story.

Dalia squared her stance, trying to do as Beth taught her. Only to hear another chuckle from beside her. "Here." Glenn stepped closer and she felt her pulse quicken. She wasn't ready to forgive him yet. She didn't want to. And yet, her heart flipped in her chest, betraying her, as he rested his hands on her hips and adjusted her stance. They needed to talk, that much was certain. Still, it would be a lie for her to say she didn't long for this closeness. That she didn't want to bask in the glow of the connection they established and make this work.

"You're not an asset, Dalia. Not to me." His breath was hot on her neck as he spoke softly into her ear. Hands trailed over her curves, tweaking things here and there. "But you're right. I did not do enough."

She drew in a soft breath at his acceptance, settling more under his touch. This was all she wanted. Ownership over what transpired.

"Is that why you are helping me with my training?" she asked. He hadn't done so since she arrived. Each morning was only her and Beth in this dusty ring. No matter how many longing glances she cast his way. Although, he was here now; maybe that was all she needed.

"I'm helping you, because I gave you my word. We would face things together from now on. And because, I don't want to lose you. Not because of what you are, Dalia. Because of who you are . . . to me."

She'd known that. Seen it when the Hunt threatened them in the Wilds. When he sat by her bedside. Still, it was nice to hear.

Dalia twisted in his arms, arching her neck to look back and allow herself to fall into those eyes that made her miss Tidesend, and evenings looking out at the swirling blue of the ocean. Swift pressure from her unruly emotions welled up behind her own eyes. This was enough. If he could only stick to those words, it would be enough. The idea of being cared for because of who she was. Being needed as a person and not a tool, it was all she wanted. The regret she felt a few days ago in the pit of her stomach about the choice she made to keep opening up to him and allowing him to get closer to her than anyone ever had slowly began to dissipate.

"Really?"

The question was so soft and fragile. Dalia felt like his answer might shatter her. No matter how far they stumbled, she wanted this to work. She wanted *them* to work.

He said nothing, just nodded before dipping his head and pressing his lips to hers. It was brief. The ghost of a kiss, but more than enough. They were not in private. Their audience was unable to be vetted. This was a public show of his affection for her. A step in the direction she hoped they could continue to go. He still had a lot to prove, but this step was a sign progress was possible.

She smiled a real, toothy grin, unsure of what to say. But nothing needed to be uttered, for her smile was met with his own. Not some half-grin, but one pulling back bright and happy. What they had, it wasn't perfect, but it was real. Tangible enough that Dalia wanted to keep trying to fight for it.

"This doesn't look like training."

Fionn's voice for once was the last thing she wanted to hear. Turning to look at the elf, Dalia expected Glenn to put space between them. Instead, he lingered, straightening but keeping their closeness. A gesture which did not go unnoticed.

"You know, it's about damn time." Glenn exhaled a groan as Fionn clapped their hands together and practically leapt towards the two of them. "Beth and I had a bet going about how long it would take for you two to finally get something going between you."

"Fionn . . ." Glenn groaned.

"Judging by the looks of it, I might very well have won."

"You only won because I helped push her in the right direction." Beth called from the other side of the ring, much to Fionn's delight.

"And thank you for that, my dear, but it doesn't mean you owe me anything less. Oh, you two really are adorable. You see, Glenn, I was right. You can be agreeable if you actually put some effort into it."

"Fionn! Is this really why you interrupted us?" Glenn raised a hand to rub at his temples.

Dalia couldn't help but laugh at the absurdity of it all. Here she had been doubting her place, but once again she felt so at ease. The general may very well not be the great man she hoped he was, but this little band she fell in with was what she needed. It was good to be reminded of that.

The elf tsked playfully. "Now now, you're going back to old, not-so-agreeable Glenn."

"Come on Fionn," Dalia said, more laughter spilling from her lips. "Be nice. He's doing his best."

Gold eyes gleamed as they returned her smile. "Well, when I see you like this, all laughter and smiles and I know it's because of him, I suppose I can go a little easier, my dear."

They pushed off the training dummy they'd been leaning against and beckoned them to come along with a wave of their hand. "Believe it or not, I didn't just come to spy on you two canoodling. I actually think I have a way to fix our problem with those pesky wolves."

CHAPTER TWENTY-THREE

"What in the world is that?" Glenn sat at the table beside Dalia His eyebrow raised and head tilted to the side as though the different angle might allow him to get a better understanding of the spherical object on the table before them.

Fionn shoved all the books usually piled high unceremoniously to the floor. Beth held back a giggle at their partner's disorderly behavior, something she clearly came to accept, and maybe even enjoy. There was something so endearing about that, seeing the two of them often celebrating each other's tics and flaws. It felt like something to aspire to.

With just the four of them in Fionn's tent, things felt so right. These were her friends. The people who took the time to get to know her. Valued her for more than just the magic in her veins. Dalia wished it was always like this, but she knew they served a bigger cause. One led by someone who saw her as little more than a tool. Fionn too.

She wondered how Fionn handled such knowledge. If they even cared. After all, just as Beth said, this was bigger than all of them. The freedom of so many people was at stake. Her mind floated back Anna, to all the children in Lilivale and how they were counting on them. Personal offenses seemed so little when held up against such a standard. Judging by all she'd seen, Beth and Fionn were able to continue their relationship openly no matter what General Lachlan thought. Maybe she'd allowed the option of someone outside her relationship with Glenn to affect her too much. She could see right before her eyes the joy awaiting her if she could only tune out the rest of the noise around them and just focus on whatever was slowly beginning to flourish between them.

Fionn could do it. Why couldn't she?

The elf enthusiastically slammed their hands down on the table as they leaned forward, nodding to the strange sphere. "This thing is how we're going to stop that icy bastard. Well, that and our little Dalia."

Her eyes grew wide, looking back and forth between the three of them. Only Glenn seemed unsure. "Me?" she sputtered. "You really do want to use me as bait?"

"Unfortunately, it's the only choice we have." Beth's voice was gruff, barely containing the anger bubbling beneath the surface at the situation. "My hands are tied. My father won't allow me to bring more men along given how many we have lost. So, we can't outnumber them. The best bet we have is to make him think you really are accepting his offer."

"This is insane."

Glenn sat back in his seat, arms crossing over his chest, as he stared down at the thing on the table. They all knew what he wanted to say. Dalia was doing her best, but she was not even remotely a trained warrior, and the last time she held a blade against the Hunt it ended in injury. Her forehead still bore the purple bruising barely hidden by her curls to prove it. Worse, the Wolf hadn't even raised a finger in the ordeal. In a fight against him, Dalia didn't stand a chance. So how was this device possibly going to give her an edge?

"We're not sending her in alone." Fionn said. "The three of us will be there too."

"Two," Beth interjected. "I told you. The general doesn't want you going."

"I don't give a damn what your father says! This is on me. You know it. I'm not going to sit back and let you all face this alone!"

Dalia couldn't help the shock on her face. Fionn raising their voice at Beth was not something she'd ever heard before. Maybe they weren't as okay with her father's behavior as she originally interpreted.

This is on me.

Fionn couldn't blame themself for the last mission going south. The thought tightened her chest. They had to know how the mission played out wasn't their fault.

The two held each other's gaze for a moment. Gold eyes ablaze against deep brown. The pair were in a standoff. A silent challenge of who would be the one to relent. It was Beth who gave a sigh, perhaps knowing this was a battle she would not win. The Commander leaned back in her chair with a thump, a few braids cascading over her shoulder. "You're going to get yourself killed."

"If that's what it takes." The elf was deadly serious. It shook her a little.

With a breath and a shake of their head, Fionn pulled back a little from the table and steadied themselves. "As I was saying. Dalia is what the Wolf wants. So, we use her to get him where we want. But I'll be damned if we let him take her."

Dalia knew that was true. She witnessed firsthand the last

time they stood off. With the three of them at her side and a plan this time, she was beginning to think this was possible.

"Okay," she quietly agreed, drawing the eyes of those around the table to her. "What do I need to do?"

The elf smiled, though Dalia could feel Glenn growing restless beside her. Discreetly, she reached under the table, taking his hand into hers. His fingers wrapped around hers responsively as she gave him a reassuring squeeze. They would be alright. They had to be. All they needed to do was trust in Fionn's plan.

"This," they explained, motioning to the device on the table, "is a bomb of sorts, much like the one I used in the temple, though far more powerful."

She remembered. It worked rather effectively; however, she doubted the same trick would work against him twice. Something she was sure Fionn knew as well. So she waited for them to continue their explanation.

"Without that weapon of his, the Wolf is just another elf. We're quick, sure. Tough, but not impossible to kill by any stretch of the imagination. So, we need to get it away from him."

"How do you propose we do that?" Glenn interjected.

"By playing to your strengths, my dear boy," Fionn replied, so warmly Dalia could practically feel the man beside her rolling his eyes. "You work best fighting in the shadows. This bomb, when detonated, will release enough smoke to give you the cover you need to get in and get that dagger away from him."

Pale eyes gleamed. Dalia knew Glenn was hungry for a taste of revenge, and this just might give him the upper hand he needed to be able to kill the elf hunting him. To take down the wolf who murdered Emil once and for all.

"Well, I've got to hand it to you," Beth chimed in. "That's

not a bad idea. Especially since the smoke cover will keep the archer from being able to land a shot if she comes along."

"So where do I come in?"

"You, my dear, just need to be convincing enough to get close to him. Make him believe you have chosen to come alone, so hopefully he will be off guard when you activate the bomb. Giving Glenn the chance to strike."

Dalia's stomach turned at the idea of it. The two times the Wolf drew close to her weren't pleasant experiences. Such a strange feeling of recognition radiated from him. Not the kind that might make her intrigued or set her at ease, but the kind that twisted her gut, making her sick. By his own claim, he knew her, which made him one of the elves responsible for putting her through more than anyone should have to endure. He didn't deserve the familiarity he tried to establish with her.

"Don't worry." Glenn's soft voice brought her back to them. "I'm good at this. With stealth on my side, I haven't lost yet. I won't let him hurt you."

"None of us will," Beth added, and Dalia looked between her comrades — believed them. They would never let her go back to that torment. Not so long as they were able to take breath. This was not the time to keep waiting. This was the time for action. With her help, they could take out the one thing standing between them and Lumiterra. Getting there and getting those crystals would not only turn the tide in the favor of humans for the first time in hundreds of years and possibly end the Withering which threatened them all, but it would also protect countless children. Without the last cache, there would never be another Keep Oharn. No more children would be ripped from their families and turned into living weapons. It was worth every risk.

"I remember all that happened. Well, at least most of it." Glenn's hand tightened in hers in support, as she spoke of the state of her memories. "It's all been coming back in flashes, ever since I found Glenn." Her eyes met his for a moment, so grateful their paths crossed and she'd been forced to leave her proverbial cage. "I think that last knock to the head put things back in place and I . . . I know this needs to be stopped. Not just by anyone, but by me. I can't keep sitting back and doing nothing. For the friends I've lost. For my sister, I can do this."

Across the table, a deep sadness fell over Fionn, and with a shaky breath they moved to her side. The elf stood above where she sat before resting their hand on her shoulder. "My dear, I understand more than you could possibly know."

She looked between all three of them — the small band she was beginning to call home — before reaching out to take the bomb, and their future, into her hands.

CHAPTER TWENTY-FOUR

Dread filled their nearly two-week journey. Belestara was cut in two by the Medan Mountains, a tall range with only one viable path through that didn't involve scaling a summit. Those mountains alone were what stood between the elves and their ability to fully conquer the rest of the continent.

The closer their little band drew towards the range, the more patches of inky black dotted the horizon. The villages they passed were still bustling, but many of the fields laid bare.

The Withering. It was the first time she laid eyes on the barren mark it stamped upon the land. It was one thing to hear of it, to see the fear in refugees' eyes, it was quite another to witness the devastation herself. This unnatural sickness which threatened their continent, the blight served as yet another sticking point to fuel her courage.

"Don't expect much from the village we're heading to," Glenn explained. Dalia's cheek pressed against his warm back as they rode together. "The villages by the mountains have either been abandoned or destroyed."

"All of them?"

The question came out so soft. So fearful.

"Yes," he replied, somberly. "The elven empire has tried to expand their control of Belestara further north of the mountains many times. Any villages in the way just become collateral."

"You talk about this like you've seen it."

"I have," he shot back. "And you have too. Remember? Don't forget Tidesend. You know just as well as I what the elves are willing to do. They'll raze a whole town just to find one girl. Damn the lives lost."

Dalia felt sick. The guilt she managed to tuck away over what happened to the place she'd once laid her head striking its way forward in her heart. Clinging to him in an attempt to comfort herself just as much as her dear Stag, Dalia closed her eyes.

"You're right. I know all too well how little our human lives mean to them."

A calloused hand gently covered her own, lacing their fingers.

"We can do this," he promised. "We can face this. Together."

"Together," she repeated.

Perhaps alone she might have faltered. But with Glenn . . . with Fionn and Beth, anything felt possible.

As much as she wished it wouldn't be true, Glenn was right. Whitehill was more graveyard than town.

Images of Tidesend burning flooded her mind. Luck blessed them there for so long. The elves hadn't cared about the goings on of a tiny fishing town so far north. Not so long as their tithes were paid. Until Glenn arrived and her secret was revealed.

A secret which had scorched the village to the ground.

She had seen so many towns destroyed, witnessed the mark of the elves' cruelty too many times. Tidesend hadn't been perfect, it hadn't been home, but the people there did not deserve their fate. Nor did the people of Glenn's village, or the people who lived in Whitehill. She wondered what crime these people committed to earn the retribution of a Hunt. Perhaps they'd hidden away someone like her. Or, more than likely, no laws were broken at all. They simply were punished for the sin of where they happened to live. Made an example of for no other reason than where their homes were located.

Her thoughts turned to Lilivale as fear gripped her. Between the elves and the spreading Withering, soon this destruction would be on their doorstep too, unless they succeeded in standing in the way.

The Wolf may have chosen this location, but it worked out well in the Stags' favor. Here they were, far from any innocents, so if things didn't go well, they wouldn't have to worry about any casualties. There were also plenty of dilapidated homes and shops for her friends to hide in. That's where they were now, ready and waiting for her to do her part. Now she just needed to face him.

Dalia's boots crunched on the broken bits of glass and wood cluttering the cobblestone streets. The size of the buildings and the streets were enough to tell her this had once been a prosperous town. She couldn't help but wonder why the Wolf would choose this town as the scene for their meeting.

She wore a cream cotton dress tied at the waist with a brown belt, hidden beneath the taupe cloak draped over her shoulders, her wild curls barely withheld within its hood. Stray wisps and strands of fire fought their way out of where she tried to contain them. A stark contrast to her otherwise muted outfit.

Her attire was just as much of the plan as anything else. Dalia needed to look like she left on her own accord. That she had, in fact, taken him up on his offer and came alone. The cloak made her look inconspicuous, but it also housed a pocket on the inside where she was able to conceal the smoke bomb Fionn provided.

The same words repeated in her head, a mantra to keep up her courage.

I can do this.

It wasn't a choice. If their cause was going to survive, if they were to find Lumiterra, they needed to end the threat of the Wolven Hunt here and now. Dalia could do this. She knew she could. After all, she wasn't alone anymore. Now she had her friends. She had Glenn. Together, they could do this.

"I'm surprised you came."

The low voice seemed to bounce off everywhere. Dalia spun, looking around her at all the abandoned shops, trying to pinpoint where he was speaking to her from.

"I was starting to think I would have to hunt you down again."

Her hands clenched at her side. Gritting her teeth, she held firm and barked out a demand. "Come out. I have no desire to speak with a ghost."

The chuckle given in answer shook her to her core. "Oh, but that's exactly what I am. Isn't it, Dalia?"

The way he said her name was too familiar. She hated it, wanting to rip out his tongue so he might never be able to speak her name again. From his response, she feared he would remain hidden, but the crunch of glass beneath boots spoke of his approach.

She whirled in the direction of the sound, finally spotting

him. He was the same imposing hooded figure as always. Her objective was clear in her head, she needed to keep him talking, get close to him. Doing so would allow her to catch him off guard and for Glenn to strike from wherever he was hiding. She was not informed of their exact spots before starting this. Not when an accidental glance off in a direction could give away the plan.

"You don't look like a ghost to me." Her hands slid up the inside of her hood, pushing it down and freeing her curls. Removing the shadows from her face as she made her point. "Just someone who hides."

He stepped closer; her eyes darted a moment to the weapon at his side. Good. Not only had he brought it, but the dagger was sheathed in a place where Glenn might be able to grab it if he was quick enough.

"Your contempt for my hood is noted, but I'm not lowering it until you and I return to the others in the Hunt." That was never going to happen, but the way he was speaking to her now was so odd. His tone bore the same calmness he employed before.

His voice shouldn't have been soothing. Not when he wanted to take her and have her body desecrated and made into a weapon to be wielded.

"Did you come alone?"

Dalia simply motioned to herself and the fact she was not surrounded by the Stags as she was in the temple. "Did you?"

From what was visible of his mouth in the shadows, she saw him give an amused smirk at the question. "No. It was never part of the deal. You really need to learn to negotiate these things better," he teased, and Dalia bit her cheek to keep herself from snapping. "My archer is hidden among the shops. I did leave the rest of the Hunt behind, but can't be too careful."

The archer. Just as Fionn predicted. Luckily, the smoke would account for her as well. Whether or not her bow was Crystalline, she would need to see her target to be able to get off a shot. At least, Dalia hoped.

"Of what?" Dalia huffed. "You claim you know me. Then you should know I'm not much of a threat."

"You're not, but I don't believe for a second you actually came alone."

It was as if he'd clenched his fist around her heart. She needed to tread carefully here. They expected him to be suspicious. He had no reason to trust her. Still, his goal seemed so singularly focused on only her. This was their one chance, and they needed to take it.

"You told me that I know you," Dalia said, playing her part and taking a few steps towards the elf before her. Dalia willed her heart to steady with each one. "My past has been largely lost to me. I'm trying to reclaim it." Truths, mixed in with the part she played. Glenn told her that was the best way to do it. The best way to tell a convincing lie was to add a little bit of the truth in there.

He seemed to shift backwards as she drew closer. Confusion shot through her. He'd been nothing but formidable and overbearing. Now that she was the one to take those small steps, his body language faltered. Dalia didn't understand, but she knew she could use this. The crack in his armor bolstered the confidence she struggled to muster. This weakness brought forth a newfound strength to push this game of theirs even farther. This was it. A few more steps. A few more inches and she would be close enough. "Who are you?"

"You don't remember?" He stood so still, yet Dalia could not make out his expression to tell what he might be thinking. His voice trembled. Almost as if he was nervous. Something

Dalia could not piece together. He was the one with the power here.

"How can I remember a man whose face I don't even know?" This was just a part she was playing, but curiosity also tugged at her fingers. She needed to know. Needed to see who this man was who hunted her. Slowly, she reached out with one hand, the other snaking into her cloak. It was a dance, a soft distraction pushed by her intrigue, and by his confusing desire for her to remember.

Her fingertips brushed the edge of his hood like a whisper. For a moment, he allowed it. The frightening figure before her transfixed on her simple act of wanting to see his face. Somehow, the Wolf seemed vulnerable for a brief second. The moment she seized the fabric with any purpose though, his hand caught her wrist.

"I said not here." Both his hold and his voice were soft. A gentle reminder rather than a reprimand. A reminder that she didn't need to see his face for this plan to work. Her curiosity being sated was not what she came for. What she was there for, she already accomplished. Dalia was close enough and his voice alone told her he didn't desire a fight.

Dalia may not have understood why, but she took her chance. Saying nothing, her thumb pressed down on the button just as Fionn instructed her to do, and she removed the bomb from her pocket. Holding it for a second hidden within the fabric of her cloak, before she opened her fingers. The only sound between them was the clunk of metal hitting the ground and then a high-pitched hiss as it started to release the smoke.

The Wolf shifted to look down at it, and then back to her, his voice catching in his throat.

"Oh, little flower, remember I didn't want this fight."

He shoved her from him, and Dalia stumbled backwards just

as the smoke started to fill the town square. She watched with wide eyes as the hooded figure before her all but disappeared, the haze swallowing them whole. Just as Fionn said it would be, the smoke was potent. A great fog settled upon them, making it nearly impossible to see but a few inches in front of her. This fact was not what caused her heart to kick against her ribs though.

Little flower.

It wasn't possible. This elf shouldn't have known to call her that. Only one person ever called her that.

All she heard were her ragged breaths and the beating of her own heart. Dalia whirled around in the smoke, trying to find where he went. The need to get to him overwhelmed her desire to follow the plan. She had to know.

Then, there it was, the thunk of something heavy hitting the ground followed by the now too familiar clangs and grunts of battle.

Glenn. The plan was working.

Her feet took off before her head could rationalize any of it. The next part of the plan was for her to hide. Let the others handle the battle and get out of there so she didn't end up being taken. But there was a part to this puzzle they missed. A piece *she* missed. If she did not discover the answer, she feared it would continue to haunt her whole life.

Following those clangs, she found them. The smoke made everything a blur. The element of surprise worked, giving Glenn the upper hand. She just made him out. His lithe form moved so quickly in the cover of smoke. His preferred twin daggers in hand, he moved more like a cat than a stag. Pouncing and striking quickly as the hooded man went to draw his dagger. It seemed to all happen so fast.

A hiss of pain. A flash of blood on a black sleeve. The kick of a boot and then the Crystalline dagger was skittering along the ground, stopping just inches from her feet. She stared at it. The truth crept in and caused panic to rise in her. It didn't look like Deathbringer. It's blade was devoid of the veins of magic as it lay on the ground before her. Without being in his hand, the blue gleam of the blade was gone.

Little Flower.

"Glenn!" she screamed, and both the men snapped their attention towards her. The all-consuming need to understand was what propelled her now. She needed to get to him. To both of them. This wasn't simple. Not anymore.

A hint of a smile appeared on the lips of a face still in the shadows.

"You do remember then," the Wolf said before abandoning his fight with Glenn, darting forward and snagging her around the waist. Taken off guard, Dalia was pulled back hard against him before she could even react. He held no weapon now. Simply held her firm with one arm around her middle and a hand wrapped around her throat, squeezing painfully to make his point.

Dalia gave out a strangled shout. Glenn cursed, readied himself, and stalked forward. Out of the corner of her eye, Dalia saw two other forms emerging from the smoke to enter the fray. Fionn and Beth. Her elven friend rushed forward, snatching up the fallen dagger and holding it before them, not hesitating to point it in the direction of their target. But a moment passed. Then two. And the elf's face fell, looking down at the weapon in utter confusion.

"Fionn!" Glenn didn't even look at his comrade, keeping his eyes locked on hers. "What are you waiting for? Use that thing!"

The answer Dalia feared the most is what came next.

"I can't . . . I don't . . . it's not working!" Out of all of them, Fionn wouldn't be the one to be confused by a magical weapon. They should have known how to use it. No, it was something else. Something so much worse, and the thought filled Dalia with unspeakable horror and rage.

Dalia stomped down hard on her captor's foot. His grip loosened just enough for her to twist herself. Still held close to his body, she spun herself around to face him, reaching up like a viper, striking and ripping his hood back.

If anyone around her was speaking, she didn't hear it. In that moment, there was nothing. Just this void, and those eyes. The same ones haunting her dreams each night. Eyes she could never escape were now staring back at her. Darker and older than she remembered, but still the same.

Slowly, the world started to filter back into place. The rush left her ears, and she realized the ploy all along. The dagger was a diversion. So was the hood. It was a trick. Their plan was rendered useless.

"Run!" Dalia whirled back around, kicking out as her captor yanked her back hard against him. "Get out of here! He's Crystalline. The dagger isn't where the magic is coming from. It's him! He's no elf!"

"What?" All the color blanched from Fionn's face. They looked down at the dagger and back up again. Glenn didn't take the moment to be shocked. He kicked off, sprinting forward and trying to reach her. It wasn't enough. It was never going to be enough.

A black gloved hand reached out before her, no weapon in it this time, but the result was the same. The air around them chilled and then, in a rush, swept forward. So cold. The very air around her hurt her lungs. It wasn't like anything he summoned before, the whole ground before them froze solid. Ice raced along the cobblestones before it leapt up, the fractals linking together to construct a barrier. The frozen wall curved and encased the Stags in a smooth dome. Where seconds before she saw Glenn rushing towards them, now stood a prison of ice, cutting her off from him. From all of them.

The man behind her slouched a little against her. The effort of creating such a large structure clearly took a toll on him. One she was able to exploit. Shaking him off her, she ran to the icy barrier and beat her fists against it.

"Glenn! Glenn! Fionn! Beth!"

The ice was so thick she could barely see through. Within the cold cage she could barely make out the distorted forms of her friends. The blurred images of another fist banging in time with her own through the barrier.

"Glenn!"

Her calls struggled out through sobs and tears streaming down her cheeks. He was right there. Just out of reach.

"Dalia."

The voice came from behind her. Low and calm as always. She didn't want to turn. Didn't want to see. Dalia knew all too well who was standing behind her, but denial felt easier to swallow. Kinder on her stomach then the idea he would have done this. That he could have betrayed her. Betrayed all of them.

"Dalia," he said, firmer this time. "Don't make me drag you out of here."

That did seem simpler, to keep fighting and allow him to be the villain. Something in her stirred and rebelled against the thought. A piece of her childhood, reaching for him through the fire, desperate not to lose him. He was right there. All she needed to do was turn around, and there he would be. She desperately wanted that, but not like this.

Dalia heard the ground beneath his boots crunch, and knew he was moving towards her.

"What did you do? What did you do to them?"

"Little flower—"

"Don't call me that," she snarled, barely recognizing her own voice. She finally turned to look at him, at Drystan. Truly what he claimed to be but moments ago. A ghost. "Get away from me."

A pained expression rippled across his face. One moment there, and then the next, nothing. Just a cold wall that might as well have been nothing but those shadows under his hood. "I did tell you that I didn't want this."

No sooner than the words were spoken, he seized her. Grabbing her by the waist, he hauled her up and threw her over his shoulder.

"No!" she shrieked, struggling and beating her feet against him to little avail. "Let me go. Let me go!"

He said nothing now, just carried her along like she was little more than the child she'd been when she lost him. The smoke cleared, and the harsh reality came into focus. Her friends were completely encased an ice dome. They wouldn't be getting out of there any time soon. The strength it would have taken to make such a thing. He held back before when he fought them. There was no other explanation.

Dalia's attention turned back to her ghost, noticing his stride, his whole demeanor. He was exhausted. Probably spent his magic for the time being making such a large structure. Even still, the job was done. She was cut off from everyone but him. But that didn't mean she couldn't fight. In his weakened state, she stood a chance.

Soft footsteps told her all she needed to know about how that plan would go. The archer. She had forgotten about her. The blonde elf stood not too far from them, her damned bow in hand. In the light of the day, veins of magic danced visibly on the curves of the weapon. At least with her, Dalia saw her ears. Her eyes and form were enough to know she wasn't Crystalline herself. Just an elf, but no less deadly with a Crystalline weapon in her hands.

"Well, that was overly dramatic," the huntress teased coldly.

"Shut up." Drystan seemed to be in no mood to deal with her mockery. With a plop, he dropped Dalia at her feet, keeping the healer between them. She looked from the huntress back to him, her chest shaking. The elf before her, Evanee he had called her, showed very little sympathy for Dalia's panic. With little more than a scoff, she stepped forward, rope in hand, and bound her wrists tight. Dalia's gaze fell, resting firmly on the ground at her feet. She didn't want to see him. Just looking at Drystan as an elf prepared her for capture was enough to make her want to scream.

"Well, we have what you came for," Evanee drawled. "Let's get back to the others. Barric is waiting."

The others. They were going to take her to the Wolven Hunt. This man, her friend, was going to turn her over to the enemy.

No.

He *was* the enemy. Her brain put the pieces together, but her heart stumbled in denial. Dalia clung to the hope the obvious was not true. Either way, there was little choice now but to go along with them and face her past.

Part Three:
Surrounded by Wolves

Chapter Twenty-Five

The short journey back to where the Hunt made camp was a quiet one. The huntress rode on ahead of them. Two steeds carried the members of the Wolven Hunt, but Dalia struggled along on foot. Her bonds were tied to the saddle of the stark white beast carrying the man who hunted her. She'd been given enough rope to walk by the horse's side. The thought of turning to try and run crossed her mind, but Evanee had threatened to shoot her if she so much as took a step out of line. Dalia would never get far. Not with the huntress wielding an enchanted bow.

Maybe she should have counted her lucky stars her captor possessed the shred of decency to keep his mount to a slow pace, so she wasn't being drug around painfully after him. It meant by the time they'd arrived, the sun was setting. Yet even that small drop of gratitude was not something she could muster. Dalia could not give thanks for any part of this. Not when everything was falling apart.

Not a single word was spoken between them. Not when he

walked her into the camp. Nor when he brought her to a tree near the edges of where their tents were laid out, tying her hands behind her back. Her arms stretched out behind her, as the length of the rope was brought around the trunk of the tree. He worked deftly to tie a knot she knew damn well would hold, even if she tried to struggle against it.

Drystan.

He was a piece of her past she only just reclaimed. The final piece to the puzzle of understanding what happened at Keep Oharn. All she lost and left behind. He never really left her though, did he? In every dream he remained. Every moment she tried to escape and rest, he'd been there. Her dreams were a constant reminder of the boy who gave his life for her.

Only, it wasn't true. He hadn't died. Or maybe he had. The Drystan she knew would never turn her over, nor wear the colors of an Elven Hunt. This man was a stranger.

It was not until he made to leave her alone, bound to the tree, that she finally found her voice. A single word erupted up through the thick weight of emotions battling inside her.

"Traitor."

It was all she could think to say. The only word she could possibly attribute to him now.

He stopped, like a rock was thrown, not a word. Slowly, he turned back to her. By some blessing he decided to keep his distance and not approach her once more. He said nothing, just stared at her.

Dalia was finally given a moment to take him in. He looked much like the tall boy she remembered, only now somehow taller and fuller. There was a weariness to him that replaced the boyish optimism he always held even in the face of terrible adversity. No ever-present smile graced his features now. Just a hard as stone expression, that looked so out of place on the boy she once knew. His hair had grown long. Black strands now half tied up behind his head, the rest spilling down to his shoulders. Even without the hood, he was imposing. His tall broad stature was not one anyone would want to meet on the battlefield, she was sure.

And then there were his damn eyes.

So familiar, and yet entirely different from her own. Hooded and deep set, so dark brown they were almost black. A strong expressive brow framed them into place. A person could get lost in eyes like his. They were kinder a decade ago. The hard expression he now wore didn't quite make it into the depths of his gaze. There, she saw only a somber exhaustion. A dark pool of sadness that was enough to make her breath hitch.

"Why?" Dalia choked out the question, tears threatening to spill with it, but she did not allow them. The things he had done, all the lives taken. Emil. Who knew how many other Crystallines. Tidesend. It was gone, and his hands were stained with that blood. Dalia could mourn the loss of the friend she once knew. The brave boy who protected her and so many others. That boy deserved her tears. The man standing before her did not. What stood before her was a monster. A weapon, just like their captors always wanted them to be.

"How could you? After everything?" Her voice raised, as she continued. Those tears fighting to come forward, but her will fought harder as she demanded again. "Why?"

If he was moved by her sudden rush of emotion, he did not show it. The tiniest flash of *something* crossed his dark gaze. A simple flicker lasting no longer than a second.

"I know it might seem confusing."

"Confusing?" Dalia choked out. "I thought you were dead. I thought you were dead, but instead you're working with them? With a Hunt?"

"Would it have been easier for you?" He spoke swiftly this time, not allowing her to work through her whole thought.

"What?"

"Would it have been easier?" he repeated, taking a single step towards her. Even that was enough to make her recoil, pushing her back hard against the tree. "If I had died, instead of doing what was necessary to survive. You would have preferred that?"

The line of questioning felt vile to swallow. Burning like acid and twisting her heart as she took it down. Would she have preferred if he died? He had been her friend. She might have forgotten until recently, but he always lingered with her. He mattered to her. Would she really have preferred if he'd been gone? It was not something she wanted to admit, but there was a seed of truth to it. Dalia already accepted his death. She had mourned it and continued to live with it. This new concept she was forced to grapple with, one that included him betraying all the Crystalline they knew as children, was more than she wanted to try and stomach.

He was right. It would have been easier if he stayed dead.

"When did you even develop abilities?" She couldn't stop herself from asking. "You didn't have magic like the rest of us."

"Turns out I just took a little longer to crack."

The implication of those words silenced her line of questioning. Dalia didn't want to think about what torture he might have endured following the fire. Torture she hadn't been there to heal his wounds from.

"So, what happens now?" she asked, her voice softer as fear started to set in. "I go back? They cut out my heart?"

His eyebrow ticked up. Somehow, he found the audacity to be confused by her line of questioning. "Is that what you really think is happening here?"

"What else would an Elven Hunt want with me?" she

asserted. "You already killed Emil and attacked my friends more than once."

"Ah yes, your friends." He drew out the last word, disgust dripping from it. "What is it your friends have been telling you?"

The question struck her. Dalia drew herself up straighter, bravely saying what she knew to be true.

"That the Wolven Hunt has been after them for a while now. That there have been casualties. Including Emil, a Crystalline. You attacked him and Glenn back north, near Tidesend. And then you destroyed the village." Laying it all out, the tears did start to fall. "I lived there. They took me in after the fire. Kept me safe. And you killed them! After everything you did to help me escape. Why?"

She still wanted to understand. He'd killed and allowed himself to become the monster the world wanted to see them all as. And the reason he'd given was just to survive. A pitiful excuse. The idea of taking so many lives so he could continue his own felt hollow.

Drystan barely flinched at her accusations, but he did stalk forward this time. Moving so quickly that Dalia sucked in a surprised breath. His one hand struck out, palm meeting the trunk of the tree above her head, as he leaned in. Loose strands of black hair fell forward across his face which was now mere inches away from hers. Her heart and breath threatened to tear her chest apart, but she held firm. Meeting his dark gaze, jaw clenched, as she summoned the strength not to back down against this man.

"Go on." His low voice rumbled in command. His ever-calm tone gave way to something else. Something laced with a deep rage. "Tell me what else I've done. All the sins they've attributed to my name."

"You won't win," Dalia spat back. "They will never let you

find Lumiterra. Those crystals will never be allowed to be used on anyone again."

A moment passed between them. A horrible mix of revulsion for his actions fought with the urge to want to be close to him. Embrace him, even, and find comfort in the fact he had not sacrificed himself for her. Her promise of finding him again was fulfilled. The only promise she could now say she was able to keep. The logical part of her managed to kick in and remind herself the boy she made that promise to was gone.

The person before her now was no boy, but a wolf.

This wasn't some magical reunion. It was a whole different kind of mourning and funeral.

"You think this is about the crystals?" His question sounded almost amused sending a jolt of confusion through her.

"That's what all of this has been leading to," she snapped back, not allowing him to make her second guess herself. "The clues, everything. It's to the last cache. So your new masters can steal more children. Kill more of us to make weapons. Well, I'm not going to let that happen." She paused for a moment, forming the insult and spitting it forth with venom. "Did you wear that hood to hide your shame? Waving around a useless dagger as a prop, for what? So people wouldn't know what you truly are? A weapon for the elves that didn't have to be cut up to be bent to their will."

His jaw clenched. Rage bubbled under the surface, threatening, their shared breath becoming visible as the air around them chilled. The deepening of his voice served as warning. "Dalia . . ."

"Don't." Her voice was quiet but almost unrecognizable to her ears in how unshakable it was. "You don't get to say my name or call me Little Flower or pretend some familiarity with me. You are not my friend. You are a stranger. A monster, just like them."

That fury bubbling forth slowly sunk down again. A cold wall of ice lifted back over his face. Only his eyes reflected the sadness possibly lurking beneath it all. Her words hit him exactly where she wanted them to, causing pain, even if he didn't want to show it.

His head hung a little, his face still far too close to hers for comfort. "You're right. I am a monster."

The admission should not have stirred pity in her soul. It should not have made her wish her hands were not bound so she might reach out to him. Yet, that stupid part of her remained. The part that wanted to heal. Wishing her power might extend to the soul, so she might be able to take away his pain. Wishing she could find the part of him that was once the boy she knew and mend it back together. But such wishes were a fallacy.

Before anything more could be said between them, Drystan pulled back, pushing off against the tree, and once again allowed space between them. It was like a weight lifted off her chest. Like she could breathe again. And yet, his final statement shook her. The fact he accepted the insults slung at him faltered her resolve.

"You're right about many things," he continued, after he put sufficient space between them once more. "I am not a good person, nor am I the boy you once knew. But I did not kill that Crystalline."

Dalia opened her mouth to protest, but then ended up shutting it again when he raised his hand, not finished with what he wanted to say. "And I did not destroy that fishing village."

She swallowed thickly, her salvia sticky in her throat. That couldn't be true. He had to have done those things. If not him, at the very least the Hunt he worked with did. So no matter what he said, their blood was still on his hands.

"Liar." It was a whisper. Not nearly as confident as earlier, but it was the only word she could find. There was no one else to blame for those sins. They were his. Even if he didn't want to accept them.

A huff exhaled from his lips. "I'm sure that's easier for you too."

She hated how those words stung. Dalia wanted to be so unaffected by him. She wanted to be able to see his face and not have treacherous pangs of longing for what once was. What a soft and stupid girl she was. They all knew it. Her sister, Nora, Glenn, even Drystan. They all knew she was not meant for this fight. A flower to be protected, not one with thorns meant to strike.

This was no place for a girl with a kind heart.

Some movement in the camp behind Drystan's shoulder caught her eye. Horses arrived, three black steeds. He glanced over his shoulder quickly before turning back to her. "I'll be back. Maybe then you'll be more willing to listen to reason."

Any remark she might have conjured up died on her tongue as he walked away swiftly. She needed to change focus. The questions she held for the man once known as her friend might never be sated. Going down that route and quenching her curiosity would only lose her precious time.

No, what she needed was to find a way out.

CHAPTER TWENTY-SIX

From her spot on the outskirts, Dalia craned her neck to try and see what was happening. Three elves arrived at the little camp, that much she could make out. The others crowded around and lowered their heads in respect. This must be their actual leader. She assumed Drystan had led them because of his trappings and the fact he wielded a Crystalline weapon. Now knowing the truth, it made sense there was someone else pulling the strings.

A few bodies moved and Dalia was finally able to catch sight of him. A strikingly beautiful elf with higher cheekbones than she thought was fair for anyone to have. His sandy blond hair was chopped just above his shoulders and the golden eyes which signified his kind were just visible from where she stood. He was dressed like anyone else in the camp, in fact, maybe even less dramatically. Each member of the Hunt wore some kind of wolf pelt adorned on their black leathers. All of them relatively the same, except for Drystan. Realization dawned on her. He was a diversion. There was no other reason to dress a Crystalline up in such splendor. It was a ploy with the help of a prop weapon bound to work every time.

Her mind tumbled, trying to wrap itself around why their leader would want to conceal his identity. It could have been to hide that Drystan was a Crystalline from the rest of the world. No, that hardly made sense. After all, the archer wielded a magical weapon as well. He wasn't the only member with magical power, just the only one wielding his own. An elf controlling a Crystalline as a soldier seemed like something they might want to scream from the rafters. Boast about the power they commanded in the form of an actual living weapon rather than one made from scraps of the dead. This elf hid Drystan away though, and Dalia felt her curiosity creeping through her veins once more.

The two were speaking just beyond the rest of the Hunt. Dalia heard their murmurs but she couldn't make out any words. The stiffening of stances and waving of hands was enough to hint they were disagreeing on something. The only indication she was the subject of their conversation was when those golden eyes met hers for a moment. A brief second, but enough to stir something within her. His face, it was so famil-iar. This couldn't be another person forgotten from her past. No, she was so sure she put the pieces together now. Still, something about him sparked recognition.

"You're the flower we've been looking for."

The elf pushed past Drystan, leaving the Crystalline standing there with a look of utter frustration on his face. The Hunt's true leader walked right up to her with a confi-dent air about him that could rival General Lachlan's. He moved as though each step he took flowed. Yet, it was the expression on his face that threatened her jaw to drop. She didn't see disgust or arrogance. Nothing like the looks she remembered which ate away at her mind and soul. Nothing like the look Mollie gave her, or even the look of reverence she sometimes got from Glenn and the other Stags. This elf looked at her with kindness and a little pity. He looked at her like she was just any other person. Not a weapon to possess and wield.

"Please, forgive Drystan's manners. This was not exactly what I had planned for this meeting."

Dalia just stood there with wide eyes, utterly confused. The elf made it sound like he'd been looking for her specifically. That didn't make sense. Fionn made it sound like, to activate the clues left by the Lumiels, any Crystalline would do. With someone like Drystan at their disposal, it didn't make sense anymore why they were hunting her at all.

"My name is Barric," he offered with a polite bow of his head, her confusion causing more pity to show on his handsome face. "And you must be Dalia."

She had absolutely no idea how to handle this situation. Having to accept the man who hunted her down was a ghost from her past was enough. The fact that he murdered innocents was enough. But the idea of this elf speaking to her just like she was anyone else . . . it was all too much. Dalia said nothing. She just stood there, completely dumbfounded.

"Can we get her untied, please?"

Behind him, the rest of the Hunt hesitated at his order. After looking between one another for a moment, Drystan finally stepped forward. "I hope you know what you're doing," he muttered, before walking behind her and starting at the knots he had tied only a few moments ago.

"Oh it's alright." Barric grinned. "She's not going to get far if she tries to run. No reason to tie her up like a prisoner."

Once her wrists were free, Dalia snatched her hands forward, rubbing the sensitive area of skin where the tension left minor rope burns. Her voice slowly started to creep back to her and fight its way over her utter bewilderment. "Am I not a prisoner?"

The elf crossed his arms over his chest, shifting his weight to one side casually. "Well, it would seem you are. Though I did ask Drystan to only bring you here if you came willingly. He assured me once he got you away from the Stags, and you knew who he was, that you would listen and follow. Clearly, he overestimated your faith in him."

She glanced back to the Crystalline who now stood slightly off to her side. A pang went off in her chest. He thought she would trust him. Maybe she would have, back when they were children. But now this was all a complicated mess, one she didn't know how to properly sift through. There were so many things she knew to be true, but they were not lining up with what she was seeing here. Or with what he was saying.

"I don't understand," Dalia muttered, looking between the two men and then eyeing the rest of the hunters watching them. "Why do you even need me if you have him?"

"Well, he's not exactly the key to Lumiterra, is he?"

Her brow furrowed. What was that supposed to mean? The clues reacted to any Crystalline's blood and abilities as far as she'd been told. It's what happened in the temple. It was how Emil revealed the writings left near Tidesend and the ones before that. There had never been any mention of a key.

Barric opened his mouth and drew a breath. His lips formed a silent 'oh' as his eyebrows raised. "They really have left you in the dark. Haven't they?" he exhaled, a twinge of amusement dancing over his words.

None of this was right. First Drystan, and now this elf, were insinuating things she could not find a way to reconcile. This was a trick. Some clever ruse much like Drystan's use of the dagger. Why they were lying to her, she didn't know. But she knew better than to believe a single word that came out of this elf's mouth.

When she said nothing in response, Barric pressed on. "I'll tell you what. Let's make a deal."

Dalia did not like the sound of that at all. Especially given her apparent inability to negotiate deals in her favor.

"I let you go. You go back to your band of humans and keep going about your way." Drystan shifted his stance uncomfortably beside her at the suggestion. Clearly fighting the urge to protest against this deal his commander was proposing. "Under two conditions. One: you will owe me a favor of my choosing. And two: you start asking the right questions."

"I won't help you hurt my friends."

"Who said anything about that? No. I suppose I should add that stipulation though. One favor of my choosing, which will not include harming any of your precious friends."

Her lips parted as she tried to steady her breath and take in what he was offering her. Nothing about this arrangement sat right with her. Giving her up would allow the White Stags to keep pressing forward after Lumiterra. The race between the two of them would be back on. The fact he would allow such a thing made her uneasy, and the thought of owing this elf, who owned Drystan's leash, sat like a stone in the pit of her stomach.

"I don't—"

"No, I imagine you're very confused. As are the rest of my Hunt." That certainly was the case. Drystan was not the only one who looked like they wanted to yell in protest. In the small crowd, Dalia could see the archer. Her eyes narrowed and jaw tight. "But you are no good to me or my plans as a prisoner. And I doubt anything we say to you while you are one is likely to change your mind."

His words ran through her head over and over and still made little sense.

"There's so much you don't understand, but I suspect it's something you need to figure out on your own *Flower*." He leaned forward then, lowering his voice to just above a whisper. His emphasis on that word stuck her like a pin prick. "Ask the right questions. Demand the truth. And when you're ready, we will be waiting for you."

The breath she took next shook. A trick. It had to be. But it was one she didn't know what to do with. Playing along meant she could go back to the White Stags, back to her friends. She wouldn't be a hostage anymore. The cage door was open, and when Barric stepped to the side and ordered the rest of his Hunt to do the same, she took the step forward. Dalia pushed herself on wobbly feet to walk through their camp, feeling their eyes on her. Looks of varying levels of interest. All except one.

Glancing back at Drystan for the briefest of moments, she saw his face bore nothing but concern. That look tugged on a piece of her heart she didn't want to acknowledge, and so she tore her gaze away, back forward, urging herself to be brave and keep moving.

"Barric, if they hurt her . . . I hope you know what you're doing." he muttered from behind her, repeating his sentiments from before.

"Don't worry. We'll see her again."

CHAPTER TWENTY-SEVEN

Everything hurt, but her feet screamed in the most agony. Dalia had no idea how long she'd been walking. The sun started to rise in the sky, peppering pinkish rays between the trees. Those soft colors were enough to tell her it'd been at least a few hours.

They may have let her go, but Dalia didn't know the way back to Whitehill, and even if she did, the chance her friends would still be waiting there was slim. That, along with so many other fears, were pounding around in her skull. Any time she tried to focus on one, her head throbbed and her throat constricted, strangling sobs which threatened to consume her. She couldn't think on those fears now. Trying to parse through all the things said back at the camp would have to come later. Thinking about how Drystan was still alive would have to come later. Right now, she just needed to find her Stags.

With a moan and a huff, Dalia fell to the ground. Plopping down and resting her back against a rock, she tried to catch her breath. Mud caked the hem of her dress, and she looked like an utter disaster as she ran her fingers over her round face. Wiping sweat off her freckles as she tried to focus herself on the task at hand.

They wouldn't just leave without her. That wall of ice couldn't hold forever, certainly they would get out. And when they did, they would start to look for her, she was sure of it. Dalia just needed to make sure she was somehow able to be found.

With a frustrated sigh, she let her head fall back and looked up at the canopy of leaves. Then she saw it. Standing out like a sore thumb among the green. The leaves of one of the trees were as black as pitch. Just like those patches Dalia saw in the distance on their travels, but this was the first time she'd witnessed the Withering up close. The tree above her was not just dying, it was decaying like something out of a nightmare.

Black pulsing veins twisted around its trunk like an infection. A sickness. Something that might be healed.

Drawing in a sharp breath, she mustered up what strength was left in her and scrambled to her feet.

When she used her power in the Wilds, the area in her vicinity had glowed. Same as when she healed Glenn. If she tried to cure this tree, maybe it could serve as a beacon. A light in the dark to lead her friends to her. Just how the Hunt tracked them in the Wilds.

Following the blackness down to the trunk and roots, Dalia knelt at the base. Holding her hands out before her, she closed her eyes and said a silent prayer to the Gods. Warmth pooled in her hands and she opened her eyes to see the tree aglow. Lines of blue raced up its twisted bark, chasing higher and higher, until the leaves themselves shuddered. Competing with the diseased lines of black.

It was unlike anything she'd done before. Healing injuries was one thing. Attempting her ability on this Withering sapped her of her strength faster than she could have ever imagined. And yet, it was working. New life breathed into the darkness and a lushness returned to the foliage. A green glow came from within the tree itself to meet her fingers, the colors twisting into something like a turbulent sea.

The forest which had been so still in its decay now teemed with light. The cries of birds broke the afternoon air, and the rustle of leaves spoke the introduction of curious wildlife creeping back to this area of the wood.

A fox emerged from the bushes not a few feet from where she knelt. No fear reflected in its yellow eyes as it ventured into the clearing and bounded through newly sprung grass. With a yip, Dalia could have sworn it looked right at her, before disappearing again into the underbrush.

The Withering was tearing their world apart. Not only for humans, or even elves, but all life. If this desperate attempt to signal her location to her friends healed even a small sliver of the scar it left of their continent, then Dalia would gladly give more of herself.

She just had to hold on, pour as much of herself into this as she could until her friends could find her. Dalia worked at it in spurts. Allowed small pieces of her strength to flow from her into the roots below her palms. She gave more and more as the seconds, then minutes, ticked by. Nausea roiled in her gut and she groaned as her head grew light.

Just a little longer. Just keep holding it.

The ground around her cracked. The great roots of the tree grew out further, as it drew from the lifeforce she poured into it. Buds sprung among the leaves, robbing her of whatever she was willing to give. Dalia's vision began to darken. Her hands shook and her body swayed, ready to give in to the darkness of exhaustion beckoning to her, wanting to swallow her whole. Then, his voice came: a lighthouse calling her to shore.

"Dalia!"

She sprung back to her senses, cutting off her connection with the tree, and wobbled up to her feet. His voice calling her name was the only thing holding her together. She heard it over and over again, until she finally saw him.

His mop of brown curls falling into his eyes as he burst through the thicket towards her.

"Glenn!"

Dalia's heart sprung to life against her chest as she ran. With everything she had left, she ran towards him. Arms outstretched until she all but collapsed into his embrace. Burying her face into the crook of his neck, she took in his warmth before finally letting out everything she fought against. Every emotion that threatened during her capture poured forth as she wrapped her arms around him and sobbed.

THEY HADN'T NEEDED to go far to get to where the White Stags were starting to set up their new base of operations. The herd was on the move closer to the Medan Mountains to finish what they started. Dalia was struck by just how different things looked as she entered the new camp, leaning against Glenn for support the whole way. If the old camp was a training ground, this was something else entirely. Gone was the large ring from the center of the tents and the happy faces that wove in and out. Everyone around her seemed to be on alert. There was so much movement, so many weapons and armor stands. It seemed the number of people had increased, too.

They were preparing for battle, an invasion, even.

The sight didn't sit right within her. Sure, the Wolven Hunt out maneuvered them so far. Their weapons, and apparently abilities, far superior to their own. But, Fionn helped to level the playing field, and even if the weapon General Fettler possessed had limited uses left, it was still in an option. Dalia wasn't even sure what power lay dormant inside of it. The sheer amount of people here seemed like far too much to simply be going to battle with the Hunt alone.

There were so few of them. She'd counted maybe ten at most at their little camp.

Wrapped up in all the hustle and bustle around them, Dalia hardly paid attention to where Glenn was leading her. Once they were in the tent and she was seated on the cot, she took a breath and a better look at her surroundings. Judging from the strewn clothing and few personal effects, it seemed he had brought her back to his personal tent. Vaguely, she heard him muttering. Something about how he was going to let General Lachlan know they were back safe and how he would alert the others as well.

Dalia remembered nodding, but honestly, the bed was soft, and sleep called to her. Even if using her powers against the Withering hadn't drained her, she was beyond mentally exhausted. Drystan still haunted her, only now it wasn't in her dreams. He was alive. He was out there, and he was the enemy. It left a hollowness, and when Glenn exited the tent, she simply laid down on the bed and shut her eyes.

Sleep didn't come. Her mind was too abuzz. Still, it was nice to have a moment to just stare at the backs of her eyelids.

"Dalia..."

The soft voice drew her from her rest. Opening her eyes, she saw the elf standing there. Fionn's face a mixture of relief and that shame they wore so well. Yet, the sight of them sparked a hint of much needed joy in her heart. A smile drew on her lips as she sat up. "Hey..."

They launched themselves at her. Long arms wrapping around her as they skirted to a halt on their knees at the bedside. Her eyes widened in surprise at the action, but it was momentary. Her smile warmed and she embraced her friend in return.

"I'm so sorry," they muttered softly. "I should have known the dagger was fake. For all my research, what good was I to you?"

"It's alright," Dalia said, squeezing Fionn before she pulled back slightly to better look at them and meet their golden gaze. "You couldn't have known. If anyone should have known, it was me."

They shook their head. Clearly not ready to let the blame be placed off them. "Glenn told me about who that was. He was your friend. I'm sorry."

Dalia's face fell instantly. This wasn't a conversation she wanted to keep having. Drystan was right. It would have been easier for her if he stayed dead. Then she wouldn't have to face any of this.

Thankfully seeing she didn't want to elaborate anymore right now, Fionn stood up. An exasperated sigh released from their chest. "I won't let that happen again. We can't use you as bait. It was stupid to begin with. We already lost Emil to them, and now we almost lost you."

Emil. Drystan's words were ringing in her head: how he claimed he was not the one to end Emil's life. It didn't make sense, and yet, they set her free. Which made even less sense to her. More so, he accepted that he was a monster. Taken every other blow thrown at him, but denied only two. Instead, holding firm that Emil's death and the demise of Tidesend were not on him. It made little sense to concede to so many horrible things only to deny a few.

"Fionn." Her voice was so soft, resistant. The condition Barric gave her ran through her head — *ask the right questions.*

"What could Emil do? The general made it seem that, unlike me, his power was an offensive one."

The elf raised their brow. "Why ask about this now?"

Dalia shrugged, deciding not to fully let Fionn in on the events which played out with the Wolven Hunt just yet. "I'm just curious. You never really talk about him, though I know you cared."

"I did," they sighed. "We traveled together for a long time, before I even came to join the White Stags. Besides Beth, he was the one who convinced me to stay here. To join the cause."

She never realized their relationship had been so close. No wonder Fionn, and even Bethana, seemed so concerned for her safety and so broken up whenever the other Crystalline was mentioned.

"He was a good man, and his gifts were extraordinary. He was a conduit of sorts. Summoning electricity at will."

Her encouraging smile faded some. "Electricity?"

"Ah yes, you humans don't know much about that do you? Elven cities use it to light their homes, where humans usually use candles." Fionn chuckled. "It's like harnessing lightning. Much like when a bolt strikes the ground scorching it. That's the sort of thing he could do. Never burned him though, it was like he was immune to it."

Eyelids fluttered. The information sat heavy on her, making it hard to breathe. Still, she forced a kind smile. "I'm sorry you lost him."

"I am too." Fionn cleared their throat. "Anyway, I will let you get some rest. We can talk more about what happened when you're feeling up to it." She nodded and they turned to leave, stopping at the tent flaps to look back one last time. "I am truly happy you've come back to us."

The smile she gave then was more genuine. Warm from the affection she had come to harbor for the elf, but it didn't last long. The second they were gone, it vanished from her face, leaving nothing but cold dread.

Gears turned in her head, replaying the night she found Glenn again and again. The wounds on his body. How foreign they were to her. Emil, nowhere to be found. Dead was all Glenn told her. He never expected to survive that night either.

She never questioned it before, never even put much thought into the matter. The Wolf had been a bogeyman. A wraith representing so much hurt in her past. She never questioned the fact that the hooded monster was the one to try and kill Glenn. Of course it was him. Glenn was a White Stag harboring a Crystalline. He was an elf in a Hunt. Only, he wasn't. He was a Crystalline himself.

One which used ice as his weapon.

Ice.

It never clicked. The wounds Glenn suffered . . . they were not from freezing. They were burns. His body blackened and scorched in patches, as if lightning came down from the sky and struck him.

Her stomach twisted, the hollowness growing and gnawing like a deep pit there. Dread replaced the emptiness as the truth slowly took form in her head.

She had asked the right question.

CHAPTER TWENTY-EIGHT

It was like tumbling. Each time she reached out to find a lifeline, or a net might open to catch her, she just kept descending. Further and further. Deeper and deeper into the dark.

Was everything she thought she knew a lie?

The act of having to question her reality was not new to her. For so long she stumbled in the dark, grasping for memories and clues to her past. Not understanding who she really was or why she so willingly gave in to her own isolation. Why she conceded to something she truly despised.

It often made her question her own sanity. Question if anything she thought she endured was real or not.

She fought through all that. Reclaimed her memories and her reality. Only to be thrown into another pit. One she wasn't sure she even wanted to climb out of. Maybe it would be easier to pretend. Pretend she never gave into an elf's request and never pursued the truth. But Dalia couldn't turn away from it now. The truth was there, staring back at her from the darkness.

Drystan was not responsible for Glenn's wounds the night she found him.

She had not done much else besides just sat there on the cot, feeling like her chest might collapse under the weight of every emotion screaming to get out. Yet, she stayed silent, staring at the flap of the tent. Once again in wait, dreading every second passing that led her closer to having to face him.

As if fate heard her prayers and decided to ignore them, the fabric finally fluttered open. Glenn ducked under the heavy material, carrying what looked like a mug filled with tea and a plate of food.

"Hey, I brought you some lunch. How are you holding . . ." His voice shifted away like sand caught in the tide when he saw her. She was sure she looked like death. A pale shell of the person she once was as she struggled to muddle through everything before her now.

"Dalia?" He set the food and drink down on the chest in the corner of the tent and came to kneel before her. "What is it? Are you alright?"

"What happened that night?" Her voice was hollow, a reflection of herself. "The night I found you. What happened?"

Confusion swept across his face. "I've told you. The Wolven Hunt attacked Emil and I."

"What happened to Emil?"

He stood up. Brows furrowed as he looked down at her. "He died. We've talked about this. Dalia, what is this about?"

"See, this funny thing just happened." A smile crossed her face when she said it. One that didn't reach her eyes. One that didn't stop the tears from hitting her cheeks. Borderline deranged. "Fionn told me what Emil could do. They told me about his powers."

She saw it then, the shift in him. The proud stag changed. That same desperation and cowardice crawled over him, just like how he had been after they met with General Lachlan. He looked like a rabbit whose leg was snared in a trap. Finding strength, she didn't even know she possessed, she stood. The hunter within her waking up, that part of her she had hidden away for so long roared to life.

"The wounds I healed. They were burns. You said so yourself. Burns like nothing I had ever seen before. Your skin was black and charred beyond recognition. Almost as if struck by lightning." Her teeth bared as she spoke, chewing through each word. She might have expected him to protest, but instead, Glenn seemed to sink into himself. Eyes wide in disbelief.

"Dalia, let me explain."

"No!" Her voice came out louder than she anticipated, and Glenn flinched at the rejection. Softer, she continued, but with no less venom. "No. Don't you dare try and feed me anymore lies. I will ask you again, what happened to Emil?"

"The Hunt killed him."

She surged forward, fingers curling into tight fists at her side. "Stop lying to me!"

"I'm not," he protested, holding his ground. His eyes darkened as he drew his back straight. Staring up at her from where he knelt on the ground, swallowing that frightened desperation with yet another mask of his. "The Hunt didn't need to make the final blow to have killed him. They made it necessary."

With those words, their dynamic shifted. Now it was Dalia's turn to feel small. She faltered, eyes widening, her lip quivered at what he just said.

"Necessary?" The word repeated from her lips like a curse. "What are you talking about? What do you mean?"

Dalia had been the only one to see his wounds. It had been so easy for him to pass off Drystan as the one to attack him. To claim the Hunt killed Emil — not him. Still, she needed to hear him say it. She needed to hear him admit to what he had done. More than that, she wanted to know why.

He rose from the ground, causing her step to back. Her calves hit the edge of the cot. There was nowhere else to go. She just needed to hold her ground and be strong now.

"Listen to me," he begged. "You have seen what one of those weapons can do. Hell, you have seen what a Crystalline on the wrong side can do. They are insanely powerful; that's how the elves keep us down. How they turn the tide of every battle. I couldn't let them have another."

An asset. It was just like General Lachlan said. Emil had never been a full person to Glenn, either. The thought washed over her and left nothing but nausea in its wake.

"We were cornered, Dalia. Running out of time. I made a choice to protect us all."

Her nails dug into the flesh of her palm as she pressed her fists tighter. "He was your friend."

"He was a weapon. One that could have been turned against us."

He might as well have slapped her. The second that passed between them felt like an eternity. Releasing her rage, she lashed forward. Her hands met his chest as she shoved him backwards. "He was your friend!" Dalia screamed the sentiment again, fists raising again to beat against his chest. "You killed him!"

Glenn moved quickly, catching her wrists and holding firm. A strangled sob left her as he contained her, forcing her hands down by her sides as he loomed over her.

"I know you don't see it like I do." He appeared calm, but

his desperation strained against every word. It sparked pity in her, but not enough to give him what he wanted.

She could not accept and forgive this. "You saw Whitehill. So many towns are like that. Run through by the elves just to keep us in line. My town. My sister. Gone. Yours too. Because they had a weapon that could do that. You need to open your eyes and realize things are not as simple as you want them to be. You needed to see what they can do. What they *will* do."

Her cheeks were already wet with her tears, and yet more started to fall. His words revealing just how far he might be willing to go. Dystan claimed he hadn't killed Emil. It seemed that was true. He also claimed he was not the one to set Tidesend ablaze. The idea that particular sin might also belong to Glenn, just so that he could make a point, choked her. The mere concept turned all her words to ash in her mouth.

Everything he was telling her right now she should have known. She should have seen the signs. They were all right there. The way he talked about Emil. The way his general talked about her. Glenn allowed him to speak about her that way. Dalia didn't want to admit it, but this was not some new side she was seeing to Glenn. It had always been there. She was just too blinded by the chance to mean something to someone that she had ignored it all.

"And what about me? Am I just a weapon too?"

"No. No, don't say that." Somehow his comfort was worse than if he said yes. She would have been able to stomach his distain, but his hands left her wrists to smooth her hair and cup her cheek; such kindness she could not bear. The affection in his touch and his voice, the sadness in his eyes, she didn't want any of it. Not anymore. His touch felt like a brand, burning into her flesh, her jaw trembling as she just stood there.

"Dalia, your power is different. You are not a tool of

destruction. You are like a gift from the Gods. You're so good, and kind, and there is no way they can corrupt you like they did the others."

She couldn't believe what she was hearing. Suddenly, every time he looked at her like she was something to be worshiped, something to be protected. Those moments she held so dear. They felt rotten. The roots of them grew from such hatred.

"Don't touch me."

Those three words were the only ones out of the hundreds she wanted to say she managed to get out. For some unconceivable reason, Glenn had the audacity to look shocked, his hands barely wavering from their place on her face.

"Don't you hear what I'm saying? You're special, Dalia. You're not like the others, and I will make them see that. I will protect you. I care about you. No one is going to harm you here. Not even my father."

Her mind was racing, and his closeness was not helping her thoughts settle.

"I need you. We need you. I will make them understand that."

They needed her, but not Emil. Much like Barric needed her and not Drystan. There were pieces still missing. Things she needed answers to. Dalia managed to get her hands between the two of them and shrunk away, getting at least a little space between her and this man she no longer recognized, much to Glenn's growing shock and dismay.

Ask the right questions.

"What did the writings say? The ones you found by Tidesend. You told Fionn you couldn't remember it all. I don't believe that, not anymore. What did it say?"

Glenn grappled with her questions for a moment. A muscle worked in his jaw as he mulled over his answer. That was all the confirmation she needed — he was absolutely hiding something from her. With each passing moment, he was looking more and more distraught. Not at the truths he was revealing. No, it wasn't guilt due to his actions. He was looking at her, at the way she moved away from him, like his entire world was crumbling.

"I was trying to protect you. If the general knew what that tablet said, if Fionn—"

"I think Fionn is the last person I need protection from!"

"Are you so sure about that?"

Dalia couldn't do this. She couldn't keep questioning her own sense of right and wrong. Learning friend was foe and foe was friend. So, she ignored his comment for now. "What did it say?"

His breath heavy, he conceded and spoke the words.

Find the flower with hair like fire
Only she can unlock the rest of this quest
Bring her to where the ruins still stand
In the Wilds due Southwest

The words hit her like a cold wave. All of them, every riddle so far included flowers. Every last one. *A flower blooms in wait.* They weren't talking about the flowers carved in the stones. No, this flower was a person. This flower . . . was her. The last riddle told them where to find the final message.

In a field of our names.

Our names.

Fresh tears burned as she started to put everything together. None of this was what they thought. This was not some path to Lumiterra left behind by the Gods to any who would find it. It was one left for her. These were implications she was hardly able to unpack as the man who stood before her was slowly and surely becoming more of a threat.

"You needed me to come with you," Dalia managed breathlessly. "Not just because I was a Crystalline, but because you actually needed *me*."

Glenn said nothing. It should have felt like a welcome change as she processed all of this. But it just felt like being kicked when she was already down. "So was it all a lie then? All of it?"

"No. Oh Gods, no." His voice was so sincere it almost made her want to believe him. It kept her in place a moment as he surged for her once more, reaching. That movement was enough to snap her back to her senses. Throwing up her hands and taking a step back.

"I said don't touch me!"

Glenn looked utterly dumbfounded. As if everything he said held some logical sense to it. Like he expected her to just excuse the murder and Gods knew what else because he had perfectly sound explanations for all of it.

"Listen to me. Please." He was back to begging. It was unbecoming and barely did anything to stir her heart. "I would never hurt you. I did all of this for you. I know you know that. You were dying in that place. Caged when you needed to be free. I set you free."

There it was. Everything Drystan said was true. He was not responsible for what happened to Tidesend. Emil's death was not on his hands. Nora's death wasn't either. Those sins she threw at him, they belonged not to a wolf, but to a stag.

Glenn continued. "We have a chance here. We can change everything. We can take away the last source the elves could use to make more weapons. It would change the tide of this whole damn thing. You are so much more than you realize."

That was the plan all along. Use her to get to Lumiterra and, in doing so, keep the elves from getting their hands on the last cache of crystals. Then, no more children would be made into Crystalline. No more weapons would be forged. It always sounded like a good plan. Something worth fighting for. But now things were so much more complicated, and the cost involved with saving those children made her stomach churn.

"You can save us. Gods know you saved me."

He reached out again. This time too fast for her to recoil. Seizing her hand, he pulled her closer. His close proximity crowded her senses, his words striking like blows despite the soft affectionate tone.

"You found me half-dead on that beach and saved my life. Not questioning who I was. You just gave yourself. I never could have imagined finding someone like you. Someone so kind and generous. Someone who gives so much of themselves without question. Dalia, you are a light in this godsforsaken place. You are my salvation, and I would never let anyone harm you. This was real. Okay? We were real."

He smiled so brightly, a gesture that only stoked horror within her.

His words somehow rang true and yet brought the sting of bile up into her throat. It had been real, but there was so much more to it than she ever knew. So much wrapped in those words that she didn't want any part of.

She signed on to be his equal. She wanted to be his partner. She had healed his wounds without question, but it was not her job to mend his broken soul.

"I don't exist to fix you." The words had so much bite behind them, landing hard and true as she watched hurt crawl across Glenn's face. "You may not care who is collateral damage in your desire for revenge. But I do. I'm not going to help you with this."

She went to move, but his hold tightened. Dalia turned to him, about to demand he let her go, but the sight of him stopped her. Head hung, brown curls spilling over his eyes.

"You know I can't let you leave."

His words were so quiet. A threat dripping off each one. She stood tall, wanting to appear at least like she wasn't also breaking. Dalia opened her mouth to demand he let her go again, but he moved before she could.

"Glenn! Stop!" He was stronger than her. No matter the training she had put in since coming here, it hadn't been enough before, and it wasn't enough now. A few weeks of learning to fight could not equal a lifetime of experience. Still, she took the one lesson he'd given her, twisting at the waist, and punched him straight across the jaw.

He staggered back, fingers reaching up to where her fist collided with bone. His hesitation giving her just enough time to scramble for the entrance. She just about reached the flaps of the tent when she felt his arm curl around her waist. One strong hand across her stomach and his other clasped over her mouth. Still, she screamed, her voice muffled by his firm grip.

"I'm sorry." His voice was heavy, like he was the one put in an impossible situation — not her. "You have to know. This is to keep you safe."

CHAPTER TWENTY-NINE

Despite her name, there were very few times in her life Dalia ever felt like a delicate flower. Perhaps one that was stinted, growing on the side of a cliff rather than in rich soil, unable to extend her roots and take from life what she really needed. Never had she thought a single hand capable of curling around her, crushing the stem there and ripping out each root as petals fell. Not since her time at Keep Oharn. Not even when she was amongst the Wolves. Now, sitting on the hard floor, hands bound to the leg of the cot with a rag in her mouth, she was well and truly broken.

There were so many moments where she'd turned a blind eye. Finding Glenn on that beach seemed like fate. A path laid out for her by the Gods themselves, and she took the leap enthusiastically, looking for every reason she could to attach herself to him. Dalia wanted nothing more than for their stories to intertwine. She'd fought so hard for something that now repulsed her. For he saw the same destiny within them, and tried to claim it in an unforgivable way.

If she was truly a flower, he had not tended to her and wanted her to grow. Instead, pulling and tugging, he'd torn her from the ground only to put her in a pretty vase and call her his. Damn the consequences.

What stung the most was not the loss of him. It was the other things tied in. This place she so desperately wanted to call home was now just as much of a cage as Tidesend. And Drystan. She had been given a chance to reunite with him. If not for Glenn's lies, she might have been able to find happiness in the knowledge her friend was alive instead of only dread. She might have even listened to him.

So many questions were still unanswered.

It seemed she truly was the key to all of this. Each clue pointed to her and her alone, all that was left to discover was who left all of this for her. The answer was right there for her to grasp. Hidden within the words and yet, she hardly allowed her mind to wrap itself around the truth. Dalia suffered one disappointment after the next since leaving the safety of her stagnant life. This one not coming true would be too much to bear.

Dalia was beginning to question if anyone at this camp was truly trustworthy. A thought which clawed away at what little hope was left in her, making her wish to flee. Where she would go was an entirely different story. The idea of going back to the Wolven Hunt was of course there, but even if they had told the truth, there was no saying they wouldn't turn on her. Or force her into some sort of servitude at best, ultimately ripping out her heart when they were done with her, at worst. As far as she knew, there really was no safe place to turn. So she sat there. Silent tears dried sticky over her freckles.

"Dalia? Dalia, are you in there?"

The voice made her tense, sitting up straight against her bonds. Before she could even decide if she would try to answer by humming against her gag, the tall elf crouched in, glancing behind them as if they did not wish to be caught sneaking in.

The second their eyes met hers, horror splashed across their sharp features. It wasn't much, but it was enough to tell her what she needed to know. Fionn might well be the last person in this camp who would fight for her. The memory of how General Lachlan only referred to them as the elf was fresh in her mind. Maybe they were in similar positions. Merely tools and not included in the darker plans. Bethana's intentions were still in question. A thought which sent a new wave of disgust through her.

"What happened?" they asked in hushed frantic tones, rushing to her and leaning down to start undoing her bonds, ripping the cloth from her mouth. "Glenn said that you needed time to rest when I asked about you. But I knew something was off. He hadn't had that bruise on his face earlier."

So, his lesson paid off. She had managed to inflict some damage on him. Good.

"We have to get out of here. It's not safe," Dalia said quickly, scrambling to her feet as she grabbed Fionn's hand.

"Whoa, whoa." Fionn tugged back. "What are you talking about, my dear? What happened?"

"He killed Emil. Glenn, he killed him."

The truth spilled out of her so suddenly and with absolutely no tact. Fionn stood there, face white as a sheet. Blinking as if the repeated motion might take back the damning words.

"No. No, that's not true. Why would you say that?"

"The night I found Glenn. He was burned. Just like you said. It was like nothing I'd ever seen before, like lightning came from the sky and scorched him. Emil must have done that to him, not the Hunt. He was trying to defend himself."

The elf shook their head. Tawny hair falling across their face unceremoniously. "That doesn't make any sense. Why would Glenn attack him? Why would he—" The question cut off as sad acceptance rolled over the peaks and valleys of their face. They knew. They had to know the sentiment of the White Stags when it came to the Crystalline. When it came to their own kind too. Why else would she have been left tied up on the floor by a man who only a few days ago might have balked at that idea? They knew it was the truth. A quiver set in their lips as they turned away for a moment, trying to compose themselves.

Her heart twisted, wishing she wasn't the one to tell them. Wishing their friend was still alive and not killed simply because of what they were.

"Fionn, why are we looking for Lumiterra?" she asked gently. "What do they plan to do with all those crystals if they find them?"

The elf didn't look back at her, but answered all the same. "Destroy them. I asked to keep a few for my research, but I especially doubt they would allow that now. The Crystalline weapon the general has . . . it works much like my bombs. It's explosive. With it, they could destroy the whole cache in a single blow."

The chill of horror crept up her spine. "We have to stop them."

Dalia almost charged right out of the tent, but Fionn's voice stopped her. "Why? I can't defend any of their actions, but maybe it would be best if the Luminites were gone. Isn't that what we have all been fighting for? To make sure that no more children go through what you did? We can deal with the rest of it after that is done."

"No, Fionn. It's not that simple."

"Isn't it?" She could see the struggle in their eyes as their voice raised. Tears brimmed there despite the resolution they proposed. "People like us. We have to be careful what battles we choose, so we can survive. Right now, maybe it's best we play along. Until the task is done."

Dalia couldn't believe what she was hearing. They needed more to be swayed, and she certainly had enough fodder. "Listen, please." Her voice was gentle, and while they might not want to admit it, Fionn looked desperate for her to give them an alternative. A reason to fight. "Glenn knew more about that tablet from the northern temple than he told you. He lied. He knew exactly what the clue said."

Something flashed in those golden eyes. Something like rage. They must have suspected all along. Finally, someone was just giving them the pieces, the reason to do something reckless.

"What did it say?"

THE CLUE ALONE WAS ENOUGH. No more pleading, no more begging. Just a simple riddle and Fionn clicked into action. "We need to get to the next clue, and fast. Just you and me. No one else will interfere or keep us from the truth."

They left Dalia in the tent but for a moment before returning with a signature White Stag cloak and a ribbon for her hair, quickly helping her braid the curls. If any of her wildfire tuffs stuck out like before, they would give themselves away. It was night, but the camp was still abuzz, preparing for the war and the mission ahead. Her blood ran cold at the thought, but it also gave them the perfect cover. Everyone was too busy to notice where Fionn might be going or that they were taking someone along with them.

"No horses," they whispered, as they moved swiftly

through the crowd. "That will draw too much attention. We go on foot."

She followed Fionn across the courtyard, keeping her head down. Out of the corner of her eye, Dalia spotted Glenn. She never thought the sight of him would make her stomach churn with such dread. Her heart pounded as he almost looked their way. A dark-skinned knight stepped into his line of sight, sparking up a conversation and preventing their flight from discovery. Relief flooded her. Beth. It seemed she too could be trusted, despite her parentage, the commander's interference allowed her and Fionn the distraction they needed to disappear into the night.

Luckily, the way was not far. Fionn pushed them at quite a pace. By the time the sun was rising, they reached their destination. Sweat beaded down her brow, muscles ached, but they made it. The peaks of the Medan Mountains rose just over the horizon, perhaps a day's ride from them. Soft white snow-capped peaks poked over the lush green horizon.

"This is where the texts say a temple once stood. If we have any hope of finding it, I would think this would be a good place to start looking," Fionn explained. But a temple wasn't what Dalia was looking for. Scanning the open terrain, her gaze finally settled on pops of reds, purples, and pinks breaking through the green.

In a field of our names.

She moved as though in a trace. Not compelled by magic this time, but by the beating of her own heart. Her steps slow at first before breaking out into a run. Pushing through her fatigue, she bolted. Feet stumbling along until she was engulfed by the vivid colors. Surrounded by the blooms, she stood there. Dropping her hood and inhaling the sweet smell, she let something like hope stir in her.

"This is impossible." Fionn stepped after her. Their voice a soft murmur as they took it all in. "These are dahlias. And these are—"

"Amaryllis flowers." Dalia finished the sentence for them like uttering a prayer finally recognizing the bloom carved on stone they found in the Tanbury Wilds.

"These two flowers shouldn't grow together."

Magic was the only answer. The final clue, not left for anyone but her to find. Dalia's breath quickened as she looked around. Within the center of it all, stood a stone. Much like the one in the Temple. Slowly, she started to move again, approaching the answers she had waited for so long, as timidly as a mouse.

Stood just short of the small monolith, she gently fell to her knees and reached behind her. Fionn didn't hesitate, placing the hilt of a dagger into her open palm, their anticipation, a weight on her back. Dalia pressed the blade to her finger and pricked the skin. A bead of red formed and Dalia extended her hand to touch the stone, her blood smearing on its smooth surface.

From deep within her, Dalia accessed that part of her she tried so hard to hide away, opening herself up and feeding herself, her power, into the stone. Eyes and hands aglow, the mixture of magic and blood shifted the world. A breeze rippled through the field as each flower sprung to life. A soft blue glow reached its tendrils out through each one until it consumed the entire field. Leaving the two of them surrounded by bioluminescence.

"It's incredible." One look at Fionn told Dalia they were doing everything in their power to stay calm and keep themselves from jumping up and down at this discovery.

There had to be more. The last stone revealed runes that shifted and given them a clue. They couldn't have come all this way just for glowing flowers.

As if sensing her desperation, the wind picked up again. This time carrying on it a whisper. A voice swirled around them, speaking so softly, and yet somehow filling up her soul.

"My dear sister. I am so sorry I could not keep my promise."

Dalia's eyes shot right to Fionn. She needed to know this was real, that they were hearing those words too. It wasn't just some trick of her imagination. Her heart begged for this to be real. As runes sprung to life in the dirt of the field, the voice grew louder. Both of their eyes locked but a second, Fionn's chin bobbing in a nod. It was real. They heard it too.

"My only prayer is that you either have broken our vow and found the path I laid for you. Or that someone else has brought you this far."

Her chest felt like it might explode; it was so full. She hadn't even noticed the smile breaking across her face until her cheeks ached from how wide it was. Her sister. Ammy. She was alive. Not only that, she hadn't forgotten her. The life she had begun to accept was all in vain, the pieces of her she'd wanted to shed away started to wrap around her again like a favorite blanket. The girl who lived off hope. The one who allowed herself to dream and pray and wait: she had never been wrong. No matter what the cynical world tried to tell her, she was never wrong.

"Dalia, the place you seek is deep within the Medan Mountains. Where the river cuts around the highest peak. That is where Lumiterra is. That is where we are."

We. There were more of them.

"My Gods." Fionn's fingers rested on their lips, eyes glistening at the discovery.

"For our protection, we have locked ourselves away there. The lock is magic and cannot be opened from the inside or the out, an extreme necessity in a world that seeks to destroy us. The spell can only be broken by you. Dalia, you are the only one who can open the

door. I love you. I miss you more than I can possibly say. If there are any other Crystalline with you, bring them to us, and come home to me."

With those final words, the wind settled, leaving the two of them to just stand there for a moment in utter silence. Trying to absorb the information and sentiments still hanging in the air. It was Fionn who finally broke their silence.

"You were right." They looked at her with such a gentle smile she almost broke down. Almost fell to the ground from the burden of all the emotions she carried. "They were for you. All of this, it was for you."

Her tears finally fell. Warm trails tracked down her cheeks. Not tears of sadness, or regret, or betrayal. These were tears of joy and hope. Home. Her sister spoke of home. That was a place she only dreamed about. Not something she was able to touch or have. Merely a wish she uttered each night before bed. That one day, she might find a place where she belonged.

The home she longed for her whole life was just out of reach, and it was in grave danger.

"We have to stop them," Dalia pleaded, turning to look at Fionn, as panic washed over her. "Fionn, we have to do something. Who knows how many Crystalline are living in Lumiterra. You heard my sister. They're locked in there. They're defenseless."

"If General Lachlan goes through with his plan, it's going to be a lot more than just crystals he destroys." Fionn's voice was hushed in determination. "He doesn't need to get in to do it. With his weapon, he can demolish the mountain itself."

If the resolve on their face was to be believed, Dalia would not need to do anymore to convince them. They both heard what was really hidden in those mountains. More importantly, she knew the truth wouldn't change anything for the Stags. They both knew all too well what they thought of her kind.

They were weapons. A bunch of hidden Crystalline would be viewed as just as dangerous as the Luminites themselves. They would destroy Lumiterra without a second thought if they knew who was hidden in there.

"It sounds to me like you two could use some help."

CHAPTER THIRTY

Dalia whirled in the direction of the new voice, fearing the worst. What waited for her was Barric, trailed by four members of the Wolven Hunt. Only his hood was down, but the trappings of each of their outfits allowed her to pinpoint the one who made her breath shudder in her chest.

Drystan.

Anger burned in her veins. Not that he once again found her. Nor that he brought his strange group of elves with him. It was deeper. Dalia couldn't help but feel like she was robbed of something. Glenn's deception had stolen something from her and her dear friend. Something she could never get back. She would never be able to take back the way she looked at him. The horror and rage she threw in his direction instead of relief and astonishment. It wasn't entirely Glenn's fault, but the guilt still gnawed at her.

Looking at the small band before her, Dalia felt no fear. Not like she had when she was amongst the whole group at their camp. Without Barric, she would have never gotten this far. It was reason enough to put at least a tentative trust in him. Or at least the want to understand why he helped her.

Her companion clearly did not feel the same way.

"Dalia, get behind me."

Fionn's face contorted into something unrecognizable. In the temple, she saw them face down Drystan without fear. They stood guard and then rushed headlong to protect her. Now, they looked terrified.

Dalia looked between her friend and the band of Wolves. It was Barric who made the first move, stepping towards the two of them, hands up in a display of nonviolence. "It's alright. We mean you no harm. It's been a long time—"

"Fionn." The elf said their own name quickly. Stopping the hunter before them from using whatever name they were about to utter. A gentle acceptance dawned on his expression as he nodded, repeating the name in understanding.

"Fionn."

Looking between them now, Dalia couldn't believe she hadn't realized it before. When she met Barric, she had found his face familiar. Now it was easy enough to see why. From the high angled cheekbones to the precise shade of gold in their eyes. These two were clearly related. And he had been about to call Fionn a name they had long left behind.

"Brother, I never expected to see you with a Hunt." It wasn't just Fionn's cold tone that cut through her, but what they called Barric. This was not some distant relation. He was their brother. They had spoken to her of a lost sibling before, but never one still living.

Suddenly, more pieces fell into place that Dalia never even realized she had been missing. Drystan could have easily killed Fionn before in the temple. The moment was at his fingertips for the taking, but he hadn't. He spared their life.

Dalia believed it was merely a ploy to get her to accept his offer to leave with him. It seemed there was more to it. Perhaps, he spared the elf's life for his commander's sake as well.

A lazy smirk pulled at Barric's lips. "Well, things have changed since you left." He lowered his hands, turning his attention away from his sibling and to Dalia instead. "Forgive me, when we last met, I did not allow us a proper introduction." With a flourish of his hand, the elf bent at the waist, dipping into a bow one courtier might give another. "My name is Prince Barric of Carrnelia. Heir to the throne and some other nonsense after your friend here decided to skip out and leave the honors to me instead."

Lips parted, eyes widened, and it took Dalia all of her strength to keep herself from just dropping her jaw completely. He was a prince. That explained so much. Of course another member of his Hunt would don the clothes of the leader. The heir to the elven throne would have a huge target on his back. Allowing Drystan to seem like he was in charge instead helped keep him hidden. And it hindered any threats from guessing who really led their band.

But that wasn't what left her speechless. No, it was another fact that came with the revelation of who he was. It was who Fionn was. They were royalty. Dalia thought back to the night of the festival and the sheer amount of elven finery Fionn offered for her to pick from. At the time, she barely questioned it. Dalia merely assumed they came from an influential family of sorts, given they mentioned being nobility. It never struck her that they were from the royal family. Even more than that, the heir to the throne.

"Barric . . . please." Fionn was clearly rattled. Their whole demeanor off, looking utterly uncomfortable with the knowledge Dalia had just learned.

"Oh what?" the elf scoffed. "Do all your new little friends not know?"

Their lips tightened, standing so rigidly. A far cry from the usually joyful elf she had come to truly enjoy being around. Barric seemed to realize he pushed too far. His expression softened and he turned his attention back to Dalia instead.

"I see you asked the right questions."

"I did," Dalia replied with a nod, taking one very brave step forward. "Did you hear the message my sister had for me?"

"I did," Barric answered, mirroring her movements.

This was it. This was her opportunity to stop the plan already in motion. Fionn and her could not do it by themselves. If the camp was an indication of the White Stag's preparations, they were going up against an army. The very idea of trusting a Hunt soured her stomach. But so far, they were the only ones who had not led her astray. The elf at her side and the Hunt before her were odd allegiances to be sure. Her very being recoiled at the thought of what she was about to ask, but it was the only option laid before her.

"Will you help us, then?"

"Dalia!" Fionn's pale face shifted, panic joining the horror there. Quickly moving to stand between their brother and her, they grabbed her arm and gave her a tug to try and get her away from the elven prince. Quick hushed tones frantically spewed forth. "Listen to me, I know you're desperate. I know what we heard. We have to stop them, we do. But we cannot trust these people."

"What choice do we have?" she asked. "Fionn, you saw what they are preparing. We can't go up against an army alone."

"No matter what they have told you. These people are not safe. Especially for you."

"And you are someone she is safe to be around?" Barric shot back, frustration apparent in the growl of his tone.

Unbridled anger flashed in her friend's golden eyes. Fionn let go of her and rounded on their brother. "You shut your mouth!"

Barric's lips twitched in what looked like amusement.

"Yet another thing she doesn't know then."

No. No, there couldn't be more. Not more secrets. Not more lies. Dalia didn't know how much more of this she could take. Her heart hammered against her chest as she stepped towards her friend. "Fionn, what is he talking about?"

"We need to go." The elf turned back to her, reaching for her hand once more. "Now."

"No!" Practically leaping back, her whole body trembled and recoiled from them. "What is he talking about? Tell me."

A painful moment of silence followed, just Dalia staring into those usually joyful eyes. The only thing in them now was sorrow. A simple wish played repeatedly in her head. Please, don't take Fionn from her, too. Beth and them were the last things she had left.

"She deserves to know." Drystan's low voice sounded for the first time since he arrived. Hood lowered, he stood next to the Prince. "There have been too many secrets. She deserves to know."

Somehow, it felt like an apology. Not near enough, but a start. Something that, maybe if she wanted to, they could build on. Yet still, Fionn shook their head. The opportunity to come clean with was there, stretching out before them, but they couldn't do it. Nor could they do much to hide their distress any longer. Practically tripping over themselves as they pleaded with Dalia once more.

"Please, don't listen to these people. You can't trust them."

"Coward." Barric sighed, shifting his weight back to his

center as the prince adopted a much more authoritative stance.

"What my sibling is failing to tell you, is they are in a way responsible for the experiments. They created the technology that made them possible."

She was falling all over again, once again descending down that dark hole. Her feet moved without her even demanding it, pedaling backwards. She wanted to scream at him. Tell the prince he was lying. Fionn would never do such a thing. But much like with Glenn, deep down, she knew it was true. Fionn said it themselves — they were the leading scientist when it came to studying the Luminites. When they tried to help her remember her past, they knew so much about the machines used. All their diagrams. Their notes. The one she saw that sent her spiraling was even handwritten within their own journal. It was sitting right in front of her the whole time. Every answer, and she willfully ignored them all.

The people she was so quick to call her friends, their secrets were laid bare, leaving her feeling numb.

"You know I never wanted that." The protest was barely a whimper. Shame riddled Fionn's face as they seemed to stare at nothing and spoke up in defense of their sins before looking at their brother desperately. "Barric, please. You know it wasn't like that. Don't twist this, I never intended any of this. You know I never wanted it to be used on humans. Not after—"

"After what?"

Somehow, Dalia found the will to speak up. The loss of Glenn had broken her heart. The image she built up of him was ripped to shreds and she was still in shock from it. She couldn't lose Fionn, too. Not her joyful friend. Not the elf who showed her that not all of their kind were hateful creatures. They protected her. They stood by her and put their life at risk to come out here with her. There needed to be more to this. She couldn't accept it otherwise.

"Please, tell me what happened."

A soft prayer. A begging for them to say something to fix this.

Finally, they met her eyes. For so long, Dalia sensed a deep sadness within her friend. She saw it the night by the bonfire. And when they rattled on about certain parts of their research, lingering somewhere beneath the effervescence that was Fionn. Now, it was on full display. The guilt and shame that peaked out every so often clouded their eyes as they found the courage to speak.

"He's telling the truth. I did create it."

Dalia had braced herself for those words, and yet they still seemed to rip through her. Fionn let this settle, before taking a breath, and speaking their truth.

"I created it because I was obsessed with understanding the power of the Lumiels. I wanted us to be able to harness it for ourselves. My brothers, they helped me."

Dalia stole a glance over at Barric. Pride beamed there, unexpectedly breaking through the veil of sorrow.

"There were three of us. Three siblings who were destined for the throne. I am the middle one. Barric the youngest. And Oryn . . . well, he was the oldest." Fionn's voice faltered as they spoke of their elder brother. Dalia remembered back to the night by the fire. The only other time Fionn had ever mentioned their family and this loss. "I developed it, a way to synthesize the liquid in the crystals into an injectable drug. I did it so that we could share the power of those who came before us. So that we could bring magic back to this world. Oryn tested it. He truly believed in what I was doing. He believed so much in me, in my science, that he put himself on the line. And I let him."

The elf paused, clenching their hands into fists at their side before closing their eyes as though trying to draw on some inner strength to continue. "It killed him. I killed him. I failed to see that the Luminite fragments would not be compatible with elven anatomy. We are not from this place. He trusted me, and in my hubris, I overlooked our own shortcomings as a species. And now he's gone."

She should have felt nothing but anger. After all, without them, none of the horrific things she endured would have happened. They were responsible. Even if they were not the person to tie her down and forcibly change her, they created the process. Yet, what stirred within her was not rage, but sympathy. For a person who was grieving. For a person she cared for.

"Dalia." Fionn looked at her now, lip quivering as they spoke. "I never meant for it to go farther than that. After my brother died, I tried to destroy all of my work. My parents, however, had other plans. They saw my research as a way to create weapons. They instituted the Crystalline program behind my back and by the time I tried to stop it, it was too late." Their lips drew back tight, fighting off the guilt that ran so deep within them. The guilt she now understood. "Please. Please, believe me. I never wanted anyone to get hurt. I never wanted this for you. I just ... I just want to make it right."

Dalia should have been the victim. The one who needed to be comforted, but somehow along the way, it switched. Once again, Fionn proved to her that the world was not how she imagined it. The truth now lay before them. But unlike with Glenn, her view of the person before her was not shattered. Time and time again, she saw Fionn trying to correct the hurt they caused. In the quiet moments they shared studying, they had been close to telling her the truth. They put their life on the line for Crystallines without hesitation, and now she knew why. They were their responsibility. Fionn didn't need to be scolded. They didn't need to be told to atone. They were doing just that, long before she ever met them. What was needed was not a judge and jury, but a friend.

Dalia moved slowly, closing the distance between her and the elf, and took their trembling hands into her own. A breath hitched in their chest as they looked at her, astonished. Tears slid down her pale cheeks as she pressed a warm smile to her face. "It is not my place to forgive you for all of us. But for myself . . . I am still proud to call you my friend."

Their chest shook with a sob before Fionn threw themselves at her. The two embraced in a bond of friendship which stood unbroken by the crimes of the past. Together they could forge a new future. Dalia saw that now. Old prejudices had not served her well. They pushed her into the arms of someone who committed evils in the name of something good when the people who might have helped her were just out of reach, hidden in the guise of those she was taught to fear and hate.

Her own experiences still rang true. There were still evil people out there. Ones who robbed her of her childhood. Those people did not deserve her kindness or forgiveness. But now, Dalia knew people like that existed on both sides. The answer for her was not in their allegiance, but in who they were individually. Something much harder to figure out. Maybe the Wolven Hunt would prove to be no better than what she was choosing to leave behind. She still didn't know if she could fully trust them. But right now, they were the better option.

It was a hard lesson to learn, that a stag could be more dangerous than a wolf.

Pulling back from her friend with one more smile, she looked to the Hunt, mustering up the courage once more to walk into the fire. "Will you help me? Help me stop them from destroying Lumiterra? Help me save my sister?"

"We will." The answer did not come from Barric, but from Drystan. She didn't know where they both stood, but his willingness to help meant more than she could say. He had stuck with her in spirit for so long. His face was still one of nightmares. One that haunted, but now there was something beneath that. A bond that could be reignited. A spark, if tended, might become something more. Dalia wished for such a thing, but she wouldn't allow herself to dwell. Her naivety caused her to entangle herself with Glenn, and it left her in pieces. She would have to pick up what was scattered to the wind before she could trust too deeply again.

For now, the Wolves were a means to an end. The only way to be reunited with the person she waited half her life for.

"Come with us," she pleaded softly with Fionn.

"I can't," they stuttered back, looking between her and their brother. "I'm sorry. I can't. I can't leave Beth. This can maybe still be stopped before it happens. I can't fight against her, but I will do my best to make her see. To try and stop this. Maybe with her influence her father might be swayed."

Nodding in acceptance, Dalia squeezed their hands. "Then this is goodbye. For now." Once more she threw her arms around them, holding tight. "Thank you. For always protecting me."

Letting go was the hard part, but she knew Fionn would never choose her over Bethana. In a swift motion, like removing a bandage from a wound, Dalia pulled away, moving to join the ranks of those she had once been so desperate to fight against.

"You take care of her." Fionn's voice shook in their plea. "Barric, take care of her."

The prince gave his sibling a long look, sadness clouding the gold of his eyes. Wishful longing playing with the metallic hues. "I will. You have my word, Fionn."

CHAPTER THIRTY-ONE

No matter the courage she showed in making this choice, Dalia still felt like a fawn in a den of wolves. They had given her nuggets of truth. Hints which pushed her towards this path she needed to walk. For that, she was grateful. For that, she would side with them, for now. How far her trust would stretch was still in question.

Fionn may have been hiding dark secrets in their past, but they were at least trying to make amends. Barric's motives were still unknown. He gave her the tools she needed, but he was also the crown prince, the heir to a throne which was currently subjugating every human on the damn continent. He stood with the people who tortured children and forced the consequences of those experiments into hiding. Fionn walked away, leaving such atrocities behind. Barric had not.

Something she would do well to remember.

Dalia could not make the same mistake twice. She would not throw her trust at people only to be left feeling like she never really knew them at all. She didn't want it to, but her heart clenched at the thought. Ached at the loss. She didn't know if it was for Glenn or merely for the fact that she lost the connection and purpose she longed for her whole life. She couldn't say she loved him. It had happened too quickly to call it love. Yet, she was still empty. Her escape happened so fast that there wasn't time to truly process the loss. Her righteous anger was fading and in its place she was numb.

There was no time to shed tears. Dalia would once again have to push her feelings aside and act. The lives of so many depended on it. The life of her sister being one of them.

She found herself once again in the Hunt's camp, but this time as a guest. She hadn't walked in with her hands bound but sharing a horse with Drystan. Arms wrapped tight around his waist to keep from falling off. The only other time she'd ridden, she'd shared a horse with Glenn, and while she wished she wouldn't, it was impossible not to compare.

She might have thought he would be cold, given what his powers could do, but all she found as she wrapped her arms around his waist was an odd comfort. A gentle warmth seeped into her bones and made her want to stay. An instinct Dalia fought against immediately, keeping her hold on him stiff and formal.

From over his shoulder, she really took in the scene before her. Before all she saw were the frightening shapes of the elves surrounding her. Now, it was in the height of daylight, and she could make out the camp much better. They were an odd bunch to be sure.

There were already the two outliers she knew about. The Crystalline she shared a horse with and the huntress. Evanee was her name. The blonde rode with them now. It seemed as though she was the only female amongst their ranks, and her presence within a Hunt was still so strange to Dalia. She shouldn't be allowed to have joined this band. Then again, nor should a Crystalline.

The rest of them were all elven males, but they didn't seem to have the demeanor or fit of the trained killers she'd been taught to expect. A skinny elf they passed on the way in had waved at them with a bright smile on his face, almost reminding her of Fionn's enthusiasm.

All her life she was taught to fear Hunts, told they housed the worst of the worst killers. Cold, evil beings who were capable of untold slaughter. In some cases, she supposed that must be true. She saw Whitehill, heard the fate of Glenn's village and all the stories Mollie brought her over the years. Something about the people who were around her now made her question if they were even capable of such horrors. Not to mention, Tidesend fell at Glenn's hands. No matter what the world might have wanted her to believe, humans were capable of equal evil. She saw that now, Glenn's reasoning notwithstanding.

Most of the happy bustle around her seemed to shift as they noticed her. It was not the same look she received from the White Stags. Not one of awe somehow twinged with apprehension, or even distrust. No, many of them even offered her smiles and nods. They didn't look afraid. They didn't keep their distance. They seemed to look almost sympathetic. Dalia supposed their ease in her presence made sense. They rode with a Crystalline already. She was not a novelty or a monster to them. Just the same as someone they might already call a companion.

Once their horse stopped, Drystan dismounted, before offering her a hand to help her down. She hated how she hesitated, wanting so much to seem brave and in control of her fate. Neither of those things were true.

So many times before, Drystan had offered her his hand.

She'd seen it then as a trap rather than the lifeline it truly was. Her fingers hovered a moment over his outstretched, gloved palm, lingering as she thickly swallowed her fears. Maybe, despite recent betrayals, she didn't need to be alone in this. Finally taking his hand, she allowed him to help her off the steed.

"It's alright. You're safe within these ranks." His voice was so soft. Dalia wondered if he sensed her fear, or if her face so easily betrayed what was bubbling inside her. But no matter his comforting intent, his words were too close to Glenn's. Far too similar to the soft reassurance her Stag gave as she'd entered another camp.

"We will have to see about that."

He touched her wrist before she could turn away, a gentle request to wait. The difference was impossible to ignore. Glenn would always grab for her. Drystan, instead, requested.

For a second their eyes caught, and if she had allowed herself, she could have drowned. Those dark wells were filled with such a deep, aching sorrow. She wanted to be swept away in it. Swim in those pools and find the boy she once knew. Find his hand and pull until they both were at the surface again, able to breathe. Maybe if he had found her first, she might have taken that plunge. She could not allow it now. Not when the acidic taste of heartbreak still lingered on her tongue.

Glenn saw her as a savior. Someone who could pull him from his darkness and envelop him in light. He tore apart her world to get it, leaving her in tatters. Whether or not Drystan would do the same, she didn't know. What she did know, was no matter how much she desired to heal others, she could not fix a broken man.

"I'm sorry," he finally spoke, clearing his throat and dropping his hand. "No more lies. I thought I was doing the right thing in keeping who I was secret to protect Barric. He means more to me than I can say, and I have often played a role as a distraction to keep him safe. It wasn't because I didn't trust you, but because I knew I could not trust the company you kept. My presence as a Crystalline within these ranks is not something well known. Or at least, it wasn't. My actions were to protect my prince, but it seems you have had more than your fair share of secrets kept from you."

"You think?"

She couldn't help but be bitter, even if now she understood why his identity needed to be kept a secret.

"I swear to you. No more secrets. At least, not from me."

It was a sentiment she was more than grateful for. Honestly, it was the very thing she needed, but she was not ready to trust it. Not fully. Not yet. Drystan would have to prove to her that his word meant something more than a Stag's.

"We don't have a lot of time," she said, brushing off the intimate moment he was attempting to share with her. He bristled, standing a little straighter and seeming to understand the boundary she put between them. Thankfully not trying to poke it, but simply accepting it was there, before he nodded and backed off.

"You're right, follow me."

THE CAMP WAS REALLY nothing like the one she stayed in with the White Stags. The scale alone was enough, but there was more to it. Everything in Camp Hart was coordinated, pristine. All clean and white and gold, a simmering fortified beacon that spoke of its might the moment she entered. The Wolven Hunt was nothing more than a few ragtag tents and a small fire pit, with a small grazing area set up for their horses.

It was hard to think of prince actually stayed here, leading this Hunt. She would have thought royalty would want to travel in splendor. Yet, everything his hunters traveled with was practical. It all served a purpose. Tents that were easy to pick up and move without much fuss, and not much more.

Standing at the center of camp beside Barric now, she could see the entirety of the force they had to work with. It wasn't much.

Dalia knew Hunts were smaller groups. Even a small group of elves patrolling the northern countryside always seemed terrifying. Now, knowing the army they were up against, her heart sank.

Ten. There were only ten of them in this Hunt, including the ones she already knew. This might not be enough.

Scanning their faces, she expected to see fear. At least some sort of nervous energy for the task at hand, but all she saw were people ready to fight. Determination sang among them, lifting even her own spirits into thinking maybe, just maybe, they stood a chance.

"We have the element of surprise on our side," Evanee chimed. She was practically perched on a log across from where Dalia stood. Her lithe form so casually folded over her knee as she spoke. "The traitor is the only other person who heard where our entrance is. They may have abandoned your family, but they didn't seem like they would talk easily."

"No. It didn't seem like they would," Barric agreed.

Dalia shifted uncomfortably. Barric accepting the title of traitor for his sibling twisted her stomach. Fionn's past might have been muddy, but she had a hard time listening to them being spoken of in that way.

"But we know Lachlan's ambitions. He's not going to stop until this is done, and he'll torture Fionn for the information if he has to."

Dalia snapped her attention over to Barric with wide eyes. "Would he really do—"

"Yes." Evanee cut her off. A coldness in her tone. "You may not want to believe it, but your precious Stags are a blood-thirsty bunch."

"Easy Evanee." Drystan's low tone rumbled.

Dalia was glad for Drystan's interference. She wasn't sure how to defend the people she once wanted to enmesh herself with. It would be so easy to point out that they wouldn't even exist if not for the elves, that they were pushed to this breaking point. Such sentiments would get them nowhere. They needed to work together now, or her sister would once again be lost to her.

"The answer is simple enough," Barric said. "We need to get her to those mountains before the White Stags get there."

"You want to open the door?" an elf with longer braided brown hair asked with concern. "Would that not just let their armies in?"

"They have a Crystalline weapon. They could destroy the whole mountainside without even getting in, if they wanted to." Drystan warned and it sent shocks of whispers through the band. Deathbringer. That was its purpose, of course. Not to fight elves, but to destroy Lumiterra. "Unlike me, those weapons don't tire. It will run out of magic at some point, but probably not before they take down the whole ridge."

"Precisely," Barric agreed with a simple nod, somehow not shaken by the prospect. "We don't know how many Crystalline are hiding in those mountains, but the best chance we have is to let them out. Let them defend themselves."

A protest died on her lips. She wanted to argue, to tell him despite what they could do, they weren't weapons. They couldn't just assume the people in Lumiterra could fight off an army, but that wasn't true. They may have been people, just like her, but even a few Crystalline would be enough to take down an army. Dalia's power may not be suited for battle, but she knew firsthand what people like her were capable of.

"You're saying you just need me to open the door?" It was simple enough, and yet the task seemed unbelievably daunting. After all, it was just opening the door to an ancient place which apparently housed the rest of Belestara's magical crystals. No big deal. "How am I supposed to get there before it's too late? For all we know, the army is already on its way."

For a moment, no one so much as moved. Silence rippled through them, as the plan started to take physical form. Dalia knew it had to be her; she truly was the key to all of this. She would fight tooth and nail to get back to her sister, even go along with a plan put forth by the heir to the elven throne. But she couldn't do it alone.

"She can ride with me." Drystan stood, ending the quiet and looking at his prince. "If they're already there, I'm the best shot we have of clearing a path."

"And if they break through and get a shot on you?" Evanee questioned from her perch.

"Well, then it's good I'll have my own personal healer riding alongside me."

An easy breath filled her lungs. It felt like hope. Dalia never thought of that option. It would be asking a lot if the time came, but it was a chance. Mixing their abilities just might keep the two of them alive long enough. "I can do it," she said quickly, trying to sound confident. "I can keep us safe."

The tip of Barric's fingers touched his lips as he seemed to play the scenario over in his head, looking at his hunters before his gaze settled on his Crystalline. "We don't have the manpower to spare if you get overrun. If you do this, if you run ahead with her, you two will be on your own. We can provide some cover from the rear and try to thin out the herd, but I can't risk every Wolf I have on this plan."

"I understand." Drystan's dark eyes bore an intensity capable of convincing the stars of his conviction. "This is worth the risk."

No truer words had ever been spoken. It was worth everything to her. Dalia would give her life, without question, to try and save her sister's. At the end of this conflict laid everything she waited an entire decade for. She would give every last piece of herself.

"We can do this." Her words were soft, but she met Drystan's gaze with equal conviction, finding comfort in the fact they would face this together. Even if where they stood was rocky, she started this journey into the unknown with him. And now she would come home with him by her side.

"Well then, you two better start riding."

That was all they needed. No more words, no more plans. They were going to end this. Two Crystalline against an army. Doing exactly what they were created to do. Only, not for the same reasons. Not to subjugate or oppress.

To liberate.

CHAPTER THIRTY-TWO

Once again, there was little time for her and Drystan to speak. Hooves thundered against the ground as they rode forth, leaving words left unspoken in their wake. If they made it through this, perhaps then they could address the things needed to be said. For now, Dalia just clung tightly to his back as the white steed raced towards the river.

The comparisons she'd made to riding with Glenn earlier flew from her thoughts. Left behind was just the pure need to cling to him with all her might as he urged their mount forward. They needed to make haste.

This plan failing wasn't an option she could even entertain. She was still breathing, still moving, pushing through all she faced in the last day or so, but so much was lost to her. Any more would tip the scales. A grain of sand would be enough to crack her now. The loss of her sister would be an avalanche. It wouldn't tip the scale; it would obliterate it, leaving behind nothing left of her.

"We follow this to the mountains," Drystan said loudly over the sound of hooves splashing as they reached the cool waters. "That's what Amaryllis said. Where the river splits the range."

Hearing him say her name aloud sent a chill down her spine. This was all real. He had known her sister, too. Bonded with her under the same trauma that bound them. Her name on his lips only made this all the more solid. At the end of this watery path were the answers she waited years for. Maybe ones he had as well.

"This is the only real way into the heart of the mountains," he continued. "Even if Fionn doesn't talk, they'll be headed this way."

It only made sense. The Medan Mountains split their continent like a scar. The path through them was narrow and treacherous. General Fettler would certainly have enough sense to send his men as far into the range as possible, even if he didn't know the exact location of Lumiterra. Confrontation was inevitable at this point. The only question remaining was when it would occur.

"Will the others follow?" Dalia asked, daring to glance over her shoulder. There was still no sign of the other Wolves.

"They'll come. Though they will focus their efforts on the main force."

So they really were alone, for now. The two of them were thrown into the fire, just like so many years ago. Only, this time, they weren't hiding. They were going to face the threat head on, reclaiming the identity of being weapons, and turning it back on those who called themselves their enemies. Dalia could only pray this time would not end in sacrifice.

"Dalia." Concern laced through Drystan's tone as he spoke. "Are you ready for this?"

"I can do this."

"That's not what I asked."

His concern was not unfounded. Drystan molded himself into what the world expected him to be — the perfect weapon. His powers that had awakened since she'd known him were formidable, and she could imagine this was not the first battle he had fought in. Dalia was always different. With the Stags, she tried to fit herself into the mold needed of her, training and pushing herself to be what they required. But she was a healer, not a soldier, and a decade of isolation couldn't prepare her for something like this.

Still, her one job was clear: keep both of them alive. That she could do. After so long of denying herself every time she used her powers felt like flexing a muscle. Like she finally allowed a part of her that always existed beneath the surface to come forth. She may not have been ready for battle, but she was ready to finally be the person she always wished she could be.

"Don't worry about me," she finally replied, her grip on him tightening. "Just ride and don't stop pushing. Trust, I will keep you alive."

"I do. Trust you."

Her heart fluttered. He had no real reason to. Since being reunited, Dalia had done nothing but condemn him. And still, he was able to cling onto the past they shared. Able to trust the girl she once was, and what they once were to each other. Maybe that was what she could trust too. Not the Wolves. Not a prince that, while confusing, served a crown which would see her dead. What she put her faith in was a boy. A boy who had once been willing to give his life for her. Somehow, despite it all, that still meant something.

~

For so long, all Dalia could hear was the thundering of hoofbeats and her own heart. Slowly, the trees started to clear, the path to the mountain side becoming visible. Where the river broke through their peaks was an open field. Nothing but a sea of grass stood between them and where the river cut through their snow peaked goal.

Dalia's heart soared. They were so close. They just needed to keep moving. That hope came crashing down when, out of the corner of her eye, she saw the tree line rustle.

She held her breath, praying it was just Barric and the others finally catching up. Flashes of white fabric broke her prayer before she could even utter it.

They were here. It was too late.

"Drystan . . ."

"I see them."

He kicked his horse and leaned forward, urging the white steed to move faster. "Listen to me. No matter what, focus ahead. Don't look back. Just focus on your part. I'll worry about them. You worry about us."

It was a hard ask. The sounds of shouting started behind them. Her heart clenched as she thought about him possibly being there, amongst their ranks. The man she once dared to imagine a future with. The idea gnawed at her. Beth and Fionn hopefully escaped, but the fact that Glenn must be among those riders only intensified an ache in her chest. As much as she wanted to close herself off to him completely, the thought of facing off against him or any of the Stags constricted her throat.

A twang sounded and Dalia knew the battle had begun. An arrow whirled in their direction but stuck in the ground far behind them. Her heart was pounding so hard it threatened to break out of the cage her ribs held it in. If Drystan was frightened, he didn't show it. He was a cold stone. Steady, hard, and ready to face the coming tide.

At the sound of clangs and more shouts, she threw Drystan's advice to the wind, and looked back into the mess of it all. Black cloaks had entered the fray. The Hunt. Behind them, they wove in and out of the trees. Using the cover to their advantage, they struck, distracting some of the advance that would have come their way. It wasn't enough. A large group of white-cloaked soldiers had taken off after them, bows drawn.

This time, when they fired, an arrow found its mark. Dalia gasped as it barely missed her, embedding itself in Drystan's shoulder. He grunted in pain, giving no other indication he had been wounded, and kept his path straight and steady.

Shit. She needed to focus. If he could keep moving, keep fighting through the chaos, then she could do this. She could tune out the rest of the world. Right now, at this moment, it was just them.

"Sorry," she muttered under her breath, before ripping the arrow from his flesh. Through gritted teeth he gave a painful groan just as her eyes started to glow. Fingers moved over his wound, piecing him back together.

A chill settled around her as Drystan called his powers into play. A slick of ice spread out behind their steed's thundering hooves, lifting up in uneven fractals around them. Low to the ground but enough to make the field behind them treacherous. A few spikes lifted higher, here and there. A shield.

"That's about as much as I can manage with having to keep it constantly going," Drystan said, not once looking back. "It'll at least keep our horse safe. Just stay focused. You're doing great."

The next rain of arrows came far too soon. Before she could really soak up his praise. Dalia cried out as one found its mark in her thigh, another in the meat of Drystan's upper arm. Jaw clenched, she just kept working. Ripping arrows from their flesh as she fought through pain and injury. Attack after attack, she kept going. Eyes aglow, hands rested on his back, her thighs the only thing holding her to the horse now. In that brief moment, she ceased to be. She wasn't a human or Crystalline, she was merely light. Clinging to her power, Dalia poured every bit of her into the two of them. She had to be enough. She had to keep them going.

A pop and a hiss sounded, followed by an oddly joyous whoop.

Pulled from her concentration, Dalia threw her gaze over her shoulder, just in time to see the flashes and the smoke billowing over the field.

Bombs.

"Go Dalia!"

Two horses cut straight across the field, the popping trail of Fionn's creations setting off behind them. Bethana's dark skin gleaming in the sun as she led the charge. It was Fionn who called out to her. A great sense of freedom settled over them.

Her friends. That word solidified in her mind at the sight of them. They'd come back for her. Even Beth was in this with her, against her father's wishes. Dalia's heart swelled as she drank in the truth of it all. They had never betrayed her, and now, they were giving her a chance. Those flashes and that smoke disoriented the majority of the troops, buying the two Crystalline much needed time.

To their left, a small group of Stags broke out from the smoke and was gaining on them.

"Hold tight!" Drystan shouted, and Dalia threw herself forward. Wrapping her arms around his waist, she held with all her might. Her breath became visible, and horror of what was about to happen swept over her.

A trail of ice shot out from them like a wave. Tearing out towards the Stags at tremendous speed before finally the cold collected around their feet, and jutted upwards. Spikes of ice impaled horse and human alike in a spray of crimson and screams.

Her breath caught and eyes grew wide at the sight. Drystan slumped forward a little. That was why he'd needed to wait for them to be closer. The attack he'd planned took so much out of him that he was barely staying upright.

"Hey!" Her palm met his back, trying to pull from her own lifeforce to keep him going. A source which was growing sparse as dizziness danced in her skull. "Stay with me. We're almost there. Don't leave me now."

His back stiffened beneath her touch, trembling as he pushed himself to sit upright. They were so close. The mountains and the path through them loomed just ahead. Just a little bit more. They just needed to keep pushing a little bit more. They had left carnage in their wake; surely the worst of it was over.

Such treacherous thoughts of safety always seemed to deceive her. Just as they'd crossed into the shadows of the mountain's heights, entering the canal, the ground beneath their very feet seemed to shake.

"What was—"

Before the question could be fully formed on her lips, the blast hit. The river rocks beneath their horse's hooves exploded into rubble, throwing them forward with a loud boom. Dalia reached out desperately for Drystan. Fingers outstretched but, much like the night when the door closed between them, he was out of her reach, and she hit the ground with a painful thud.

CHAPTER THIRTY-THREE

All Dalia could hear was a high-pitched ringing in her ears as the world came back into focus. Pushing through the blur and haze from the blast, she tried to make out her surroundings.

They had made it to the pass, the throughline where the river split the mountains, but that wasn't enough. The door wasn't open yet. Dalia didn't even know what she needed to do, only that she was key. More importantly, the fact that she was alone struck her harder than any physical blow could. Drystan was nowhere within her line of sight.

With a cry, Dalia tried and failed to push herself up onto her feet. Everything ached, and she only managed to make it up to her hands and knees, her body fighting against the movement the whole way. She'd been so focused on just keeping her and Drystan breathing, she hadn't realized how much of a toll using so much of her power had taken on her. She didn't have much energy left. Standing was a challenge —

she could hardly imagine giving more of herself to use her magic again.

Just as the ringing started to dissipate, someone caught a handful of her hair, yanking back hard, forcing Dalia up onto her knees as she thrashed against their hold. Fearful screams caught in her throat and pain shot through her scalp, as she was pulled back against the kneeling figure behind her.

"After everything they've done. You still stand with them?"

A sob wracked through her chest at his voice. She should have known this was inevitable. Glenn would fight the hardest to get to her, of course he would find her. Once she might have admired such devotion. Considered it part of how they were intertwined. Now, it was a curse.

His wrist twisted, forcing her back towards him so that his lips practically brushed her ear. "I know you're confused. I know you're scared. But I need you to believe me. This is for you. For us."

This couldn't be happening. He'd believed in their destiny just as much as she had. She told him of her sorrows. He had been a protective blanket wrapped around her, keeping her from the cold. Promising her vengeance for what was done to her, and she let it seep into her, thinking that was exactly what she wanted. His rage infected her until she could no longer see the monster he was.

Her eyes were open now.

"There is no us," she spit back at him, ramming her elbow back hard into his stomach and trying to struggle away.

Despite a grunt, Glenn held fast. Folding over her, his hand releasing her hair, as his arms wrapped around her. Squeezing her limbs down to her sides. Dalia didn't stop thrashing, not until she saw a glint of gold in his hand by her waist.

Deathbringer. He was armed with the Crystalline weapon. That was what stopped them. She froze, knowing that if he wanted to, he could bring everything down in an instant. Lumiterra would be lost. Amaryllis would be lost.

"Glenn . . . please . . ." Her sudden shift in approach seemed to catch him off guard. His hold loosened slightly, and Dalia drew up her courage. She needed to use this. She needed to appeal to him. "Don't do this. It's so much more complicated than you know. Just, let me explain."

The rogue deflated. Leaning more into her, his face practically burrowed into the crook of her neck. Dalia just looked straight ahead, stifling the sick feeling in her stomach and forcing herself to be still.

"It's okay," he muttered against her skin, his sword hand starting to move. "It's okay, this will all be over soon."

"No!"

Her scream pierced the air as she threw herself forward, nails digging into his wrist, hard enough to draw blood, trying to stop him from activating Deathbringer, just as ice raced along the ground towards them.

"Get your hands off her!"

Tendrils unfurled and grabbed hold of Glenn's ankles as Drystan limped into view. A look of pure fury colored his face, washing away his usual cold calm.

With a snarl, Glenn shoved Dalia aside. Her chest collided with a rock hard enough to steal the air from her lungs. The White Stag pulled himself up, easily breaking the ice's hold on him.

"Not so powerful now are you?" Glenn spat back.

Drystan ignored his taunting. "Don't you touch her!"

His abilities were too drained in their race across the field. That one massive attack left him and his powers weakened. He couldn't hold Glenn now. Nor did he stand much of a chance in a fight. Yet, he kept moving.

Drystan put himself in the path of Glenn's wrath gladly. So long as it kept her out of harm's way.

"Glenn! Stop!" Dalia begged as she tried to struggle to her feet. The blow from the fall and the drain on her lifeforce from all of the use of her own magic made everything fuzzy. "Please, stop!"

Neither of them heeded her pleas. It was like the world around her held its breath. Everything just slowed. Drystan was barely on his feet, and yet, still he was fighting. For her. Once again, she felt like she was thrown back to that night. Just as helpless as she was when she was a child. Watching him face down death in her stead while she could do nothing.

In his current state, Glenn was able to outmaneuver the taller man with ease, landing a kick to his chest which caused the Crystalline to tumble backward. The rogue pounced forward, not missing a second.

If anything was said between them, she didn't know. All Dalia could hear were the sounds of her screams echoing throughout the canyon as she watched Glenn drag that accursed blade across her friend's throat. Red spilling forward before Glenn dropped his collar; Drystan left limp on the ground, blood gushing from the maw of a wound.

He was all she could see. His face fallen towards her. The look there so like the one which haunted her at night. Those dark eyes resigned to death. It was happening again. Only this time, he would actually die for her. She was just as weak as she was a decade ago. Still relying on everyone else to take care of her, and once again, she'd lost everyone.

No. Not this time. She was not a child anymore. She had laid in wait for too long. Now was the time to act. Now was the time to rely on only herself.

Through her cries, she moved. Not able to do much more than crawl, she just kept pushing. One more inch. One more stretch forward. Just one. Over and over, she made her body listen.

All she needed to do was reach him. Dalia did not know how much she had left in her. She didn't know if she could save him, but damn the Gods if she wouldn't try. Twice, he gave his life for her. Twice. Then lost to whatever torment turned him into the weapon he was today. It was for her. So she might live, and what had she done with that chance? What was she living for?

The answer was so clear now. It was for them. For Drystan. For Fionn and Beth. For Ammy. For anyone else who escaped the Keep from her nightmares. Dalia wouldn't stop pushing. She wouldn't stop fighting.

Movement towards her left flank alerted her back to Glenn's presence.

"Oh Dalia," he drawled, scolding. "You're so predictable. This is just what you do, isn't it? Give far too much of yourself to others."

His words cut. A horrible reminder that none of this would have happened if not for her. If she hadn't saved Glenn or trusted him. Her fault. All of this was her fault.

Fingers dug into the fabric of her dress and ripped her back, pulling her away from her desired target as she cried out. "You know I can't let you do that."

Dalia reached out her hand. Fingers stretched as far as they could, but she wasn't close enough. She couldn't reach him. Couldn't touch him and heal his wounds. What filled her now wasn't despair. It wasn't helplessness or some numb void.

It was rage.

Drystan's eyes were all she could see, fading before her. The one lifeline that had always stayed with her. Through everything, she never truly forgot him. She would not lose him. Not again.

And so she exploded.

Dalia screamed. Primal and deep, it dug to her core and released. The glow of her powers started in her eyes and then ripped out. Running through her veins until each one was alight. All she saw was him. All she knew was him.

With a singular need coursing through her veins, she reached out and pulled. Not from herself, but from everywhere. There was a flash. Light blossomed from her and rippled outward, then suddenly, she wasn't the only one screaming.

For a moment, there was nothing but blinding blue light and a crack which sounded to the heavens, and then it all just faded.

Everything started to come back into focus. Dalia was somehow kneeling now. One hand on her knee, barely keeping her from toppling over, and the other stretched out towards Drystan. A fissure ran along the curve of the mountainside before her, radiating from the spot where she was transfixed, and ending near her fallen friend. A gasp sounded as she took in the sight before her.

Drystan was still covered in blood, but he was sitting up, his hand moved to his neck, checking his now completely unmarred flesh with astonishment on his face. She had healed him, without even being close to him. That wasn't all. Around him the grass now sprung up high. Flowers bloomed where before there was nothing but barren rocks around the riverbed.

Her breath echoed in her ear. Fear coursed through her as she took in the cost of such a miracle. A black strain stretched out as if death itself swept from her body. Every tree, every blade of grass. Every single sign of life reaching a few feet back was drained. Withered to husks.

All except Glenn.

The man had been thrown; now lying on his back, he'd propped himself up with his elbows. Across his face a burned scar struck across his nose, a reversal of what she once healed for him, his brown curls now a shock of white. He stared at her, horrified. All reverence, all sickening devotion, gone. He looked at her like she always feared someone would — like she was a monster.

Trembling, Dalia stood. Staring down at the man she once hoped to love. She did this? That couldn't be possible. She was a healer. Her power was to heal not to . . .

But that was what she had done; Dalia had healed Drystan. She saved his life, but to do so, she stole life as well. Not drawing on herself but stealing from what was around her. Glenn included.

The sound of horses approaching broke her from her haze. This wasn't over yet. Most of the army still stood and they were finally approaching.

A gentle hand rested on her shoulder. Drystan, back on his feet, stood beside her. The look on his face was something unreadable. It spoke of awe and thanks, and something else she couldn't bear to let herself identify. Not just yet.

What she did know was they would keep fighting, together.

They stood, side by side, ready to face down the world.

Then the mountainside erupted in flames.

CHAPTER THIRTY-FOUR

If there was a single constant in her life, it was flames. A wall of fire nearly twice her height erected itself as if out of thin air. This was not what the Stags' weapon was able to do. This was something else. Someone else.

Dalia's heart raced. Tears caught on her cheeks as the flames danced before them. Panic did not set in like before. The only thing in her heart was a desperate longing. She needed to find her. Needed to see her.

"Wait! You're going to get yourself killed!"

Drystan's cries fell on deaf ears as Dalia took off towards the flames without fear. The energy she drained had done more than just heal her friend. Only a small limp remained in her gait. She wasn't crawling along the ground now but running.

The fire in her dreams had always been nightmarish, but a small part of her always knew it meant more. Back when her memories were lost to her, she never fully understood why, assuming it was just a human instinct of being drawn to what kept you warm. Especially on the frigid northern shores. But that wasn't it. It never was.

It was always her. Her sister was fire. Just as Drystan was ice, she was flame. What flickered before her wasn't death and destruction, but every hope she could ever hold onto.

As she kept moving, the flames seemed to dance, almost as if they recognized her, withdrawing to let her pass. Once she moved beyond the entrance to the canyon, she could see how far the fire spread. The field once covered in the soldiers of battle was split in two. Flames devoured the half by the mountainside, burning and tearing through whatever parts of the army came close enough. On the other side, stood the rest of the White Stags' troops.

Horses in neat lines looked out over the destruction, not moving. Not a single one dared to come forward. All of them were looking at one fixed point. Dalia turned, following their line of sight, and her heart leaped.

There, at the center of it all, stood a woman engulfed in flames.

Dalia couldn't move. She couldn't speak. All she could do was stare at her. Wrapped in fire and a bright red gown, her blond hair tugged by the wind, was the most beautiful sight she ever beheld — Amaryllis Arrowood.

Where she was soft, her sister was bold. Now, she burned brighter than Dalia ever remembered. She stared down an army like they were nothing, an inferno answering to her beck and call. Ammy always had a courage Dalia could not even fathom, but this, this was something else entirely. Her sister was a beacon, a being of power she never thought possible.

"You are trespassing on the sacred ground of the Gods," Amaryllis said, and fresh tears peppered Dalia's cheeks. Her familiar voice made it seem all the more real she was standing before her now. "You have seen what I alone can do. We have far more power than just me here. This is your only warning. Leave, and never come back to this place. We want no fight with you. Only the right to exist."

Her lungs burned as she held her breath through Ammy's speech, fearing what might happen next. General Lachlan was not a man to take threats lying down. Though, the main forces appeared to be subdued. They couldn't cross such a blaze. No matter the general's resolve, he must have known this battle was lost. The only threat left was behind her.

Sucking in air, Dalia quickly turned. Drystan might have been healed, but he didn't have much fight left in him, and when Glenn rushed forward, he managed to shove the dark-haired man to the ground, Deathbringer drawn and ready to be activated. Dalia did the only thing she could do. The only thing that might be able to reach him.

"She's my sister!"

The man's whole body froze. He stood there, sword ready, and yet, he was still as a statue. Dalia stood between him and Ammy. Arms held straight out at her sides; the surrounding flames played around her, licking at her extended arms. As though she and them stood in tandem against the threat.

"Please," she begged, her voice soft, as she repeated herself again. "She's my sister, Glenn."

Those three words pierced him as she knew they would. His own sister being taken from him was what pushed him on to dark path. His stance faltered. His gaze met hers, and he crumpled.

Sword dangling next to his body, he just stood there. Her once proud Stag, nothing more than the broken man beneath his mask all along. One who had made terrible choices. He did not deserve her pity. Yet, her heart stirred. His hair and face were not the only changes upon his person. Glenn was hollow, his blue eyes somehow faded gray. Damage she'd inflicted upon him. She had stolen greatly from him and left behind a shell of the man she once allowed herself to care for.

Drystan moved. Not needing his abilities now to overpower the man. Grabbing Glenn by the collar, he shoved him to the ground. Claiming the Crystalline sword and holding its blade to the Stag's throat.

"This won't go how you think," Glenn pleaded, his desperate gaze jumping between her and the Crystalline pinning him down. "Dalia, we have to destroy the crystals."

"No."

She would not be swayed by his emotional words now, but she couldn't allow his life on her conscious either.

"You said you wanted me to save you. This is all you'll get. A chance to save yourself," she said, turning her attention to her old friend. "Let him go."

"What? Dalia—"

"Please. Just . . . let him go."

Rage burned in his dark eyes, but Drystan listened all the same. Releasing the stag but holding tight to Deathbringer. "I'm keeping this," he growled.

Drystan didn't have to understand. No matter the horrible acts committed, Dalia could not deny that what happened between her and Glenn was real. It was wanted. She couldn't let him die here. The bits of life she stole from him were penance enough.

Glenn stood on shaking legs, looking between the two of them warily, before stepping forward. He stopped just before her. Hollow eyes searching for something. His gaze so pleading and penetrating that Dalia shuddered.

"You were supposed to be different from the rest of them." Glenn's voice trembled, and Dalia steeled herself against his quiet insult as she moved aside for him.

"Go." Her soft voice wavered, but one simple word was enough. Maybe in a way, she *had* saved him, allowing him a second chance and a different path to walk down. What he did with that path now was up to him. It was not her job to hold his hand and guide him. No matter how much he might have wanted it, she was not his guiding light. He needed to be his own.

Things between them felt like they were finally unraveled. Whatever fate tied them together slipped away. For Dalia it was a relief, while Glenn's face spoke a different story. The look of anguish upon those scarred handsome features was one she didn't know if she would ever be able to forget. The fear in his eyes as he turned and walked away with his life sparked an unwelcome pang in her heart. The fire itself, as if understanding her intentions, allowed him a narrow path to leave unscathed.

"You're going to regret that."

"Maybe," she replied, her eyes never leaving Glenn as he disappeared into the flames. "But I would have regretted killing him more."

TIME CRAWLED by as the scene before them played out. Side by side, the two Crystalline sat, looking out as the army withdrew and the flames dissipated until there was nothing left but an ashy field. Her sister disappeared along with her inferno, leaving Dalia alone once more with a pang of longing in her heart. There had to be a way in. Ammy came out from somewhere, that could only mean Dalia had been successful in breaking open the door.

"I owe you my life."

The two had been content to sit in silence, processing. But

now, Drystan turned his head to look at her. His voice low and soothing.

"Thank you. For what you did. I don't know how you did it but . . ."

"You would have done the same for me."

Dalia pulled her knees up to her chest, wrapping her arms around her legs and leaning the side of her cheek down upon them. Her braid had long since become unruly, and tufts of bright copper curls spilled over her torn skirts and face.

Drystan merely nodded. He didn't need to say anymore. They both knew he would have. They both knew he'd risked his life time and time again for her. Only now, she'd proven she was willing to do the same.

Silence once again settled over them. Comfortable. Filled with years of longing and unspoken truths. In the stillness, Dalia just watched him. She watched as he slowly removed his gloves, pulling at each finger of fine leather before tucking them beside him.

His hand now bare, he reached forward and Dalia's eyes fluttered.

With careful, deliberate strokes, he brushed the wayward hair from her eyes, before his fingers caught the curve between her jaw and neck. His thumb dared to be bolder, brushing the corner of her mouth.

"I searched for you. For so long."

Dalia didn't know what to do with his confession. She just stared back at him before allowing herself to lean into his touch. Relaxing onto the support of his hand and breathing in his evergreen scent. She was too tired to fight against the confusion bubbling in her since she saw his face again. Too battered to care about the consequences.

A sense of absolute calm washed over her, even when he grew bolder. Even as he leaned forward and pressed his forehead to hers. Even as they stayed there, sharing breath, wondering who might be the first to chase after something more.

"Well, there you two are."

The sound of the familiar Wolf filled Dalia with dread. She half expected it to be just like with Glenn. For Drystan to snap away from her in sight of his commander, but . . . he didn't. He lingered, growling his annoyance. His fingers pressing into her flesh as if he wished nothing more than to stay there with her. As though his prince would have to rip him away.

No, it was not Drystan who broke away — it was Dalia. Knowing full well the magic of the moment was gone, and that duty and logic needed once again to dictate her next move.

Her lips grazing the inside of his palm, she untangled herself from the man who had haunted her so thoroughly and faced Barric.

Riding beside him was Evanee. An unreadable look plastered firmly on her pretty face. Something like disgust curling at the corner of her lips.

Barric leaned forward in his saddle, half a smile playing on his lips. Unlike his companion, he seemed quite amused at the scene they'd stumbled upon. "I'll give it to you. Your sister, she packs quite the punch."

A shaky breath shook her chest as she managed to stand, unsure on how to feel about the compliment.

"Do you know where she went?"

The prince shook his head, and the desire to simply flop back onto the ground almost consumed her. This was a victory. Yet what she fought for was nowhere to be found.

"I saw two steeds safely flee into the woods," Evanee offered in her usual cold manner. "A certain traitor and warrior on their backs. I thought perhaps that might comfort you, little weapon."

Despite the horrid nickname and her delivery, Dalia did find comfort in the words the huntress gave her. She prayed that would not be the last she saw of her friends. But to know they were safe. That they hadn't fallen taking up arms in her name brought more comfort than she could say.

Her icy companion finally rose to his feet and walked over to his comrades, Deathbringer sheathed on his belt. The prince's eye caught on the sword, before he smiled.

"You look like shit."

Drystan huffed in reply.

"Shut up and move forward. I lost my horse to those bastards, so you're going to have to share."

"Oh no, not Snowflake!"

"Please, for the love of the Gods, stop naming my horses that."

Dalia snorted, though their banter struck her as odd. Here was the crown prince of the elven throne joking with a Crystalline as though they were friends. Not whatever their designations would demand they be. Yet, no matter how warm that was to her heart, the realization hit her that Drystan was leaving with them once more.

"Wait." She stepped forward, confusion riddling her face. "You're leaving?"

Drystan's only answer was a nod. The simple motion constricted her throat. He couldn't. Not after she'd just found him again. It was Barric who gave any sort of explanation.

"Drystan is a Wolf. I highly doubt any Crystalline in there will be open to speaking to a member of a Hunt, even one that helped them. But that, my dear, is where you come in."

My dear. It sounded so like Fionn that, for a moment, she almost saw her friend in their brother.

"I made you owe me a favor, and here it is. Tell whoever lives within this mountain what we have done. Tell them that

Prince Barric of Carrnelia wishes an audience. That he wishes to broker peace. If they refuse, remind them we now know where they are, and we have a stolen sword capable of destroying this whole place." Tension hung heavy in the air. It was a parlay, but also a threat. One she did not relish having to deliver. "This is goodbye for now, but I look forward to working with you in the future."

She wanted to say more. At the very least to be able to properly say goodbye and thank Drystan, but the horses were moving before the words came. Her dear friend stole one final glance at her, and once again, it was just the two of them. Staring at each other as they parted. It was not until the horses were out of sight, that she allowed herself the luxury of tears.

Once again, she was left alone. Once again, waiting for her sister. Only this time, she knew she would not be waiting in vain.

Still, as each moment passed her heart churned treacherously. Spinning anxiety that she might once again be abandoned.

"Dalia?"

The sound of a voice she didn't recognize caused her to whip around. There was a man in the canyon. A stranger. He stood just outside the crack in the rock wall her power created. Now, at a second glance, she could see what she hadn't noticed before: a seal. An ancient glyph had appeared on the now broken stone. In healing Drystan, she'd done more than steal from around her, she opened the gate.

"How do you know my name?" she demanded softly, feeling so utterly alone. Like she was once again just the girl from Tidesend.

The smile that broke across the man's face was confusing. Relief shone through every crinkle in his face. There was so much joy, but he didn't know her. At the very least Dalia was sure she didn't know him.

"I know your sister has been looking for you for a long time," he explained before beckoning for her to follow him. "Let's get you inside. She's waiting for you."

Skipping heartbeats broke across her chest. Inside. It was all real. Her sister really was out there fighting an army, and the door to a legendary place was open to her.

All she needed to do was step inside.

CHAPTER THIRTY-FIVE

Dalia had grown accustomed to people looking at her like she was some kind of spectacle. Be it because she was some sort of symbol of hope, or a monster, or anything in between. The stares were just part of the scenery around her now. Coming into Lumiterra was no different, except, it was a celebration.

Knowing Lumiterra was in the mountain, she expected it to be fully underground or enclosed. Instead, it seemed to be built into the side of the range itself. Rooms and corridors within the rock were connected by hanging bridges which stuttered her breath as they crossed them. All along the mountain side, lined on those bridges, were people. There was no fear to be found, only joy. Elation carried by their cheers into the wind. Dalia couldn't believe all of this could be for her.

Every step, every clue. And now, she was finally here. A lost flower finally coming to take root.

"You said you knew my sister?" she asked softly, still following the man who led her.

"Yes," he answered, his tone hinting at amusement. "I would say everyone here does."

There were just so many people. Dalia thought there might be a few. A handful of Crystalline hiding away, but what she was looking at now was a city. One that weaved in and out of the mountains themselves. Every part of it seemed to fit perfectly, as if nature itself erected it, and bustling within it all was a shocking amount of people. More than she could count, maybe hundreds of them. They couldn't all be Crystalline.

Looking upward, Dalia tilted her head in confusion. The sky gave off some kind of odd purplish haze to it. As though understanding the question on the tip of her tongue, the man leading her on spoke.

"Magic. A barrier created using runes. Keeps people on the outside from seeing in. Some of my better work, to be sure."

His work. Dalia stopped. Her hand clutching the railing to her side as she looked at the man before her with a new understanding. "It was you. You were the one who left the clues."

He looked over his shoulder at her. Short chestnut hair swinging over the bronze of his forehead as he smiled. "That I did. It was the only thing your sister ever asked of me."

He did it for Ammy. Her heart swelled. All those years of waiting were never in vain. Her sister searched for her after all.

"Are you Crystalline? A Lumiel, even?"

"By the light no, I am no God. No, I'm just a man. One whose family has looked over this place for centuries." He looked out over the mountainside, peace resting upon his pleasant features. "You may call me Luken Amos, or the Guardian of Lumiterra, although I think just Luken rolls off the tongue better."

Per usual lately, so many questions demanded to be answered, and it seemed Luken was happy to oblige. The man motioned for her to continue following as he explained.

"Centuries ago, this was the home of the Gods. When the Lumiels left us, they left behind this sanctuary, and many humans rushed here for safety from the coming horrors of the elves. One of the Gods left my family with the knowledge of how to use runes to protect the people here. The symbols from their lost language can connect with the ley lines of magic, but they are limited in their powers and scope. The magic doesn't come from me, unlike your own abilities."

The runes . . . it did make sense. Each clue was engraved with them. It wasn't his own magic then, but the magic of the writing itself which spoke to them.

"We did not used to be so isolated. People could come and go as they pleased so long as they knew of our secret. Then ten years ago, when I heard about what the elves did, I left the safety of my home to find the children affected. I saved as many as I could, including your sister." The look on his face was enough to tell her the memory was a grave one. "I then locked Lumiterra away, a measure to protect the Crystalline now living within. Unfortunately, my own limitations made the lock impenetrable from both sides, except to one person. It was the only spell I knew that might do. Before I set the lock, your sister made me promise to try and find you, and when I could not, I left a web of clues. A trail of crumbs to bring you home. Making you that person who could open the lock, so I might fulfill her one wish."

Home. That word again, only this time, she started to believe it.

"You looked for me?" Her voice was so soft, soaking in the warm feeling of knowing she'd been wanted all those years.

"Yes. It was shortly after the fall of Keep Oharn. I went to the north, stayed as long as I could, but I could not find you."

It took her months to get there. A frightened seven-year-old traveling alone across the continent. It was a miracle she'd been delivered safely to Tidesend. After so long of scraping by, she was merely skin and bone when she arrived. Tears threatened, thinking of Nora. She was gone, and simply for the choice of taking her in. Tidesend, it was gone too. What stood before her now was where she was always meant to be.

"Come, let's get you cleaned up, and then I think it's about time you and Ammy were reunited."

She still had so many questions, but for the first time, she felt like she was finally going to get answers.

It seemed the act of getting cleaned up in Lumiterra was very different from what she was accustomed to. Dalia was not led to a bath, but a cavernous room with glowing crystals jutting out of the walls. Luminites. Dalia never expected there to be so many. This wasn't some small cache. They seemed to be everywhere. Embedded in the very foundation of the city.

The room was like nothing she ever imagined. Water fell from the ceilings, running down into a natural drainage system to the bottom of the mountains. Dalia tried not to be too memorized by the whole thing and focus on the task at hand.

Scrubbing away the blood and filth of battle, Dalia stood under that warm stream, and for the first time in days, she just breathed. Drystan's thumb brushing the corner of her mouth kept playing in her head. The way he clung to her, and the look on his face when he left her behind. At least she didn't have to ponder on whether or not she would see him again. The favor she owed the prince was also fresh in her mind. Dalia supposed seeing Drystan again would be the upside to that whole endeavor.

Once she was done, Dalia was led to a small living quarters. A change of clothes waited for her there, and she slipped into the dress. It was closer to elven fashion than human. All gauzy and draped fabrics, though the bodice was more fitted. Pressed tight with princess seams and boning against her bust and hugged her curves down to her waistline where it then hung looser around her hips. The steely blue of the fabric was a nice compliment to her pale skin and blaze of curls. Such a fine dress she hadn't seen since Fionn allowed her to borrow their clothes.

No sooner had she started to look around at the space, taking in the rather ornate wooden furniture and plush bed, than the door opened.

Pushing forward to reveal a sight Dalia could scarcely believe.

It was her.

Amaryllis.

Her beautiful older sister stood in the door frame like she never left her. She bore no signs of just fighting a battle. Her blonde locks hung in looser waves than Dalia's hair was even capable, draping down a blood red gown that fit her generous curves like a glove.

She didn't move. Didn't speak. Just stared at her. If Drystan had been a ghost, her sister was a memory come to life. All Dalia wanted to do was rush to her, but she just stood there like a statue, round blue eyes brimming with tears.

"Dalia."

A sob escaped her as Amaryllis spoke her name, and suddenly the two women were moving, rushing forward until she was encased in warm arms and were the two crying against one another.

"It's really you. Gods, I can't believe it." Ammy pulled back, hands on her sister's shoulders, scanning the young woman before her. "Look at you. Look how you've grown. I can't . . ."

"I know." It was all that needed to be said. This was it, the end of the long road she started walking when she was only seven years old. From a promise between two frightened sisters, to a journey that led her through more than she ever thought possible. Dalia was finally in her sister's arms again.

"I should have never left you."

Her sister's tear-stained words touched her heart. How long had she wanted to hear her say that? To admit it was a mistake? Dalia grew up alone; and yet, none of that seemed to matter now. All the years wasted. All the time lost, all of it still led her here. Back precisely where she wanted to be.

"I'm sorry I didn't keep my promise," Dalia said, sheepish grin.

A laugh escaped her sister's lips, and it sounded like the sweetest music. "Gods, I'm so glad you didn't."

Her own laughter came up to meet her sister's. It should have felt strange to be in her presence. After a decade, it should have felt like so much had changed. Instead, she was just at ease. Childish in a way, looking at her big sister like she was the only person in the whole world who mattered.

"Come." Amaryllis took her hand. "The people want to see you."

Dalia raised an eyebrow but allowed her sister to lead her along all the same. Watching her pull back a light gauze curtain at the end of her room to reveal a balcony. The two sisters stepped out onto that precipice hand in hand and were met with a cacophony of cheers.

Dalia's eyes widened, taking in the sea of people gathered.

"Is this all for me?"

It didn't seem possible. Dalia was no one important. A Crystalline sure, but they had at least a few of their own here. Such celebration was something she expected, even from the small glimpse she'd gotten walking through the city, but it was still hard to imagine it was for her.

"Yes." Her sister beamed. "They've been waiting a long time for their lost princess."

Her heart stumbled and breath drew in far too quickly. "What? I'm not a princess."

Amusement danced on Ammy's face. "No, I suppose you're not. But you are the sister of a queen so it seemed the only fitting title to give you."

Dalia turned to face her sister fully, eyes wide sweeping over her impeccably put together attire. The way she carried herself. The way she looked out over the people below them with a similar affection to what she just showed her moments ago. A queen, that was what became of her over the last ten years. She didn't just live in Lumiterra, she hadn't just hidden away there. She was ruling it.

Dalia's hand in her own, Ammy rose up her arms, much to the elation of the crowd below them. "My sister is home! Our time of hiding has come to an end!"

More cheers rang out. The crowd hanging onto every sylla-ble. It was dizzying. Dalia spent so much of her life being seen as nothing. To have gone from invisible to a beacon of hope to now, whatever she was here. It was a rush she was not prepared for, and one she didn't know how to swallow.

"What was all that?" she asked once they were back alone in her room, the cheering masses behind them. "What do you mean you're a queen? We're not royalty, Ammy."

They were nobodies. Until the elves captured them and took the pair to that keep, mutating the sisters into weapons. But even then, that did not make them anyone important. It only made them tools to be sought after. Ammy was powerful, sure. Dalia saw firsthand how much her powers had grown.

She singlehandedly held an army at bay. Strength alone did not make someone a ruler though, there was more here.

"Dalia, this place is not like the rest of Belestara." Ammy's face was a beacon of joy as she spoke. "Here Crystalline aren't just accepted, we're practically worshiped. And I was chosen to lead, to protect these people."

She didn't know how to wrap her mind around what was being said to her. The idea of a place where Crystalline were seen as anything besides a weapon should have felt like a miracle, but something about this made her pause. The very idea of being seen as somehow better for the experiments done to them made Dalia worry at her lower lip.

Amaryllis stepped forward, scooping her sister's hands up in hers. Dalia didn't know if it was an attempt to try and quell her nerves, but it worked. The soft touch from her lost relation bringing her head out of whatever anxiety was brewing and back down into the moment she so longed for.

"When Luken couldn't find you. I almost lost myself." Her voice was barely a whisper, but an anchor for Dalia all the same. "I wanted nothing more than to scorch the very earth to find you. Leave nothing behind but ash until you were returned to me."

Her devotion spoken into existence sparked something within Dalia. So many nights as a child that was the very thing she imagined. The fire of her nightmares coming for her. Yet, it never arrived, and she'd waited. Waited for nothing more than this simple reunion, and to know her sister loved and wanted her all these years.

"Well, I'm glad you didn't do that," Dalia said. "You probably would have gotten yourself killed."

Ammy's nose crinkled at the mocking jab before continuing. "It was Luken who convinced me to stay, who laid the groundwork for you to find us. There were so many nights I almost gave up hope. But now . . . here you are. And here, you will never have to be feared for what you are ever again. You will be loved for it."

The foreign concept washed over her. Here she could be loved, not in spite of what she was, but because of it. There was so much to tell. A favor to ask. Friends to find. A new role in life to fill and understand. But for now, it was just her and her sister. Two girls ripped apart by cruelty only to be melded back together within a crucible. A long trial finally come to an end.

Ammy's arms were around her again, squeezing. "Welcome home."

There was that word again. She almost forgot that's how it started. That all she wanted was one elusive word. A place to belong. Somewhere she could find meaning. It had been there all along. In the stories she enjoyed. The legends she clung to. Home was not among the people of Tidesend, and it wasn't among the Stags. It had been a place only she could unlock. A secret meant only for her.

Amaryllis was her home.

Dalia tried to tell herself to let go. Tried to convince herself Ammy was lost to her. She almost allowed the world to change her, to steal her hope. But it was hope that led her here. Trust ripped apart the net holding her captive and set her free.

Free into a world she couldn't have even begun to dream about.

Finally, Dalia relaxed into her sister's arms, giving into the comfort and safety there. Here, her roots finally stretched. Entangled with the roots of another, more stable flower, wrapped in the arms of her sister.

Dalia Arrowood was finally home.

ACKNOWLEDGEMENTS

It is an odd and wondrous thing to see your dreams come true. First and foremost, I need to thank my parents. I cannot be more grateful for all you have given me, and the support and encouragement you constantly exude. I would like to say especially to my father, thank you. Thank you for never letting give up on this dream and for asking me over and over again since I was fourteen, "When are you going to finish that book?" Well Dad, I did it. I finally did it.

To my agent Jennie, I cannot thank you enough for believing in me. In an industry where it is so easy to feel alone and isolated, you have given me the great fortune of always knowing there was someone on my side.

To my editor Lauren, you were the first person to ever give me that elusive, "Yes" and I will be forever grateful for your faith in me and in this story. Developing these characters and rounding out this story with you was my great honor. And to everyone at Inked in Gray, especially Kota, thank you for answering all my baby author questions and for making this experience just so positive. The entire team cares so much for their authors and I am so grateful my story found its way to you.

I certainly would never have published this book without the love and support of so many amazing author friends. Alex Kennington: thank you for listening to all my querying woes. I'm so glad we are March debut buddies. Sydney Shields: I would have never made it through querying without you. I am so thankful for your friendship. Thank you for helping me to be a better author and grow my craft. Rachel Burroughs: My dear friend, number one hype squad and co-founder of the "I hate Glenn" club. I'm so eternally grateful to you. And to all the authors in the Reylo Discord: You are the best author community I could ever ask for. Thank you for your constant enthusiasm and for making this journey a little less isolating. "You're not alone."

I would also be remised not to thank every single amazing writer I rped with over the years. Without you, I would never have grown or developed my voice enough to get here. To all my beta readers, thank you for pushing this story to be better and for your encouragement. And a huge thank you to Dani Kay. Not only for being one of my best friends in the world but for making the most amazing cover I could have ever asked for. Thank you for literally making my dreams come true.

Ann Darby, there's more than I can fit in this section to thank you for. You're my best friend and I would never have made it here without you. To Sam Wagster: thank you for being crazy and amazing and cosplaying a character of mine before you even read the book. Sorry he turned out to be kind of an ass. Kim Cicconi, road trip extraordinaire. Thank you for being such an amazing friend and supporting me on this crazy journey. To my siblings: Tori and Kae. I love you. Thank you for listening to my rants and for supporting my work!

To my beautiful daughter and dear little miracle, Cirilla. Your smile kept me pushing on any day I ever doubted myself. I love you more than I can ever say.

Can't forget the cats! To Shallan, Adolin and Kaladin: thank you for snuggling me through the best and the worst of my writing days.

To Phoenix: this book quite literally would not exist without you. From watching our daughter so I could write, to spending hours brainstorming and helping me edit, you are my rock. I love you.

And finally, to every soft girl: you don't have to harden yourself in order to be strong. This was for you.

About The Author

Ria Parisi has always found her joy in telling stories. Now she has finally evolved from writing fan fiction to her own work. She is a debut YA Fantasy author who is eager to write stories with the representation she wished she had in books growing up. When not writing, she can be found having fun in cosplay and posting to Booktok. You can find her across social media @riathewolfwrites.

Also By Inked in Gray

If you enjoyed *Of Wolves and Stags*, please consider also reading *With Love, Juniper*, or any of the other Inked in Gray novels and anthologies. Support our small business by buying direct at InkedinGray.com

We also appreciate any and all reviews! You may leave a review on Goodreads, Amazon, or on our site at Inkedingray.com

www.ingramcontent.com/pod-product-compliance
Lightning Source LLC
Chambersburg PA
CBHW051437190726
48289CB00001B/228